The good girl he'd accused her of being was nowhere in evidence as she responded to his invitation to pleasure.

She sucked on his tongue before biting his lower lip with her teeth, the wanton invasion making him dizzier than an entire bottle of whiskey to his shoulder ever could have.

Who was she? This willing partner on a sensual exploration of just how far they could push each other. Hell, they were both fully clothed and he wasn't sure he'd ever been more turned on in his life.

"You're not one to let a gunshot keep you down."

Knox knew he should resist—knew he should pull back and walk away—but so help him he was rooted to the chair. Murmuring against her mouth, he smiled against her lips. "Consider it the power of your healing touch."

"Hmm." Gabriella smiled against his lips before nipping a quick kiss. "Maybe I need to start stitching up men instead of turkeys, and I might get a few more dates."

Whether it was the playful banter or the mind-numbing power of kissing Gabriella Sanchez, Knox didn't know, but as he felt himself falling under once again, he struggled to surface.

Moray was still out there. The rubies were still out in the open. And she was still in danger.

So he pulled back, willing himself to look away from the dark, molten depths of her eyes and the lush, pink lines of her mouth.

Walk away, boy-o. It's the only way.

**Be sure to check out the previous books in the
Dangerous in Dallas miniseries:
*Danger and desire fill the hot Texas nights...***

* * *

**If you're on Twitter, tell us what you
think of Harlequin Romantic Suspense!
#harlequinromsuspense**

Dear Reader,

Welcome back to the world of sultry Southern danger with the fourth and final book in my Dangerous in Dallas series, *The Royal Spy's Redemption* (following *Silken Threats*, *Tempting Target* and *The Professional*). Gabriella Sanchez has built an incredible business on sheer grit and moxie. The only girl in a tight-knit family of boys, she's spent her life frustrated by the overprotection and general nosiness of her loved ones.

Knox St. Germain is a man on a mission. A member of Britain's MI5, Knox is in Dallas to secure the Renaissance Stones and keep them from falling into the wrong hands—namely his boss, whom he suspects of going rogue.

Knox and Gabriella have only known each other a few days, but there are definite sparks and a simmering attraction when they get together. When Knox goes to Gabriella for help after sustaining a gunshot wound while recovering the rubies, he inadvertently unleashes a larger problem that forces them on the run—together.

I have so enjoyed sharing this series with you and hope that Knox and Gabby's story brings you as much joy reading it as I had writing it. It's so much fun as a writer to take two people who seemingly have nothing in common and show how well-matched they truly can be. And when the hero is as sexy as Knox St. Germain, well...don't say I didn't warn you!

Enjoy!

Best,

Addison Fox

THE ROYAL SPY'S REDEMPTION

Addison Fox

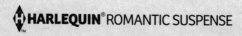

Recycling programs
for this product may
not exist in your area.

ISBN-13: 978-0-373-27984-5

The Royal Spy's Redemption

Copyright © 2016 by Frances Karkosak

Printed in U.S.A.

Texas transplant **Addison Fox** is a lifelong romance reader, addicted to happy-ever-after. There's nothing she enjoys more than penning novels about two strong-willed, exciting people on that magical fall into love. When she's not writing, she can be found spending time with family and friends, reading or enjoying a glass of wine.

Contact Addison at her website—addisonfox.com—or catch up with her on Facebook (addisonfoxauthor) and Twitter (@addisonfox).

Visit the Author Profile page at Harlequin.com.

For Roxane

I know we say Tank brought us together, but I believe our friendship was fated even without canine interference.

You are the sister of my heart. I love you, Mary Poppins.

Chapter 1

Growing up with five brothers, Gabriella Sanchez assumed she'd experienced everything the male of the species could throw at her. From the gross to the ridiculous, she was quite sure she'd seen it all.

That was, until a sexy British cop with a gunshot wound stumbled through the front door of her shop.

"Knox!" Gabby screamed his name as the man stumbled into her, a solid wall of heat and flesh as he wrapped his arms around her in an awkward hug.

She screamed his name once more and half staggered, half dragged him a few more feet before spreading her legs and resetting her grip. Whatever adrenaline had carried him to her shop door had given out, and he'd passed out judging by the deadweight that pressed against her.

A large stack of wine boxes still stood where she'd left them earlier; she'd been unable to get to the inventory for an upcoming tasting series after the excitement of the afternoon. Her friends, Violet, Cassidy and Lilah, had needed her help after they'd accidentally come into possession of a cache of rubies.

And clearly they weren't the only ones who needed assistance.

Knox St. Germain was a British MI5 officer who had shown up recently and inserted himself into the whole mess with the rubies. Although she didn't fully understand his job, Gabby had expected his influence and, frankly, his interference would have made the evening's events—a sting operation in a downtown park—go more smoothly.

The blood currently covering his shoulder suggested otherwise.

Her friends had only discovered the cache a few weeks prior. And it had taken them several days to let her in on what they'd found. Gems, buried in the concrete floor of their shop, placed there more than fifty years ago when they were hidden away by their landlady, Mrs. Beauregard.

Mrs. B's father had moved them from Britain after World War II under the auspices of the Crown.

So how did MI5 even catch wind of their rediscovery?

Cassidy, Lilah and Violet hadn't shared, nor had the men who'd come to their aid. Gabby certainly hadn't told a soul.

Yet Knox St. Germain had found out anyway and had been dispatched with all haste from Mother England to recover them.

Shifting Knox once more, she used the thick line of heavy boxes to support him as she shuffled them forward. Settling his weight against the wall of wine cases, she held him still to avoid his falling.

"Knox!" She added a light slap to his cheeks along with his name, pleased when it pulled him from the faint.

"Just need...some downtime." He tightened his arms, the move was enough to pull her off balance, and she staggered beneath his weight, glad she'd traded the day's heels for a pair of slippers.

Something warm covered her bare shoulder; the tangy, coppery scent of blood only added to her awareness. "What happened?"

"Park. Drop. Rubies."

His voice faded on the last word, and she struggled to keep him upright. "Stay with me!" The sharp order was followed immediately by an image of her friends. Violet, Cassidy and Lilah, along with the men who'd come to their rescue, had planned a sting operation for that evening to finally capture the evil Tripp Lange, the man at the heart of all the violence they'd dealt with since discovering the gems. Since Knox's arrival in Dallas, Gabby knew he had inserted himself into the operation and had gone along to the park.

Although they'd already texted her they were fine and had promised to share details in the morning, she now began to wonder. "Violet? Max? Are they okay?"

"Fine. Away." Knox seemed to right himself, his arms tightening briefly before he stopped and summoned himself to his full height, stepping away from the supporting boxes. She had a quick flash of something she intimately recognized—sheer, stubborn, gritty will—before the pain he was dealing with returned to his crystal-blue gaze. "They're fine. This isn't about them."

Not about them? Hadn't that been the whole purpose of the private meet at Klyde Warren Park? Her friends had come into possession of three matched rubies—the famed Renaissance Stones of legend—and they needed to ensure they stayed out of enemy hands.

Gabby had done some quick internet research after Violet had shared the discovery of the gems. The rubies had a nasty history. Since their initial discovery as one large stone by the British East India Company in the seventeenth century, the gems were cut down into the trio they were today. The stones had led men to vile acts of depravity and madness, and murder trailed the stones, leaving blood as red as the rubies in its wake.

And now there was more blood.

A fresh stack of kitchen towels she'd set out early for the tasting caught her eye and she snagged one to press against his shoulder. "Take this and try not to bleed all over my clean floor."

He took the towel without question and as he staunched the wound, a wash of red filling up the white towel, a flash of reality battled the surreal that had settled over the scene.

Instinct—raw and surprisingly well honed—had her moving into action. She shot a quick glance around her business and pointed him toward a long bar she used for class demonstrations and wine tastings. "Here. Hold on to this counter."

His reluctant agreement almost had her smiling in victory but she tamped it down, well aware a quick gloat wouldn't sit well with a wounded—and decidedly alpha—male.

Satisfied he had his balance, she raced back to the front door and flipped the lock, then hit the light switch. Darkness flooded the room, leaving nothing but the eerie glow of the streetlamps outside, visible through the glass doors.

Had someone followed him? Who had shot him? And why was he here?

The questions tumbled over themselves, one after the other, even as something small and quiet and a lot like satisfaction whispered through her mind that she was pleased he'd come to her.

"Get a damn grip, *chica. Hello.* Highly suspicious gunshot wound." She muttered the words to herself, well aware a call to the police would be a far better choice than helping the man with the enigmatic gaze.

And then she turned toward the silhouette she'd left at the bar and fought the light flutter in her belly. Knox didn't appear to have moved. His large hands still clutched the edge of the thick stainless steel counter.

Khaki cargo pants hung low on his hips, while a stretch of gray cotton spread across his back. A large red stain marred his left shoulder, rapidly turning the T-shirt black in the darkened light.

"Can you walk?"

He lifted his head from where he stood stock-still, his gaze focused on the counter. "Yes. Bullet just nicked the flesh."

The ice-blue eyes that had already done a solid number on her insides in their previous meetings had a glazed, unfocused look, and she knew he wasn't nearly as good a judge of his condition as he should be.

Men.

To be fair, her reasoning seemed to have taken a sizeable detour, even as she cycled through her mental Rolodex. She could call her cousin, Isabella, who worked nights in the ER, to come take a look. The idea had merit—and Isabella was discreet—but something held her back.

Wrapping an arm around his waist, she pulled him close, careful to avoid pulling too quickly and forcing him off balance. "Do you have me?"

"Yes."

"We need to get out of the front area here. Even with the lights off, we're too easy to see through the windows."

He nodded, the motion exaggerated enough to put pressure against her body as she forced him to walk.

"Easy. Step by step."

"I shouldn't—"

"Shhh. Focus on getting back to the kitchen."

While her catering shop—a renovated warehouse in Dallas's Design District—was sizable, the trek to her kitchen wasn't anything she'd ever considered. Suddenly, the door to her kitchen—and safety—seemed a mile away.

Using the stubborn streak she'd honed since birth, she moved them forward. One foot. Then the other. They walked, slow and plodding, as she fought to maintain the press of his body and the increasing pull of shock and gravity that was determined to drop him to the floor.

The entire shop was maybe twenty yards from the front door to the back. Despite the relatively limited space, the distance to her industrial kitchen seemed interminable. Gabby cleared the two of them through the swinging door that acted as sentinel to her inner sanctum just as the screech of tires echoed in front of the building. "Damn it."

"What?" Knox's head tilted upward.

"I locked the door, but forgot to set the alarm."

"You can't go back out there."

"I've got a keypad back here, but you're weaker than you were. Can I leave you unsupported?"

He grunted at that—whether in acknowledgment or irritation, she wasn't sure—before standing straighter. "Go. Now. I'll be right behind you."

Although that imperious tone usually set her teeth on edge, she ignored it in favor of expedience. And a funny sort of relief that he'd want the property armed.

Ignoring the odd mishmash of thoughts, Gabby hot-footed it to the back entrance and keyed in the code— her grandmother's birthday—and prayed she wasn't too late. The blinking green light that said all her doors and windows were closed flipped to red just as she slammed the last number into the keypad. Instantaneously, the piercing siren that accompanied a breach lit up the interior of the kitchen, growing louder as the stainless steel surfaces deflected the sound, pushing it back into the atmosphere like a living, breathing wall of energy.

She shoved Knox toward a large pantry, ignoring whatever cleanup would no doubt be involved in having a large man bleed all over her food before racing back toward the swinging door. She tipped it open slightly to view the outer room of the shop and could see a man fleeing down the front steps of her business, his large silhouette and strained gait highlighted by the streetlamps that lined Slocum Street.

"Is the bastard gone?"

Even with the unceasing clanging, Gabby heard the question. "Yes."

"Then turn off the bloody alarm."

For the second time in a span of moments, ire tickled the back of her neck at his imperious words and snappish orders. It was time to set things to rights. She stalked back to the alarm keypad and reset the code. The cell phone she'd left lying on the counter rang, and she snatched it up, answering the alarm company on the other end.

"No, I'm fine. False alarm." She added the required password to confirm she wasn't actually being held hostage and thanked the man on the other end.

"*Beef enchilada* is your password?"

Knox's sultry voice held the unmistakable notes of pain, but she didn't miss the veneer of humor underneath. "I make damn good enchiladas."

"I curse myself for not sampling them. It's still an odd password."

"It's as good as any other." She shrugged and fought down the natural swell of concern working its way through her defenses. She might be the youngest child in a family of boys, but she had a damn fine mothering instinct.

Not that she'd put it to good use, of course. A fact her mother reminded her of on a near-daily basis. Especially since it had been two—no, three?—years since her last serious relationship.

Had it really been that long?

Gabby shook off the embarrassing answer, well aware it *had* been that long. She'd been so focused on getting her business off the ground, the ninety-hour weeks more joy than punishment, but her personal life had paid the price. Just that evening, in fact, her mother had reamed her out for not having a date to her cousin's engagement party.

Shaking off the remembered conversation and the maudlin thoughts she'd spent far too much time dwelling in lately, Gabby sized him up. "Are you okay?"

"I've had worse."

"That wasn't my question."

"It's like I told you—it's a surface wound. The bark is far worse than the bite."

Could she say the same for him? With a hard turn on her heel, she headed for the front door. She hated to leave him, but an unlocked door left them exposed. "Let me see what damage they did to the lock, and then I'll be right back."

His protest to stay in the kitchen echoed off her back, but she ignored him, already halfway to the front door. She knew how to protect herself, and she'd be damned if she was going to leave her business to the whims of some nameless, faceless threat. She also knew how to move around the room to avoid a direct line of sight to the front door.

The street outside remained devoid of life, and she walked along the edge of the demonstration area until she'd almost reached the front door. At the last minute, she put herself in full view of outside, her form visible in the glass door. The lock she'd so recently flipped had been unlatched.

"Someone's damn quick with a pick."

Brushing off the small shiver, she turned the lock once more, then leaned down and latched a second small bolt at the bottom of the door frame. It was invisible from the outside, and the only way anyone was getting in now was by coming through the glass.

"I said I'd handle it."

The dark tones, rich and cultured, slithered over her skin as she straightened. For the first time, Gabby was forced to wonder if the real threat was already inside.

Knox St. Germain ignored the shot of heat that sizzled through his veins at her glorious ass still pointing heavenward. He loved women—all of them, regardless of age or size—but there was something about Gabriella Sanchez that gripped him with fierce claws.

He kept a hand over the towel at his shoulder, but a combination of steady pressure on the wound and a few moments of downtime had gone a long way toward restoring his equilibrium.

Sadly, the same couldn't be said for the temptation standing before him.

His vision cleared as Gabriella straightened, and he didn't miss the wary expression that filled eyes the color of a rich espresso.

"You don't appear capable of handling much right now."

He couldn't quite tell if the statement was meant to put him in his place or reassure her she wasn't in danger.

Don't let the gunshot fool you, love.

The words were on the tip of his tongue, but he held them back. He was in pretty bad shape. But after a few more hours of downtime he'd be ready to move again.

He *had* to move again.

And he had to figure out how Richard Moray had gotten the jump on him.

He'd come to Dallas under the auspices of MI5, to retrieve the recently recovered Renaissance Stones, but the mission had gone sideways barely before it had begun. His boss and leader was attempting to secure the stones for his own selfish gain.

Knox had suspected Moray—the intelligence they'd gathered was pretty clear—but until he'd actually come face-to-face with Richard, some small part of him had denied it. Had ranted and railed that it simply wasn't possible.

But no longer.

Reassessing, Knox took in Gabriella's tall form, still standing before the door. "Get away from there. This area's too dodgy to be standing around all night looking for trouble."

"My brother's a cop. He patrols this dodgy area—" She broke off with a small smile edging those lush lips. "Regularly."

"As someone who grew up in plenty of dodgy areas, trust me—things can change in an instant."

He saw the curiosity flash in her eyes and cursed himself for the slip. Why in bloody *hell* did he offer up that tidbit? He'd worked damn hard to leave his Manchester background behind. And now he was offering it up on a platter?

It took a minute for the bigger part of her comment to register, and Knox took in the admission that her brother was a cop.

More good news.

He already knew he was in deep with Reed Graystone, Dallas PD detective and the fiancé of one of the women caught up in this whole mess, Lilah Castle. Reed's stepfather, Tripp Lange, had been revealed as the local mastermind behind the initial theft of the stones.

The moment Graystone got word back to his cop buddies that Knox had taken the stones during the exchange in the park, they were going to hunt him down.

And no amount of arguing that he was working under the authority of MI5 was going to change that.

"Are those my thousand-thread-count catering napkins you've got wrapped around your shoulder?"

He shrugged and paid for the wave of fire that lit up his wound. "Are those the ones in the cabinet nearest the counter you left me against?"

"Yes."

"Then these are your thousand-thread-count catering napkins."

"I can't serve anyone on those ever again!"

"Then I'll buy you some new ones." He pulled a second pilfered napkin out of his pocket and made quick work of wrapping it over the layer at his shoulder, fashioning a makeshift bandage. With a final tug on the tie with his teeth, he lifted his head. It stung—flesh wounds always did—but the blood had already stopped.

His hands now free, he reached for his back pocket to give her some money. As his fingers closed over a pair of handcuffs, he remembered he'd left his wallet and ID back in his hotel room. "When I get my wallet back, I'll give you the money to buy some new ones."

"You need to go to the emergency room."

"No."

"But you're hurt. I saw the blood seeping through my napkins, and that's on top of the one I gave you from the front counter."

"The bullet was clean, and I'll get to it later. I'm not going to the hospital."

"But you could barely walk three minutes ago! And now you're up and around and—"

The fear that had flashed when she'd turned from the door lit up her gaze once more before those dark eyes shot around the room. Gauging the distance to the back door, no doubt.

He wasn't sure why the real evidence of her fear struck him like a spear low in the gut. She was an inconvenience—an incredibly attractive one—and nothing more.

"Look. Gabby. I need your help for just a little while longer."

A string of rapid Spanish fell from her lips, and he

smiled in spite of himself. He quickly translated the prayer—an appeal for help and the strength to maintain her patience.

"And while I appreciate the request to a deity, you're sort of stuck with me for the moment."

Fear morphed to anger in the space of a smile. "You understood me?"

"Every word."

"Why me?"

Why had he come here? He could give himself any number of excuses—namely, that she'd been handy since her shop was a safe place to regroup and close enough to the park where the events had all gone down.

But that wasn't the full truth.

He knew he was a bastard of the highest order, but Knox made every possible effort not to lie. Especially not to himself. "I needed help."

"Try again." Her gaze flashed once more toward the back door before it shifted to him. He felt her perusal as clear as a brand, from head to toe and back up again.

Damn if it wasn't the sexiest thing he'd felt in a long time. *Too* long.

Focus, man.

He had a she-cat on his hands and he'd do well to remember that. This wasn't a woman who backed down. "It's the truth. I needed somewhere to lay low, and I remembered how to get to your shop. I'm just lucky you were still here." Something unsettling flashed across her face like an ephemeral mask, and Knox stilled at the dark cloud that seemed to hover over her.

But it was her words that revealed even more than the look. "I'm always here."

Was that pride? Resignation? Perhaps an odd mix of both?

He'd made a rather successful career at reading people, yet he couldn't quite get a grip on this woman. Everything about her screamed confidence and competence, even as vague disillusionment tinged the edges. They'd met a few days before, and he'd gotten a nebulous impression of the same, but it had taken this comment for the impressions to form into a more cohesive thought.

She's not your problem, mate.

The thought beat a rapid tattoo in his mind, but even a thousand warnings to himself couldn't still the curiosity that had begun to run rampant about the luscious caterer with the long, curling hair that made a man itch to grab several fistfuls.

Her brother's a cop.

He tried that internal warning on for size, and even the promise of a gun-wielding, protective sibling couldn't quite eradicate the image of running his mouth over those generous breasts or burying himself at the apex of those long, long legs.

And then he nearly groaned as he pictured the spiky high heels she normally sported still capping off those long, long legs.

Voice harsh, he pressed his earlier point. "Look, I just need a few hours. You don't even need to be here. Set the alarm and leave, and I can head out in a bit."

"I'm not leaving you here."

"Well, I'm not leaving, so we're at an impasse."

A triumphant note was layered beneath her sexy voice. "Then you can deal with my brother on his next set of rounds through the neighborhood."

"Or you can do as I asked."

Before he could check himself for being such a raging bloody idiot, he snagged the handcuffs from his back pocket and had one over her wrist. In a matter of heartbeats, he had the other cuff over his own wrist.

"What did—"

He cut her off, wiggling his fingers in a small wave as he lifted their conjoined arms. "Looks like you've got company for the evening."

Gabby stared at the large hand that waved so near her own.

He'd handcuffed her? *To* him?

Shock had quickly given way to anger, and she fought to keep the upper hand. Or, hell, any hand. Preferably a free one. "What is wrong with you?"

"Desperate times, love." He added a wink, and even though she knew the cheeky move was more an act than sincere, she couldn't stop the shiver at the endearment. "I need to lay low for a few hours and I'm doing it here. Get over it."

"Knox." If she thought using his name would make her plea more personal somehow, she hadn't given any thought to how it would make *her* feel. It slipped from her lips, wrapped in the breathless frustration of the moment, and she couldn't deny she liked the sound of it on her lips and tongue.

The single syllable was hard and unyielding, like the man. Add on the unusual *X* at the end, and she had a sense of the wild and raw.

Also like the man.

"I can't be a part of this."

"You were anxious to be a part of things a few hours ago with your girlfriends."

"I've been worried about them. Giving good friends moral support isn't aiding and abetting a man with a gunshot wound."

"I'm one of the good guys."

"Are you sure?"

She'd seen his government badge and knew Lilah's fiancé, Reed, had checked Knox St. Germain out through the Dallas PD database. So when had the whispers that the British officer wasn't all he seemed taken root?

"Quite sure. You'll be reimbursed for your time, trouble and your thousand-thread-count napkins." He tapped his bloody shoulder with his free hand. "But for now let's get out of the doorway."

He'd cuffed the wrist of the same arm that had the gunshot wound, and no matter how hard she'd like to make him suffer for his asinine tactics, she reluctantly followed him back to the kitchen. The cuffs ensured there was minimal distance between the two of them, and a rush of awareness filled her at their nearness as they moved in lockstep with each other.

She'd dragged his body inside, pressed against hers, not more than fifteen minutes ago, yet even that hadn't seemed as intimate as the small links of metal that bound them to each other.

"What are you doing here so late?" he asked.

"Cooking and finishing up some paperwork."

"It's almost midnight."

"It's a lot of paperwork."

The words came out on a snap, and she decided to let them linger. While it wasn't his fault she spent nearly her entire life focused on her business, she wasn't done being irritated with him. And she certainly didn't need the inevitable lecture he'd feel honor-bound to deliver about the evils of working too hard.

"It must be a lot to run your own business."

Her gaze flew to his at the gentle comment, and the

swinging door to the kitchen nearly hit her before he reached out and caught it with his free hand.

"Sometimes."

"But worth it, too. Hard work is its own reward and all."

She continued on through the door as he held it open and fought the urge to shake her head. She'd already spent far too many precious hours this month arguing with various family members about the *high personal cost* of starting a business, the latest just this evening with her mother. It was strangely unsettling to have a conversation in the exact opposite vein.

"I'm building a future for myself."

Knox ran a finger over the counter. "Looks like you're off to a stellar start."

"You know catering?"

He grinned at that. "I know eating. Cooking the food is another matter entirely."

"You don't cook?"

"Love, I've never even turned on the oven in my flat."

Again, that persistent shiver at the endearment fluttered over her nerve endings. "Ever?"

"Gas company keeps sending me notices asking if I want to turn off the line."

Unbidden, a small giggle bubbled in her throat, especially as she recalled grumbling at the size of her gas bill the previous month. "So what do you eat?"

"Takeaway and sandwiches are my speed. Occasionally, if I get really ambitious, I'll scramble up a few eggs."

"Good thing you've left the gas on."

"No doubt."

He settled onto one of the stools she kept lined up

against the large countertop that made up the center of her kitchen. Although the pasty sheen of white had receded from his features, pain still tightened the corners of his eyes and mouth, and she took the seat next to him without argument.

Unbidden, a wave of compassion hit at the mix of pain and exhaustion that she sensed even more than she observed. But it was that softening that had her going on the offensive.

"Why are you really here?"

"A gunshot wound isn't enough?"

"I don't mean here at my shop. I mean here in Dallas."

"I'm doing my job."

The urge to call him out was strong, but a quick glance toward their joined hands made her reconsider. Although she didn't feel physical danger in his presence, she'd be rather shortsighted to ignore the barely leashed strength she sensed in him. And gunshot wound or not, Knox St. Germain looked like a man who could take care of himself and anything that got in his way.

So she'd wait and watch. And continue to puzzle through the issue on her own. Although she'd kept her own council, she'd questioned his arrival from the start, showing up at her friends' store, Elegance and Lace, and claiming the auspices of Britain's MI5.

"Those are awfully serious thoughts flitting through your mind, Miss Sanchez."

The lilting, cultured tones of his voice seemed to fill up the darkened room, spreading out like a warm flow of lava. He was an attractive man—virile, strong and incredibly self-possessed—but add on the accent and he took on a sort of lethal sexiness.

She met a lot of people in her line of work, and few—

if any—of them had ever churned her insides up in a whirl of nerves and need.

But maybe she could use that to her advantage…

Because in that moment, as her insides went to liquid at his voice, she sensed a solution to her two most pressing problems. She wanted to uncover the secrets of the man beside her. And she desperately needed a bit of relief from her family.

The question was, could she pull both off?

"I'm in a serious situation."

"I won't hurt you. And I'll be out of your way soon enough."

Gabby shot him her most beautiful smile and went to work, laying it on thick. "I know that. But—" She hesitated another moment before offering up a small sigh. "I wonder if you could help me in return."

"What do you need help with?"

"I need to get my mother off my back."

The words were out, floating around in her darkened shop like heat-seeking missiles with no place to land. Had she really just opened up on the most embarrassing thing in her life? And was she actually thinking of blackmailing an injured man, no matter how suspicious he seemed?

With a glance at the hard jaw that showed the lightest sheen of stubble and her mother's earlier litany still echoing in her ear, Gabby knew the answer.

Yes.

A million times yes.

"What, exactly, does getting your mother off your back entail?"

"My cousin's engagement party. Tomorrow night."

Chapter 2

"Who has an engagement party on a Wednesday night?"

Gabby supposed it was a fair question, but in an extended family of more than one hundred, you didn't wait solely for the weekend to get together. The Sanchez family often spent time together. "My aunt is hosting dinner tomorrow night at her home. We'll celebrate then."

"I've never been engaged, but isn't that something people do on weekends?"

The knowledge he'd remained perpetually unattached only added to those sizzling hormones that seemed to spring to life in his presence, but Gabby resolutely ignored them.

She had him on the hook.

"I have a big family. If we waited only for weekends, we'd never fit in all we have to celebrate."

"And you want me to go to a private family event?"

"As my date."

He stilled at that, his earlier humor settling into the craggy grooves of his face. The color had returned to his cheeks, and he no longer looked on the verge of passing out, for which she was grateful.

"Your date?"

"It's my lack of a love life that has my mother so upset. Bringing a date for the evening will give me some breathing room for a few months."

"Why does she care?"

"How many brothers and sisters do you have, Mr. St. Germain?"

"One. A sister. And it's Knox."

"Is she older or younger?"

"Older."

"Does she get up in your business?"

Something flashed across his face. She saw it in the brief tightening of his jaw before it was shut down. Firmly. "She's my sister. Of course she does."

"I have five brothers. I also have forty first cousins, more than half of whom are women. And I have my mother. And my grandmother. And too many aunts to count. Trust me when I tell you interference is a way of life in my family."

"If that's the case, why do you need to get your mother off your back? Isn't that the definition of her job?"

"Mine's gotten worse since this cousin got engaged. Maria's the third in three months. Add on that three of my five brothers are married and giving her grand-children…"

He shrugged. "Okay. So they're living their lives and you're living yours. So what?"

"I'm her daughter. I should have given her no fewer

than three grandchildren by now." She leaned forward and offered up a conspiratorial whisper. "You know. Because I'm over thirty."

"And that's some sort of tragedy?"

"It is to Elena Sanchez."

He studied her for a moment, and she wanted to squirm under the perusal. His gaze was raw—unyielding—and in that moment she knew why Knox St. Germain was so good at his job. He missed nothing.

"And she's fine with you bringing just anyone?"

"You're a man and you're breathing. You fit the bill."

Gabby fought to keep her gaze on his face, even as she imagined the hard chest and tapered waist that reinforced her point in every line of his fit male form.

A small light glinted beneath eyelashes to die for, and he leaned closer, his already deep voice dropping into a husky register that she suspected had removed more than one pair of panties in Knox's past. "Will there be kissing?"

"There can be. It *is* what dating people do."

"And touching?"

Oh, my.

She fought the rising wave of pure lust that thundered through her midsection at the idea of Knox running his hands over her body. The heated response did serious battle with the self-righteous anger that still lingered over his handcuffing her.

She'd brushed off unwelcome advances before; she'd do it again. He meant to get a rise out of her and nothing more. "It's hard to kiss if you don't touch."

He moved a fraction closer. "What about hand-holding?"

You are aloof and unaffected. You are a rock. You see through his act. "Isn't that touching?"

He leaned back abruptly, the sudden movement jarring her from the vision of them kissing on her aunt Corrinda's back patio.

"I'm not sure you're up for it."

The vivid lights rimming the scene faded from her mind as Knox's words registered. "Excuse me?"

"You heard me. I can't swoop in like some conquering hero, kiss you and love on you, and then leave. What will your family think of me? And you by extension."

"They won't think anything."

"I'm hard to forget."

"You're a pompous as—"

The words hadn't even fully left her lips when Knox struck like a cobra, swift and immediate. His lips were on hers, warm and soft, and she had the abstract thought that the man ought to have a warning label tattooed onto his forehead.

Sexy voice, sexy abs and sexy lips are not to be toyed with.

Even as alarm bells hit every note on the scale, she refused to pull away. Her mother wasn't the only one who lamented Gabby's lack of a significant other. Gabby was the one who went to bed alone each night. And she was the same one who opened the front doors of this shop between five and six o'clock every morning.

She knew what she was missing.

And she was damned sure she wasn't going to miss a shot at a few make-out moments with the British god who'd shown up at her front door.

Heat radiated through his T-shirt in delicious waves, and she pressed her free hand to a firm shoulder—the one not currently sporting her catering napkins—while her other hand lay against his, somewhere in the vicinity of their laps. The attachment that had felt intrusive and insulting only moments before suddenly felt like a bond. A tight bond with slightly wicked overtones.

Just like his tongue. Strong and sure, he'd invaded her mouth as neatly as he'd invaded her shop, and Gabby was hard-pressed to push him away. Long, sure strokes against her own tongue had her seeing stars, the intrusion welcome and increasingly urgent, and she responded in kind, unwilling to give him the upper hand.

His fingers tightened over her back as their breaths mingled in the cool air of the kitchen, the slightest reprieve before they both dived back into the moment.

Had she ever been this wanton before?

The thought whispered through her mind as Knox took her under in another soul-searing kiss. Hot, carnal and full of sensual promise, he was a man who knew what to do with his mouth. And whether it was the increasing discomfort building in her body or the realization that it would be so very easy to fall for this man's conquest tactics, she knew she had to put a stop to things.

The hand she'd laid on his shoulder drifted up to his neck, the tips of her fingers threading through soft wisps of hair. She shivered at the strength she felt in the corded muscle, the physical confirming what she already knew: he was a powerful man.

And she'd have to be content with the knowledge she affected him, especially if the hard beat of his pulse beneath her palm was any indication.

With a final stroke of her tongue over his—one for the road, as it were—she pulled back, her gaze on his in the dim lights of the kitchen.

"You're still a pompous ass."

"I work at it."

The cocky smile was nowhere in evidence, but Gabby didn't doubt his words.

Knox held himself very still, unwilling to turn away from the dark gaze of the woman beside him.

What the bloody hell had just happened?

He'd wanted to kiss her from the first moment he'd laid eyes on her—those lips were too lush and gorgeous to ignore—but he'd never anticipated he'd lose his damn mind.

And bloody hell, the woman could kiss. Those gorgeous lips hid secrets he'd never imagined, and it was humbling to admit his head was still reeling. She was every fantasy he'd ever had, yet sweetly innocent all at the same time.

How was that possible?

Was this the real reason he'd come to her place? Because, if it was, he needed to do himself a favor right now and get the hell out. Who cared if Moray was out there waiting for him? He'd be a lot safer with his enemy than he was with Gabriella.

He'd accepted long ago commitment wasn't in the cards for him.

Ignoring the strange shot of remorse that wormed beneath his skin, Knox focused elsewhere. His eyes drifted over the hard beat at the base of her throat before moving on to the generous swell of her breasts.

A hell of a lot safer with Moray.

"So we have a deal?"

Her words were laced with the slightest tinge of something he recognized immediately. Victory.

"We have a deal."

"Then uncuff me. I'm not going anywhere, and you can stay as long as you need, but I've got work to do."

"What work?"

"I've got to get going on five oversized trays of enchiladas, and I'm burning night-light."

The swift change in topic when his heart still thundered with wild beats in his chest chafed against his sense of equilibrium, but he refused to show any sense of vulnerability or all-around pissiness. "That's why you're here?"

"I've been a bit behind with helping Violet, Cassidy and Lilah. And it wasn't until tonight on the phone that I got roped into the enchiladas for tomorrow night. So while you were running around downtown getting shot at, I've been doing paperwork and food prep."

"Are these the same enchiladas you brought the other day to Elegance and Lace?"

"My grandmother's world-famous recipe." She shot him a dark stare before pointing toward a row of disposable pans stacked along the counter on the far wall. "Which I need to get to."

"Baldwin dived into them like he was a man dying of starvation."

"Max Baldwin is a man with good taste."

"They looked good."

And he'd wanted a plate, surprised at himself for the hard ball of need that had lodged in his gut at the savory meal. He'd learned to go without at a young age, and it had served him well as an adult with an unpredictable schedule. He wasn't particularly enticed by food as a rule, but something about the pan of hot, cheesy enchiladas had made him wish for a few cracks in his armor of self-control.

It was a ridiculous reaction to a plate of food, but

even with a solid line of logic and reasoning, he hadn't quite convinced himself he hadn't missed out two days ago.

"They are good. Too bad you didn't take any."

"I was working. Trying to get a handle on what the seven of you have been up to."

He'd admitted to himself it was a hell of a story. The Renaissance Stones had lain buried in the concrete floor of an old Dallas warehouse built in the late 1950s and owned by the daughter of one of London's greatest jewelers. Joseph Brown had been commissioned to create the fake crown jewels during the war and after the bloodshed was over, when he decided to move his young family to America, he'd been asked to take both the false and real gems with him.

The story was fantastical, Knox knew, even for someone who had significant levels of clearance to some of the world's most revered secrets. Yet here he was. In the city that was known for sheer grit, beautiful women and the death of JFK, priceless gems had been smuggled out of England and lay buried for decades in the floor of a bridal boutique.

"The seven of us weren't up to anything. Those gems have brought nothing but heartache and danger."

"They seemed to do quite a job on everyone's love lives."

He didn't consider himself a fanciful man, but the evidence was hard to argue with. The three women who had discovered the jewels each ended up with the three men who came to their aid. If the Renaissance Stones didn't have such an ugly history, he'd be tempted to think they carried something special.

Which went beyond fanciful, veering straight into superstitious.

But seeing as how those same rubies lay in one of the pockets of his cargo pants, warm against the same thigh that had recently pressed to Gabriella Sanchez as he kissed the ever-loving hell out of her, Knox figured he couldn't be too careful.

Gabby stilled, the feisty spark in her eyes morphing with a strange light. "I suppose there is that."

Unwilling to dwell on any of that nonsense a moment longer, he dug the key to the cuffs out of his pocket and went to work on their metal tether. He unhooked her first, then his own, shoving the cuffs back into his pocket. He'd ignored his shoulder up to then, but it burned like the very devil.

"Can I clean up?"

"I've got a full first-aid kit in the back bathroom. Help yourself. I also have a stack of T-shirts in the storage room next to the bathroom from some of the vendors who call on me. Help yourself there, as well."

He lifted his eyes at the idea of a full kit. "You encounter much danger here, Miss Sanchez?"

"It's an industrial kitchen, and I regularly have students in my cooking and wine classes. Accidents happen."

That much was likely true, but he still let out a low whistle a few minutes later when he investigated the full set of medical equipment she had stored in her back bathroom. Everything he needed was in the stockpile, including gauze and the required materials to stitch himself up.

Knox inspected the flesh wound in the mirror, the red slash a straight graze across the thick roundness of his shoulder. It still hurt like hell, but it was relatively easy to manage.

The heavy scent of cooking meat had already wafted

his way when he finished taping on the last piece of gauze. He'd had worse, and he counted himself lucky Moray had such rotten aim.

Grown soft sitting behind a desk, old man?

Although the thought wasn't entirely off base, Knox quickly banished it. He'd suspected Moray was up to something, but he had sorely underestimated just how deep the man's corruption ran. He'd do well not to assume a paunch, and a penchant for issuing orders equaled a lack of skill.

The T-shirts Gabriella had mentioned were stacked neatly on a shelf in a large closet—as ruthlessly organized as the woman's kitchen—and he snagged one on the top. The name of a vineyard covered the upper-left corner.

He recognized the vineyard—had just had a glass of their wine with room service, as a matter of fact—and marveled again at what she had built. Although he'd been out of it when he first arrived, he hadn't missed her impressive setup. A large class area in the front of shop, with the industrial kitchen in the back.

He'd done his homework on Dallas before coming here, and the area where Gabby and her friends had built their businesses—the Design District—had caught his attention from the first. Old warehouses, built along the banks of the Trinity River, had lain empty or underused for many years. The design community had brought the area back and turned it from decrepit to a bit dodgy about two decades before, using the large spaces as a place to sell wholesale furniture, fabrics and art. But it was the past five years or so when the area had really come back to life, even more vibrant than its roots.

Storefronts, ad agencies and several restaurants had turned the Design District into a successful business community. The addition of apartments had turned it into a home.

He'd heard from several old friends the same was happening in Manchester and that he should come see for himself, but he'd managed to avoid a trip thus far. He had no desire to go home and wanted even less to see how the near slums he'd grown up in had gentrified through outsiders' money.

"You okay?" Her voice drifted toward him from the kitchen.

The question pulled him from the images he still carried of gray-washed factories that matched even grayer air. He didn't care how much money had been put into an update, he had no desire to see it.

"I'm good." He'd already taken one of the plastic medical waste bags in the first-aid kit and wrapped his bloody T-shirt, her cloth napkins and the waste from his stitch-up job into the red plastic.

As he glanced at the still-open bag, he caught the light scent of her on the air—a mix of vanilla and maybe lavender?—before his gaze roamed over the crumpled bloody shirt.

Why had he come here?

He'd exposed her, as surely as if he'd sent an email straight to Richard Moray with her name and address. That damnable voice tickled the back of his mind once more. *Don't underestimate Moray.*

Not only had he done that, but he'd dragged an innocent into battle right along with him.

He wrapped the package into as small a ball as he could, then shoved it into another of his cargo pockets. He wouldn't leave Moray's stench anywhere near Gabriella Sanchez.

And if he weren't such a bastard, he'd remove himself, as well.

* * *

Gabby kept her eye on the chicken sautéing in a large pan while she pounded the flank steak for the beef enchiladas. She could still remember her grandmother's gentle voice, instructing her in the old kitchen on Castle Street on how to prepare the steak before cooking.

"Pounding the meat's better than pounding your grandfather."

She smiled at the old flash of memory and the giggles that had erupted at the imagined image of Tito Jorge beaten under her grandmother's meat tenderizer. Gabby still grieved the loss of her beloved grandfather, more than a decade now, and she knew her grandmother grieved, as well. Theirs had been a love for the ages, and Gabby had believed herself destined for the same.

Yet here she was.

She'd spent her twenties lamenting her inability to find someone and had sworn to herself on her thirtieth birthday that she was done with sulking and being disappointed. But the memories of her grandparents—so in love—still managed to grab her by the throat every now and again.

On a sigh, she brought herself back to the moment. The kitchen on Castle Street had long since been renovated, the near-decrepit appliances updated with brand-new ones, and her grandmother had moved back with her youngest daughter and son-in-law in Mexico for the majority of the year. Gabby still missed her every day, but she knew her grandmother loved the quieter life in Guadalajara more than the increasingly frenetic pace in Dallas.

"That smells good."

She turned to see Knox, clad in a gray T-shirt that was a size too small, and she struggled to keep her footing. What was it about this man? He'd invaded her business. Hell, he'd *handcuffed* her.

And she still couldn't quite shake the raw interest he managed to gin up.

She also couldn't deny the sheer exhaustion she saw in his liquid blue gaze.

"I've got a cot in the storage room, as well. You're welcome to pull it down and set yourself up in my office."

"I'm good."

"You're dead on your feet. I thought you *were* dead on your feet an hour ago."

"I'll recover. This isn't the first—" He broke off, and she turned back to the meat, a small smile tugging at her lips. He might not want to admit how tired he was, but the abrupt cutoff was indicative of his exhaustion.

Now the real question was, how much could she get out of him?

Avoiding the twinge of guilt at the deliberate hunt for information, Gabby settled in to find out all she could. "Okay, big, strong man. Then go sit down and get out of my way."

"Do you mind if I put on a pot of coffee?"

"Along the wall. I've got a single brew, and you can pick whatever you'd like in the top cabinet."

Knox busied himself with the task, and she snapped off the gas, transferring the heavy pan to the counter and a waiting rack. Her grandmother had taught her many things, and the draining of the meat was key to keeping the enchiladas soft but not soggy.

"Would you like a cup?"

"No on the coffee, but I'd love one of the green teas in there."

Knox settled across from her a few minutes later and pushed over her mug. "That really smells good."

"It'll smell even better wrapped up in fresh tortillas and cheese."

"Don't tease me."

"Maybe if you sit there nicely and keep your hand-cuffs in your pocket I'll give you some."

He did perk up at the mention of the cuffs, a small spark of mischief alighting in his eyes. "I'll be good."

The promise was about the enchiladas—rationally, she knew that—but she couldn't quite dismiss something else in the words.

I'll be good.

Did she really want him on his best behavior?

Ignoring the flight of sexual fancy, she refocused on the man before her. He might wear it well, but she had to admit exhaustion still painted his face in craggy lines.

Once more, that slight twinge of guilt pinched the back of her neck, but she resolutely ignored it as she changed the subject. "You're MI5, right?"

"Technically, we're the Security Service. MI5 is no longer our formal name, but it is what we're known as."

"I thought the jewels were originally removed out of England under the direction of MI6."

His heavy-lidded gaze widened before he caught himself, his normal poker face snapping into position. "How'd you come across that information?"

Gabby shrugged, playing it cool. While she sensed she should parse out what limited information she'd gleaned, she was more than willing to speed up the information exchange if it would ensure her friends stayed safe and the danger they'd all experienced was firmly put behind them.

"Lilah, Cassidy and Violet have told me what they've

been dealing with," Gabby offered up. "And don't forget, the rubies belong to my friends' landlady, Josephine Beauregard. Her father was given the gems fair and square and asked only to remove them from England."

"Why?"

Why?

Although she knew she'd started this, his questions held something more than simple curiosity. *He didn't know.*

"Because they're cursed." A low snort was her only response, so she pressed him, curious as to his response. "You don't believe in curses?"

"No." He took a sip of his coffee before something seemed to register in his mind. "Do you?"

"Of course."

When he only continued to stare at her, his cup midway to his mouth, Gabby continued on. "I absolutely believe in things beyond our control. Forces for good. Forces for evil. They exist."

"And you think the rubies are cursed?"

"I think the Renaissance Stones carry a force inside them, imprinted from years and years of greed and avarice. I think the Queen Mum was smart to ask them to be removed from England, and I think my friends are well rid of them."

"Why did she ask for their removal?"

"I thought you knew all this. Isn't that why you're here?"

Knox only stared at her, that unyielding blue giving nothing further away. With icy fingers, a whisper of premonition skated over her spine.

"Why are you here?"

"I'm a member of the British government, assigned to deliver those gems safely back to England."

She wanted to believe him—and not because he was the first man in an age and a half who'd managed to hold her interest longer than five minutes—but she refused to accept blatant lies. With careful movements, she settled her carving knife down on the counter and moved toward the large drawer at her hips.

"Not buying it."

"It's the truth."

With lightning-quick reflexes honed from being the only sister in the midst of a horde of rough-and-tumble brothers, she had her handgun out of the drawer and pointed toward Knox in a handful of heartbeats. "I'm only going to ask once more. Why are you really here?"

Chapter 3

Knox stared down the barrel of the impressively steady semiautomatic and figured he had exactly thirty-three seconds to make up a plausible story. She'd gotten the jump on him; that was for sure.

Maybe he was more exhausted than he'd wanted to admit.

Cycling through what he knew, Knox tried to figure out what pieces of the truth he could use to distract her. There was no way she could know about Moray or where he suspected the man's influence extended. But he also needed to give her something.

Hell, after a midnight arrival that included bleeding all over her kitchen supplies, he owed her that much.

Gun or no gun.

Gabriella glanced toward the door, and he was reminded of her earlier statement. *My brother's a cop. He patrols this dodgy area regularly.*

For his money, he wasn't sure she needed the additional surveillance, but he pressed on.

"Those gems belong back in England."

"Says who?"

That gun stayed remarkably steady, but the fierce notes of protection had faded slightly from her stance. His first inclination was to disarm her, but he was too damned tired to try anything. And while she'd surprised him with having the gun in the first place, he wasn't actually concerned she'd shoot.

Her brother was likely another story, so he'd do well to avoid police interference.

"Says the British government."

"The government doesn't control the royal family's possessions."

"No, but they should have some say and influence over a political gift. And regardless of a decision made decades ago, those gems were given to England. They belong back in my country."

She seemed to waver slightly before she let out a hard sigh and lowered the gun. "Possession is nine-tenths and all that."

Knox fought the urge to squirm, the rubies in his cargo pocket suddenly like lead weights beneath the countertop. "A delightful American colloquialism to indicate you can take whatever you want."

"It was a gift that was subsequently turned over to Mrs. B's father. Cassidy even found a letter from the king and queen that thanked her father for taking the gems and removing them."

Knox stilled at that. "A letter?"

"Or more to the point, provenance."

He filed that detail away. Moray's behavior was deeply rooted in a lack of ethics, but something that denoted such clear ownership made the Security Service's claims on the gems far harder to justify. Considering a different tack, he pressed an earlier point. "You said yourself your friends are well rid of the gems."

"Perhaps I was too hasty."

Unbidden, a kernel of panic took root in his belly. Her friends were lucky. And from what he knew and a few other aspects he'd pieced together, they were all fortunate to have escaped with their lives. "This isn't a problem for civilians to concern themselves with."

"Too late."

"Or just in time."

Although she didn't reset her aim, Gabriella's gaze drifted toward the gun before snapping firmly back to his. "That doesn't mean your arrival isn't worrying and suspicious. No one knew about the gems three weeks ago. Since then, my friends have discovered the rubies, uncovered corruption in the police department and dealt with a horrible threat from a well-respected business-man. Now MI5 shows up? How is it all connected?"

He'd figured out about three minutes after meet-ing her that Gabriella Sanchez wasn't a woman to be underestimated. The gorgeous exterior and lush body was an easy distraction, but a whip-quick mind lived underneath.

He couldn't tell her they'd kept tabs on Josephine Beauregard for years. Nor would he share that the high-est levels of British intelligence had information on all of Tripp Lange's nefarious dealings, a catalog that began when they caught wind a few years back he was nosing around about the gems. That one got awfully sticky be-cause they knew about the man's unsavory side prac-tices and hadn't bothered to share the information.

Avoid sharing that one with the class, mate.

Although he wasn't going to provide extensive details about Lange, he could use the man to his advantage. "Tripp Lange's involvement is being dissected now."

"What's there to dissect? He betrayed his wife and stepson, lying to them both. He manipulated his position as a wealthy businessman to buy off members of the police department. He even put out a hit on Reed and Lilah."

Reed Graystone had been as suspicious of Knox's presence as Gabby, but Knox's badge had gone a long way toward reassuring the cop. Reed had taken the time to fill Knox in on his stepfather's activities and the hit Gabby spoke of—cut brake lines that had caused an accident Reed and Lilah were lucky to walk away from—was proof positive of Lange's mania to possess the gems.

A mania that seemed to extend to Moray, as well.

Was it even possible the jewels were to blame?

Although he didn't doubt their value, the hysteria surrounding their retrieval bordered on obsession.

Dark obsession and a desperate need to possess.

Again he was conscious of the weight against his thigh, and if he focused on the gems he could feel their hard edges. Each was roughly the size of a strawberry— small in the scheme of things, yet massive in the gemology world—and he knew from their history many had killed to possess them.

The ringing of her cell broke the moment, and Gabby eyed the device. On a small sigh, she flipped the safety and shoved the gun back in the drawer she'd pulled it from, then answered the call.

"I'm good."

Although Knox only got half the conversation, it wasn't hard to piece together what was being said.

"I'm working late, that's all. Mama wants enchiladas for the party tomorrow, and I couldn't get to them earlier." She paused a moment before quickly talking over whatever was being said on the other end of the line. "There's no need to stop by on rounds. I'm almost done and trying to get out of here."

Knox watched, fascinated, as she worked her way around the kitchen. She was a full participant in the conversation with her brother, but she managed to multitask her way through the conversation, pulling a large metal bowl from the fridge, then hip-bumping it closed.

She added several quick comments—barbs, really— in Spanish and it was hard to miss the small layer of frustration beneath.

"I'm fine, Ricardo. And I already made you an extra batch, so you can quit bugging me already. Good night. I love you, too."

She shoved the phone in her back jeans pocket and walked toward a stacked set of trays on the far wall. The trays settled onto a base that rolled, and she dragged the entire set back to the counters along with the bowl.

"Your brother?"

"Who else?"

"Does he always call you this late?"

"When he's on rounds and he sees my lights he does." Gabby looked up from where she carefully pulled light towels off the top of a tray of fresh tortillas. "You're lucky he didn't just show up."

"Why didn't he?"

"He was called to an accident during his earlier drive-by. Something going on downtown in the park. You wouldn't know anything about that, would you?"

"No."

As the lie tripped off his tongue, Knox was suddenly glad Gabby had put the gun away.

"No?"

"It's the same answer you'd give your brother if he asked you what's going on here."

"I don't lie to my family."

"You sure about that?"

Something small ticked behind her eye, and Gabby focused on uncovering the chicken mixture she'd prepared earlier for the first batch of enchiladas. She snatched a fresh tortilla from her tray, muttering a low curse when the soft disc tore down the middle. "I don't lie."

"Would you prefer omission, then?" He extended a finger toward the bowl of meat she'd drained off, but she was quicker, smacking the back of his hand.

"You were bleeding over the floor an hour ago. Don't touch."

"I cleaned up."

"You're still not sticking your fingers in my food. Grab a plate and a fork if you'd like some. Third cabinet from the sink. Forks are in the drawer below."

He followed her directions and snagged a large spoon, as well.

"That's more like it. Take as much as you want."

He tucked into the food, and she was pleased to see he ate well—rushed even—before catching herself. How, where or what he ate was none of her business. Nor was the increasing color in his cheeks any of her business, either.

"This is good."

She added a few tortillas to his plate. "Those'll make it even better."

His words still rattled around in her brain with increasing discomfort. She wasn't a liar, but the sin of omission had increasingly become her friend of late, and she wasn't quite sure what to do about it. Her family hadn't given her a choice, their increasing pressure on her personal life like a vise, squeezing out all the air.

So she filled tortillas like her grandmother taught her and lined them up neatly in a greased pan. She'd save the sauce for tomorrow before she headed out for the party, keeping the tortillas as fresh as possible.

"You're fast."

"I've been making these since I was seven."

"Impressive."

"My grandmother saw I had an interest, and she both indulged me and taught me."

"You miss her."

"I do. I still see her fairly often, but it's not the same as every day."

"She's the one you tell the truth to, isn't she?" That quiet voice was silky, weaving its way through her thoughts like wispy puffs of smoke.

His understanding struck her as an almost absurd counterpoint to his earlier statement. "I thought you said I lie to my family."

"Omit." When she only raised an eyebrow at him, he continued, "To the rest of them, but not to your grandmother."

How did he *know* that? Lucky guess? Or was it something more?

Gabby had never believed herself to be a sensitive sort. She respected the talents of others—and believed in the things she couldn't see—but she didn't have any personal skill for sensing the supernatural.

Knox struck her as possessing a strong streak of practicality, in no way prone to the psychic, so how did he know that about her family? Or, more specifically, about her grandmother?

Even without a sensitive bone in her body, she couldn't deny the stones had wrought major changes since their discovery. Was it really possible there was something deeper at play?

Ever since Cassidy, Lilah and Violet found the Renaissance Stones buried in the floor of their business, nothing had been the same. Yes, each had found love— Cassidy with Tucker Buchanan, Lilah with Reed and Violet with Max Baldwin.

Each woman had narrowly escaped danger, too.

Was it all because of the mysterious rubies?

While none of them could deny the danger that had come as a result of finding the stones, she wanted to believe her friends had found men they truly loved. Their loves weren't simply heat-of-the-moment flings. No, they had something real.

Something permanent.

Gabby glanced up, her swirling thoughts vanishing as she realized Knox's gaze hadn't wavered. He continued to stare at her with that enigmatic blue fire that seemed to light up his eyes. The man was compelling, no doubt about it. And when she finally figured out what she thought about that, there was no doubt she'd mention Knox to her grandmother.

In the meantime, she acknowledged his words. "No. I don't omit anything with my grandmother. She's the one I talk to about anything and everything."

But she hadn't mentioned the rubies.

She dropped the last rolled tortilla into the tray before wiping her hands. Although her grandmother was a vault, the story of the Renaissance Stones hadn't been hers to tell. It wasn't omission so much as privacy.

And a very real fear that by talking about them she'd bring the same danger to her family's door that had already been laid on her friends.

Richard Moray hunched down in his car and scanned his phone, plotting out his next move. The device carried the absolute latest in government encryption software and he'd added a few tweaks of his own. Even if someone back at HQ had wanted to track him, all of its data continued to transmit as if he were sitting at his desk in London, bright and early Greenwich Mean Time.

He was an early riser—everyone knew it. Besides, no one was tracking him. He'd covered his plans well—webs woven within webs—and he'd spent his life cultivating a personality that was part civil servant, part Security Service cheerleader and part purveyor of justice.

But he was always—*always*—100 percent for queen and country.

Until bloody Knox St. Germain started digging beneath the facade. He'd hired the damn boy, for the love of all that was holy. Hell, even for that which wasn't. He'd trained him and ensured the Manchester street rat had a future. And Knox had turned on him.

Moray rubbed at his knee, the hasty tourniquet nearly as uncomfortable as the grazed flesh. Oh, how his protégé had turned.

Moray flipped through the web pages he'd already bookmarked, including the catering shop owned by one

Gabriella Sanchez. *Taste the Moment.* The sultry dark-haired beauty smiled back at him from the web page, and he fought the small shot of interest that sparked at her beautiful face. She was a siren, no doubt about it. But that long mane of curly hair and the thick, lush lips were a distraction, nothing more.

She was helping Knox.

Although, if he knew his boy, he also knew Knox was a sucker for a pretty face.

Moray glanced down at the image once more, considering how he might use this to his advantage. He'd been focused on circumventing Gabriella, pulling Knox away from her business to get him out in the open.

Perhaps he needed to rethink his strategy.

Ignoring the throbbing in his knee, Moray tapped into the architectural plans for the area. The work of a few keystrokes, he marveled to himself as he caught sight of a slow-moving police cruiser in the rearview mirror. He cycled through what he already knew of Gabriella and her family and realized the answer was nearly in front of him. Never one to miss an opportunity, he went to work.

With a hard shove, he pushed on his car door and fell to the ground.

Gabby finished stuffing the last of the enchiladas and had put Knox to work at the sink washing her pans. Admittedly, she was surprised when he'd said yes to the job.

Even more admittedly, she'd admired the sculpted fit of his cargo pants over slim hips and a high, tight ass as he worked over the sink. It was late, and he was the one who'd made himself at home. The least she could get out of this entire situation was a chance to enjoy the view.

When he stiffened, she was pulled from her thoughts. "Is your shoulder okay?"

He shot her a grin over his good shoulder. "Nice of you to ask me now, sweetheart. I just finished the last pan."

"Just because I want you to earn your keep doesn't mean I'm not concerned."

His smile never wavered as he turned back to the sink and flipped off the tap. "Whatever helps you sleep, love."

She ignored the endearments—she would *not* be affected by the patter of a serial dater—and snorted as she covered the last pan with foil. "I sleep just fine. And will sleep even better knowing I conquered five pans of enchiladas."

The task had gone quicker with his help, and as she rubbed the tension out of her lower back she had to admit it had been nice to have company beyond the radio or one of her telenovelas she kept perpetually recorded on the kitchen DVR.

"I'll be out of your hair soon. Go ahead home, and I'll take the cot in your office."

"I told you I'd see you through until morning."

"So share the cot with me."

The thought struck so hard—so deep and low in her belly—Gabby had to catch her breath. She *would* like to take him up on that all-too-enticing offer more than she could describe.

And far more than she'd even realized.

Admiring a well-sculpted body was one thing. Contemplating sleeping with said body was another matter entirely.

Quickly tamping down on the images that flooded her mind's eye of the two of them entwined on her small sleep cot, she didn't miss the sexy blue gaze that zeroed in on her from the sink. "We'll just sleep."

"You are running a fever."

"Of a sort."

The desire that edged his gaze was heady, and she felt herself being reeled in by the hot body, the late hour and the attraction she'd already fought for a few days now.

Fighting the urge for all of the above, she walked the large pan toward the fridge and resolutely kept her gaze from his. She would *not* spar with him on this. It was self-preservation, she promised herself as she pulled open the door and allowed the cool air to flow over her heated skin.

Yep. Self-preservation.

She'd nearly had herself convinced when that sultry voice of his—lilting with the devil's own music—whispered in her ear. "You're not curious?"

"No."

She meant to sidestep the advance. Truly, she did. But as the heat of his body covered her back and the heat of his words filled her, something inside her simply rooted her feet to the spot.

"Not even a bit?"

"No."

He didn't touch her, but she felt his body move a fraction of an inch closer. "You sure?"

The urge to close the gap between their bodies nearly overwhelmed her; the mix of cool air at her front and hot, wicked heat at her back was nearly her undoing.

It was only the hard rap at the back door that had her coming out of the trance he'd woven around her.

"Who the bloody hell is that?" Before she could even

turn around, Knox was halfway to the door. "Get in your office. Now."

"No!" She slammed the fridge door closed and followed him to the delivery entrance, reality quickly intruding. "It's probably my brother. He can't see you."

She rushed in front of him, anxious to cut Ricardo off at the pass. Her fingers flew over the alarm pad and she sideswiped Knox when he tried to stop her.

"He sees my light. Just let me deal with this. Go get back in the office."

"You don't know who—" His voice echoed behind her, calling her back, but she already had the door open, swinging it wide on its hinge.

The warm tension that had filled her system only moments before vanished, replaced with black ice. A small scream crawled up her throat as she took in the sight of her brother, a gun pressed to his forehead, standing before her on her doorstep.

Chapter 4

Knox moved immediately, the instincts that spiked at the knock on Gabriella's door going into overdrive. He'd clearly underestimated Moray's determination to possess the rubies.

Or just how far around the bend his old boss was.

"Ricardo!" Gabriella stumbled away from the door before straightening, clearly intending to hold her ground. "What is this? Who—"

Knox dragged her away from the door, well aware the semiautomatic pointed at her brother could just as quickly be turned on her. The ready image of the gun she'd pulled on him earlier had Knox calculating the odds, and he almost made a break for the small drawer in the kitchen.

But he couldn't leave her side. Couldn't leave her exposed. Even if he was the bloody damned reason she was exposed in the first place.

He never should have come here. Never should have sought sanctuary with the sexy cook with the broad smile and the hot body and the storm clouds behind her eyes she tried so hard to hide. But there were a lot of things in his life he regretted, and he'd just need to add this one to a very long list.

Ricardo struggled against the hold, his focus on his sister. "Gabby. Run!"

Knox took quick stock of his opponent. Gabriella's brother Ricardo was a solid man, and Knox put him around five-ten. Although Moray didn't have the man beat in thickness, he had three more inches and a background of lethal training that obviously still served him well. The position of his chokehold and the steady pressure of the pistol brooked little argument.

Ricardo whispered a hard stream of Spanish, and Knox did the translation in his head.

What's going on here? Who are these men?

Moray answered for her. "You're not my focus, Officer. I want what I came for, and then you can go on your way."

Knox knew better.

They basically stood inside a shooting gallery, and no one was walking away save Moray. He had to get him away. *Get Moray's focus off Gabby and her brother and on the man's ultimate goal—the rubies.*

"These good people don't have what you want."

"They're the conduit to it, which is all that matters."

Avarice lined Moray's face like a mask, and in that moment Knox finally understood what he was truly up against. His boss—a well-respected, multigenerational member of Britain's Security Service—had fooled them all. "They're not a part of this."

Moray pressed the tip of the gun harder into Ricardo's forehead. "They are now."

Ricardo shifted his feet at the steady press, and Knox knew the man had already calculated how to disarm his captor. While he'd normally give a man of Ricardo's size and expertise a wide berth, he knew the stakes Moray played for. Priceless gems and a trio of people he couldn't afford to leave alive.

Understand your opponent's goal.

His Security Service training had given him all the tools he needed, and now he had to disarm the man who'd taught him all he knew. Ignoring the deep remorse at that thought, Knox focused on execution.

The gems he'd retrieved earlier that night were heavy in his pocket, as if history, greed and violence were layered over their endless facets like lead weights. His fingers drifted to rest at the edge of the largest thigh pocket in his cargo pants, and he quickly cycled through every other option available to him.

No time to get to Gabby's gun.

No range to disarm Moray without compromising Ricardo.

No way out.

"I have what you're looking for."

"Show me." Moray's voice remained as steady as his gun, but something sparked beneath the menace that already lined his gaze.

"Let the man go."

"Show me!"

Knox flipped open the small button that kept the pocket closed, then slipped his fingers inside. Even with the heat of his body, the three gems had retained an odd coolness, as if nothing could warm them. Shaking off the odd impression, he drew the gems from his pocket.

He'd placed the rubies on the same side of his body as his injured shoulder and the flesh burned at the movement, a match for the fire that burned in the stones' facets as they caught the light. Gabby's heavy inhale shimmered in the air, but Knox kept his focus on Moray.

Understand your opponent's goal.

Ricardo had stilled at the sight of the gems, as captivated by them as his captor was. But it was Moray who held Knox's sole focus.

He had one try to get this right.

One opportunity to keep Gabby and her brother safe.

Moray had done a fair job of hiding it, but he clearly favored his left leg. Proof Knox's shot earlier that night had hit its goal. The fire that lit up his shoulder had to have a match in Moray's knee.

Time to let it rage out of control.

"You'll take the rubies and go?" Knox asked.

"Of course. As you said, these good people aren't a part of this."

"Then prove it."

Knox moved in a blur of motion, his foot kicking out toward Moray's knee as he moved forward in a bull's stance. He nearly cried out as his injured shoulder connected with Moray's chest, but he pressed on, the fire shooting through his midsection suitable punishment for the havoc he'd brought to this doorstep.

Moray cried out like a wounded animal at the kick to his knee, and the man's sudden pain acted as the conduit Knox intended. The man let go of his tight hold on Ricardo, his arms windmilling as he attempted to right himself. The added weight of Knox's tackle had the gun flying into the air, fully freeing Ricardo as Moray stumbled over his feet out the back door.

"Get her out of here!" Knox screamed the order at Gabby's brother as he followed his opponent down toward the gravel driveway.

Gabby dragged Ricardo from the door, relieved to feel his solid—and whole—form in her arms. "You're okay."

"Gabriella." Her name fell from his lips before he turned toward the door. A series of loud grunts and groans echoed up at them from the back entryway. "What is going on?"

A heavy grunt sounded from a few feet away. Her gaze fell on Knox as he struggled on the gravel with the heavy press of the stranger's body.

She'd bet anything the man who'd captured her brother had been the same one she'd seen earlier skulking outside her business. Knox rolled over the ground with the man, shouts and screams building in the night air.

And the rubies! He had the gems he'd sworn he wanted to protect.

Why did he have them?

While she wanted to watch the drama playing out on her back drive, she needed to get her brother out. Hell, she needed to get herself out.

So why wouldn't her feet move?

Her brother spoke behind her, his voice urgent as he barked orders. She heard the distinct request for backup and whirled to face a fresh threat. "No, Ricardo! No police."

Ricardo already had her arm, pulling her away from the door. "What is wrong with you? These men are criminals."

"They're—" She broke off, the hard truth as plain

as the struggle on her back drive. They were supposed to be protectors. Men of the law.

Yet they fought over the rubies. Were clearly prepared to kill for them.

"Get out of here!" Knox's shout carried up to her, the lilting tones of England doing nothing to hide the clear set of orders.

Even with the direct order, she couldn't walk away. Couldn't leave him.

"Gabs?" Ricardo had his gun drawn, indecision painting his features in the soft wash of lights reflecting through the door. "What is going on here?"

"I'll explain later."

He tugged on her arm once more, pulling her away from the fight even as she tried to walk forward. "You'll explain now."

"You won't order me around like I'm seven."

"Then don't act like it. This is hardly the playground. Who are those men?"

"This is none of your concern."

"You're my concern!"

She knew her brother's anger was more than valid—and were the situation reversed, she'd feel the same—but she didn't need his interference or the overprotective routine right now. Knox was in danger.

Dragging her arm from Ricardo's, Gabby moved back to the door, the violent tableau still playing out like some strange movie come to life. Knox grappled with the other man, and, despite what had to be nearly debilitating pain in his shoulder, he fought on.

A hard grunt rose up as Knox fully divested his opponent of his gun. The lethal piece flew across her service driveway just as the distinctive sound of backup filtered out of the communicator Ricardo wore on his shirt.

Her brother screamed out orders, his service pistol in hand. She had no interest in getting between her brother's hard-pumping adrenaline and the enemy that had shown up at her back door, but she couldn't let him take a shot.

Knox and the man he fought continued to roll over the back drive, another hard grunt rising up into the hot August night as Knox's opponent slammed a fist into Knox's shoulder. At the impact of the punch, the rubies flew through the air, landing a few feet away.

Without wasting any further time, the man leaped up, racing toward the stones where they lay glittering in the soft light of her garage lights. He scrabbled to pick up the stones, hesitating for the briefest moment before he took off, running out the back alley.

Gabby raced to Knox. His chest heaved with labored breaths as a fresh wash of blood stained his shoulder. "Are you okay?"

"Need…" He coughed hard. "Need to get out of here."

He struggled to his feet, another hard cough racking his chest before he stumbled in the direction of his opponent. "You need to sit down," she said.

He ignored her, pointing toward her car. "Give me your keys."

Her brother moved closer, his arms outstretched, his gun pointed at Knox. "Hands up!"

"Ricardo. Enough of this. He's not the problem." Gabby summoned up as much menace as she could, placing herself between Knox and her brother. "The problem is racing down the alley, and you're letting him get away."

"Gabriella Elena, move your ass now!"

She had a split second to decide her next move and offered up a quick prayer she was making the right choice. "I'm sorry, Ricardo. I'm so sorry."

With a hard flip of her hand, she employed a move Ricardo had taught her himself. Her foot slammed into his instep as her forearm slammed into his gun hand, rendering him unarmed and immobile all at once. As he doubled over toward his feet, she added the final blow—a hard knee to his solar plexus.

Refusing to look back, Gabby ran for Knox. "The car."

Her thick key ring felt heavy in her pocket as she dragged out her keys, flipping open the remote locks.

Knox's voice floated on the night air, his demands as infuriating as her brother's. "Give them to me."

"It's me or nothing. So move it."

He hesitated, struggle stamped clearly in his features. For the briefest moment she thought he was going to stay, his feet planted firmly on her back drive. And then he moved, diving into her car like a drowning man reaching for a raft. "Drive."

She could see her brother still bent over from where she'd debilitated him in the driveway, and a hard shot of remorse turned her stomach over in sickness. Ricardo wasn't a part of this, and she'd literally added insult to injury by turning his protection methods against him.

But…

Knox breathed heavily in the passenger seat, his gaze focused straight ahead as she navigated the alley, then turned onto the main drag of the Design District. Each storefront she passed was dark for the night, the various businesses blessedly free of the strange curse that had descended since Gabby's friends discovered three priceless gems.

"You need to go back."

Knox's voice punctuated her sober thoughts, and she turned toward him, surprised to see how intently he stared at her. "It's too late for that."

"No, it's not. The cops will be following soon, and it'll go much easier if you head back."

"I'm not heading back." She wove past the sports arena, keeping to the streets she'd known for a lifetime and prayed she had enough of a head start on Ricardo's backup.

"They'll find us quick enough. Between traffic cameras and your no doubt very determined brother, we're not going to make it another mile."

"You don't believe I can do this?"

"I think the odds are stacked against you."

His words lodged in her mind, their meaning taking root beyond the situation she found herself in.

Weren't the odds always stacked against her?

Your cousins have all met nice men, Gabriella. Why can't you?

Why do you want to run your own business?

Late nights by yourself at work are no place for a young woman. You should be out, meeting someone, instead of stuck in with your ovens.

With a hard right, she swung east and headed toward her grandmother's old house. Although there was always a chance someone was bunking there, as far as she knew the place was empty tonight.

"Where are you going?"

"My grandmother's old house down in the Cliff. We've kept it for family events, but it should be empty tonight."

"Good. I'll call a cab from there."

Her cell rumbled from her back pocket like a warning, just before the Bluetooth connection in her car rang. Her brother's name came up on the dash but she ignored it, sending the call to voice mail.

"He's obviously gotten his wind back."

The wry comment wasn't lost on her as another shot of remorse tilted her stomach at the remembered image of Ricardo doubled over. "My brother's made of tough stuff."

"So, apparently, are you. Those are some moves you've got, Miss Sanchez."

"They should be. With five brothers, I've had no choice but to keep up. Ricardo was the one to teach me that particular sequence."

"I suspect he regrets that choice right about now."

"I suppose so."

She brushed off thoughts of her brother, unwilling to let the creeping guilt swamp her or change her mind. Knox was hurt, and while she had no idea why she felt this bone-deep urge to help him, she did. It was that simple and that complicated, all at once.

"Will he follow you?"

"Probably. But he's not going to think of where I'm taking you."

"Why not?"

"He won't." Gabby didn't know how she knew, but somehow she did. She had a connection with her grandmother, and while her brothers loved their *abuela*, they didn't have the same kinship—or affection—for the family home.

She sped over the Margaret Hunt Hill Bridge, a relatively recent addition to Dallas's skyline. She'd lived there her entire life, but the past decade had seen more physical change to the landscape than the prior four combined. Industry. Construction. And a constant evolution marked the city she called home.

"I've seen this bridge from my hotel but haven't been over it. Impressive."

Gabby cleared the bridge over the Trinity River and pressed on, tearing through the roads that led into Oak Cliff. The bridge probably wasn't the brightest idea. Its newness meant it had a far higher likelihood to have state-of-the-art cameras, but it was too late to worry about that now. A few more turns and she'd be at her grandmother's old house.

"The bridge gets me there in half the time."

"Clever."

"And it gives us Dallasites one more statement by marking the skyline."

"A race with London, then? Between the Shard and the Gherkin, we're well set with our own landmarks."

"A pickle?"

Knox laughed, the warm sound filling the car with subtle humor. "A relatively recent addition. It's hideously ugly, but a part of the new London. The building is officially called 30 Saint Mary Axe, but had been dubbed the Gherkin before it was even finished."

"I didn't think there was anywhere left to build in a city that old."

"The prior site was destroyed by the Provisional IRA in the early nineties. The Gherkin is the outcome of rebuilding."

Although she couldn't imagine any sort of destruction on that level, modern realities were such that nothing stood empty and barren for long. Much of Dallas's renaissance was tied to that very fact—valuable downtown land that was being slowly reclaimed from disuse and disrepair. "I guess not much can stand in the way of those pushing for growth. Even if it blots out what used to be."

"We humans are a determined lot." The humor vanished from his voice. "As evidenced by tonight."

"You want to tell me who that was? The man who attacked you."

"Not particularly."

"How about why you have the rubies?"

"*Had* the rubies. And the answer's the same. The less you know, the better."

While she'd managed to control her temper for much of the evening, she had no qualms about letting her feelings known. "You think keeping me in the dark will somehow keep me safer? Because now that your friend knows who I am and where I work, he's coming back after me."

"You don't need to worry about that."

"Why not?"

"Because I'm going to kill him."

Knox took little satisfaction in the sudden snap of Gabby's lips—their lush form had gone from open to firmly closed in a heartbeat—with his pronouncement of how he'd handle Richard Moray. He spoke fact, nothing more.

Even if she weren't involved, Moray had made his choices and put himself on this path. He'd gone rogue and proven himself more than willing to take out his fellow agents in his pursuit of his own goals. He needed to be put down.

Knox might have considered doing it within proper channels, capturing the man for eventual trial in London, but no longer. Gabriella was 100 percent right. Richard would come back after her.

No loose ends.

And there was no way he'd let Moray get close enough to her to hurt her.

But no matter how determined he might be, none of it changed the fact that she was in danger at the moment. He trusted her brother could take care of himself as well as depend on his backup, but the damn fool woman had decided to stick to Knox like glue, and he still didn't know what to do about it.

You're the only one who can protect her.

The thought had whispered through his mind since he'd climbed into the car with her.

Protection. Right, boyo. That's your only goal.

He ignored the nagging guilt and focused on the matter at hand. He needed to get his wound repaired, and he'd kill for a few hours of downtime.

And then he had to figure out a way to get her safe and secure before he went after Moray.

Knox knew MI5 kept several safe houses in the area, but he had no illusions Moray wasn't either already using one or would discover him if he attempted to utilize one. He had a few people he believed were untouched by Richard's stench back in London, but hated the idea of communicating their boss's betrayal from nearly five thousand miles away.

What a bloody, buggering mess.

He leaned his head back against the seat but kept his eyes open. He'd followed the series of streets she navigated, impressed at the ease with which she traveled her hometown. He figured he could reverse the drive if he needed to, even without the nifty GPS on his phone.

Gabriella took the last turn before Castle Street and

let out a small sigh. He recognized the relief for what it was—a mix of stress and fear—but refused to let her lower her guard.

"Don't relax now. Just because they're not here yet doesn't mean they're not coming."

She put the car in Park and turned to face Knox. "How'd you know that?"

"You checked your mirror every two seconds for the cops." Knox leaned in, the subtle scent of her catching his voice in his throat. He could still smell the food she'd cooked, and never in his life would he have thought peppers and onions could make such a tantalizing aphrodisiac. But it was the hints underneath—subtle notes of lavender that reminded him of a job he'd done in France—that caught him by the bollocks.

Now who was the damn fool?

Irritated beyond measure that she'd once again caught him off guard, he shoveled menace into his tone so that it bordered on a growl. Then he reached out and ran a finger over the high bone of her cheek, before drifting down to trace the firm line of her jaw.

Make her hate you.

"And you don't strike me as a bad girl, Miss Sanchez. I suspect this is the first bit of excitement you've had in some time."

"I'm doing just fine." Her comment held the slightest hitch, as if she fought the breathless quality that tinged her words.

"Are you? A good girl who lives under the protection of her family? Not much time for any naughty adventures, is there?"

Her pulse fluttered at her throat, and she swallowed hard but didn't move away from his touch. "I know how to take care of myself."

"You sure about that? Because one touch and you're falling at my feet. Willing to drive me anywhere I want to go." His thumb drifted over the thick fullness of her lower lip. "I wonder what else I can get you to do."

The hazy wash of need that filled her dark eyes vanished in an instant, and she smacked his hand away, the sound inordinately loud in the quiet, intimate confines of the car. "Don't underestimate me, Mr. St. Germain. I'm far more capable than I look."

He knew he was the worst sort of bastard and figured the tightly coiled need that had centered in his groin was his own personal punishment for the dirty playboy routine. But he was on a job, and he needed to use every weapon at his disposal. Even if his fingers still bore the imprint of her soft skin and hints of lavender still filled his nose with a sensual bouquet.

Gabriella slammed out of the still-running car and walked to the closed garage door. She bent at the waist and Knox added sick and twisted voyeurism to his list of sins that evening as his gaze traced the gorgeous lines of her backside before following the long lines of her legs.

Even without five-inch heels, the woman was a vision.

And she was no one's fool.

She hefted the garage door by the front handles, revealing a gleaming floor of concrete, empty save for a few lingering oil stains. Willing himself to look away from her and get a sense for his surroundings, Knox took stock of the garage, surprised to see a shiny black motorcycle in the far corner.

Was someone there?

Gabriella climbed back into the car and slid into the garage, hogging the double width straight up the middle. He nearly made a comment about the motorcycle but held his tongue. No use planting any ideas.

The ring of her cell phone echoed off the garage walls as they got out, and he tossed a glance over the top of the car. "You going to answer that?"

"Absolutely not." She shook her head before muting the ringer and shoving the phone back into her pocket. "Ricardo's pulled our oldest brother into this, and Miguel's not nearly as nice or understanding."

Nice? Understanding?

Knox knew damn well her brother Ricardo had put a target on his back. And the cop was the understanding one?

Although he'd teased her about being sheltered, using the taunt as a weapon to keep her off-kilter, he couldn't deny what a challenge that must be. To live with such oversight would be oppressive.

Was it because she was a woman? Or was it something more? He already understood, more by what she had hinted at than actually said, that she didn't meet some arbitrary set of expectations set by her family. He'd never considered himself a fanciful man, but had always assumed actually having a family meant they accepted you. Clearly the two concepts—family and acceptance—didn't always go hand in hand.

If she was still bothered by the call, it wasn't obvious as she crossed back to the garage door and pulled it closed with a firm tug on the inside handles. While he knew he needed to keep his focus on the end game— getting Gabriella to ditch him and never look back— Knox gave himself another moment to observe her.

She was self-sufficient; he'd give her that. If she wanted something done, she did it. The trek here at top speed. The multiple trays of food. Even something as simple as dealing with the garage door. If it needed to be done, she did it. No simpering or whining.

Just action.

It was an appealing quality. He knew several women who worked with him in the Security Service, and all had that proficiency of action and economy of motion, but he'd seen it very rarely in the average person.

Determination.

Many claimed what they wanted out of life, but too few went after it. Even at what appeared to be significant personal cost, Gabriella pushed ahead, focused on her goals.

He followed her up three small steps to the door into the house. She plucked a key out of her enormous key ring with unerring precision and had the door open in moments, gesturing him to follow. The house was dark, further reinforcement they were alone, and Knox wondered again about the motorcycle.

There weren't any keys sitting with the bike, but they'd likely be somewhere handy inside. A basket by the door or hanging on a peg. He'd considered appropriating her car, but the cops were looking for them, and the traffic cams would likely give him away before he got outside the city limits.

The motorcycle was his ticket out of there.

"The bathroom upstairs has a first-aid kit. I'll go get it and be right back. Sit at the table and don't bleed on anything."

"I'll do my best." The pain he'd managed to ignore on the drive over roared anew at the mention of his injury, and fire ate a path from his shoulder down his arm. Ignoring the instruction to stay put, he flipped on a small light over the stove and began rooting through the cabinets. His search produced a stash of liquor on the third door.

After dragging a nearly full bottle of whiskey out of the cabinet, he moved to the sink and pulled off his makeshift bandage of Gabriella's good catering napkins. Dropping each soiled piece into the sink, he took stock of the wound. As he expected, his stitch job had come undone. His bulldozer move on his boss had ruined his earlier work.

Recognizing there was no hope for what came next, Knox grabbed a wooden spoon from a ceramic container next to the stove and put it between his teeth. Then he leaned forward and poured the whiskey over his shoulder.

Stars exploded behind his eyes at the raw pain that threatened to knock him unconscious, and he bit down harder on the spoon to keep his focus. Unwilling to give the pain a chance to subside, only to start again, he poured another splash of whiskey on his shoulder.

"You stubborn ass!"

The dim lighting in the kitchen flickered on and off as he struggled to focus through his whiskey bath, but her voice and the gentle hands on his back pulled him from near oblivion.

"Imbécil!"

He translated the insult in his head—yes, he *was* the stupid idiot she accused him of being—even as he leaned into her steadying touch. She took the whiskey from his hand, then rubbed a steady path up and down his spine, the soothing motion at direct odds with her terse tone and dismissive insult.

"I figured you had to have a death wish to do what you do, but even I didn't guess just how much."

Those magic hands continued their steady press, up

and down, up and down, and Knox hung his head, the
weight of all he fought pulling him down. He hadn't
slept in who knew how long—not real sleep—and the
physical and emotional tension of the past day had taken
their toll.

He'd believed himself immune to Moray's betrayal—
he'd taken on this job, well aware his suspicions would
likely be proven correct—but somehow the reality
was worse than he'd imagined. Moray had been a role
model—a multigenerational member of the Security
Service.

And his betrayal stung worse than the whiskey.

"Better?"

Gabriella's voice penetrated the pain—in his shoulder *and* in his mind—and he wanted to sink into that
voice. Dark and sultry, the rich notes were a match for
the beautiful woman who bore them.

"I'm fine."

"Then sit down while I stitch you up."

"I can do it."

"So can I, and my hands are steadier." She exerted
light pressure on his back to get him moving and helped
him settle in one of the kitchen chairs.

Again, he was caught up in her efficient movements
as she busied herself around the kitchen. Two fresh
towels were pulled from a cabinet next to the stove,
followed by a long lighter from the next drawer over.

"What's with the lighter?"

"Sterilizing the needle."

In moments, she'd snapped on gloves and went to
work with the bright yellow flame, sterilizing one end,
then the opposite after giving the first enough time to
cool.

"You've done this before?"

"No." She winked at him, and he blinked, not entirely sure what he'd seen. "But I know how to stuff and sew up the hind end of a turkey, and I figure you can't be much worse."

"I require smaller stitches."

"I'll keep that in mind."

Her hands were gentle once more as she took his elbow firmly in hand. Knox closed his eyes and let her work. That lavender scent of hers drifted lightly over his senses while the heat of her body seemed to cradle him in her aura. The sensation was new—he hadn't been this close to a woman without touching her since he was fifteen—and he was oddly grateful for the steady pain of the needle and thread that kept him grounded.

This wasn't a seduction routine, nor was it a prelude to a night of passion, and he'd bloody well remember that.

The motorcycle.

The thought had his eyes popping open with the realization that now was his chance to scan the kitchen for the keys. His focus earlier had been on the cabinets, so he gave himself a moment to assess the rest of the room. The cabinets made an L shape along two walls, and a window sat opposite the table. Next to it was a phone that looked like it had been installed sometime when Elvis was alive, but it was the corkboard next to the ugly olive-green rotary dial that held the answer to his search.

Keys. Dangling off an emblem key chain advertising the motorcycle's brand plain as day.

A tug on his arm pulled him back to the task at hand, and he glanced down to see Gabriella putting a small knot at the end of his wound. "Nice job."

"You're tougher than a turkey, but the motions are the same."

Knox heard the slight quaver at the same time he caught sight of the subtle shake in her hand, and he laid his on top of hers. "You did a great job."

"Like I said, just like a—"

He caught her chin with the tips of his fingers before bending to close the gap between their mouths. The heat that had surrounded him while Gabriella stitched him up leaped straight to his groin, a transmission of raw need and broken defenses.

What was it about this woman?

She was beautiful, of course, but he'd never lost his head like this. Never put an assignment in jeopardy over his base emotions.

Her mouth was open, as if she waited for him, and he filled her with his tongue. The pain of only moments before vanished as if it had never been, as a wave of adrenaline pumped through his system, urging him on to brand her with his mouth.

The good girl he'd accused her of being was nowhere in evidence as she responded to his invitation to pleasure. She sucked on his tongue before biting his lower lip; the wanton invasion made him dizzier than an entire bottle of whiskey to his shoulder ever could have.

Who was she? This willing partner in a sensual exploration of just how far they could push each other? Hell, they were both fully clothed, and he wasn't sure he'd ever been more turned on in his life.

"You're not one to let a gunshot keep you down."

He knew he should resist—knew he should pull back and walk away—but so help him, he was rooted to the chair. Murmuring against her mouth, he smiled against her lips. "Consider it the power of your healing touch."

"Hmm." She smiled back before nipping a quick kiss. "Maybe I need to start stitching up men instead of turkeys and I might get a few more dates."

Whether it was the playful banter or the mind-numbing power of kissing Gabriella, Knox didn't know, but as he felt himself falling under once again, he struggled to surface.

Moray was still out there. The rubies were still out in the open. And she was still in danger.

So he pulled back, willing himself to look away from the dark, molten depths of her eyes and the pink lines of her mouth.

Walk away, boyo. It's the only way.

Forcing just the right amount of cocky, snotty Brit into his tone and manner, he began the campaign to piss her off and remove the persistent attraction that had a grip on both of them. "Do you have any painkillers?"

The sensual haze vanished as quickly as her smile as Gabriella sat back in her chair. "Like aspirin?"

"My shoulder hurts, love. A few minutes of mind-numbing snogging can't quite compete with a bullet wound."

Her body had gone liquid while they kissed, but at his request for aspirin her shoulders had gone poker-straight once more. The competent, confident woman, layered in full battle armor. "Right here in the kit. Let me get you some water."

She crossed to the sink, and Knox used her brief absence to head for the keys. The darkness outside the window made a perfect reflection in the dimly lit kitchen, and he made a big show of inspecting her handiwork in the soft light. "You did well, Gabriella."

His hand snaked out and snatched the keys. He was

careful to keep the ring still before he shoved his ticket out of there into the top pocket of his cargo pants.

"Take the aspirin." She held out the water, then ripped open one of the small two-capsule packets from the first-aid kit. "Here."

Knox downed the medicine, abstractly wondering if he'd do better with a chaser of what was left of the whiskey, then thought better of it. Driving through sleep deprivation and a buzz while navigating unfamiliar streets made about as much sense as going to Gabriella's in the first place. Since he was now unraveling that mistake, it wouldn't do to add another one.

"Any chance you've got a spare shirt lying around?"

"Likely several. I'll get you one."

She moved around him, stumbling as she pushed off the counter to give him a wide berth. Her body pressed full again his, her breasts outlined in exquisite detail against his biceps.

That same heat—the one that still branded his skin like an iron—covered his flesh. For the briefest moment Knox reconsidered his next move. He didn't want to leave her to fend for herself, and that was effectively what he was doing by ditching her at her grandmother's. She'd have family here in a matter of minutes, but none of it changed the fact that he was leaving her to deal with his mess all on her own.

More to the point, he didn't want to leave *her*.

"I'll be right back."

He counted to three in his head, then moved. Remorse dogged his heels, but he resolutely tamped that down, too. She was better off with him gone from her life. And the sooner he got on his way, the better.

The knob to the garage door was cool in his hand as

he twisted the handle, suddenly aware of the lightness in his pants pocket.

Slamming a hand against his thigh, he felt for the telltale sign of keys and came up empty.

"Going somewhere?"

As he turned toward the entrance to the hallway, Knox already knew what he'd find.

Gabriella leaned against the frame, the motorcycle keys dangling from the tip of her finger.

Chapter 5

Gabriella had learned long ago that besting the male of the species felt damn good. She made no bones about how much she enjoyed beating her brothers—at anything—and considered herself a fairly good sport when they defeated her in return. She'd seen Knox eyeing the motorcycle when they'd pulled into the garage, and it wasn't a major leap to getting left behind the moment he could make a break for it.

She just never expected the victory to feel quite as visceral—and shockingly sexual—as it did staring down those sky-blue eyes.

"Hand them over."

"I might be risking the wrath of my family by helping you, but there is no freaking way you're taking my grandmother's hog."

"Your grandmother? That motorcycle belongs to her?"

"It's her house, isn't it?"

"Yes, but—"

She fought back the smile and instead jangled the keys with a taunting jingle. "It's her pride and joy. And while she might not live here full time, she rides when she's home."

At the sheer shock that painted his face, she fought back another shot of pleasure. That would show him to think twice about making assumptions. About her or just how *good* she was.

The T-shirt ploy was as obvious as the kiss gambit, and she cursed herself for the knees that still shook from his mind-numbing lips. The man was lethally sexual, and no matter how many different ways she told herself to stay away, she couldn't stop dancing near his flame.

But none of it erased her personal victory with the keys.

"You're not a part of this. Hand them over, and I'll replace your grandmother's ride as soon as I'm able."

"Nope." She shoved the keys into her jeans pocket. While she enjoyed her victory, waving it in his face was tantamount to taunting a charging bull. She'd place her body between him and the keys and let the odds roll however they may.

"Gabriella. You're better off without me here. I shouldn't have come to your shop, and I'm sorry for that. Now it's time to correct that foolish action. Hand over the keys. I promise you, I will replace the bike."

Her stomach muscles tightened at the delicious sound of her name on his lips. She'd been Gabby or Gabs or even Rella to her small nieces, but very few used Gabriella. The syllables seemed to roll off his tongue with all the smoothness of velvet, and she couldn't deny how sexy it made her feel.

Which was dumb.

She was as *estúpida* as she'd accused him of being a short time earlier. Worse, if she were honest with herself. He was only attempting to repair a wound, whereas she seemed diligently focused on wrecking the world she'd built around herself.

He was a highly trained professional, comfortable with a gun and the seamier side of life. She catered parties and taught wine-tasting classes. Besides teaching kindergarten, she wasn't sure she could have found two lives further apart on a spectrum of danger, deception and risk.

Even the way he looked screamed lethal weapon. His cargo pants and thickly booted feet telegraphed his comfort with combat. He still wore the gray T-shirt, now covered in so many shades of dirt, driveway gravel and blood it was difficult to tell the base color. And when she'd sat next to him at the table their legs had brushed against each other, and she felt the distinct lines of a gun strapped to his calf.

Oh yes, Knox St. Germain is most definitely a lethal weapon.

"Why did you come to my shop?"

"You're a looker, love. And I didn't miss the heat you shot my way while we worked with your bridal shop friends. Figured it would be easy to get what I needed."

"Healing?"

"Downtime." He shot her a malevolent grin. "You added a bit of side entertainment with those healing lips."

His words once again bordered on rude—even crude—and not for the first time she questioned the odd decision to drive him away from the police. Yet even as she wanted to toss some pithy words back at him, something in his gaze held her back.

Was it remorse? Guilt even?

Maybe she could use that in her favor.

"Why did you have the rubies? I thought you were going to the park last night to help Lilah, Cassidy and Violet deal with Tripp Lange."

"A convenient cover."

"So you wanted to steal them."

"*Steal* is a nasty word. It suggests I had no right to them."

"You don't."

"On the contrary. Those rubies belong to the royal family. They were a gift to my country. I'm here to get them back."

She'd been round and round with her friends the other day after Knox's initial arrival at Elegance and Lace, and no one had quite agreed on the rightful ownership of the three gems.

Cassidy and Lilah resolutely argued for their landlady, Mrs. Beauregard, as it was her father who'd spirited the gems out of England at the Queen Mum's request. Max and Tucker had argued for England, their military training going a long way toward dismissing a rash decision made in wartime. Reed and Violet had seemed the most levelheaded. Both had suggested a solution to the immediate problem—namely, eliminating the threats that had sprung up around the stones' rediscovery and then making some sort of deal with the British government. Violet had even suggested pushing for a museum exhibit that featured Mrs. B's father's work—including the fake crown jewels he'd created during the Second World War—so his legacy could be properly celebrated.

"You seem awfully convinced of their ownership."

"Why the hell else would I be doing this?"

Although she knew Knox's statement was rhetorical, she did stop and pause. Why *was* he doing this?

The gems were historically important, but worth risking one's life? Absolutely not.

"They're valuable jewels."

"Priceless."

"I'd say your life is worth more."

He stilled at that, the hard lines of his body outlined in the door frame. "The work comes first."

"If you believe that, then your death wish is even more pronounced than I first thought."

Richard Moray worked his way past a highway overpass, ignoring the redolent stench of piss in the hot August night. What was it with this country? Bums that slept under the highway juxtaposed against the bright, glittery high-rises that made up the cityscape in the distance. He'd seen the same in New York and Philadelphia, but he had mistakenly believed a city as relatively new as Dallas wouldn't suffer from the same blight.

How wrong he was.

He patted the rubies he'd shoved in his pocket and continued his slow, steady limp onward. He needed a diversion to get into his hotel room and was debating between claiming an attack and a car accident when inevitably questioned by the concierge. While most hotel desk clerks granted a man his privacy, all were trained to know that gunshot wounds were serious business.

Damned St. Germain. He'd underestimated the whelp, convinced the boy would fall in line when he realized who'd been pulling the strings.

Did leadership and authority count for nothing any longer?

Memories of his own upbringing so many decades before at the hand of his father and uncle assailed him. "Multigenerational leadership," it was called nowadays, but he'd always just thought of it as the family business.

One that came with expectations of fidelity, commitment and discipline. And a relentless focus toward keeping Britain's interests intact and protecting what was rightfully the Crown's.

With a few nips for himself on the side.

He suspected his father and his uncle might have looked askance at his choices, but both had been gone a long time. Besides, things were different from back then. The gentleman's way of doing things had long passed, given up in favor of hunting terrorists who possessed not a shred of morality or decency on a global stage that grew more and more corrupt by the day.

He knew his limits—and he knew where his loyalties lay—so what real harm was there to take some for himself now and again?

Of course, the Renaissance Stones were rather more than "some." Although they were spoken of as priceless, he'd already investigated a few elite criminals who could find a way to fetch a rather tidy sum now that he had them in his possession. He patted his pocket, the stones still neatly nestled where he'd placed them earlier.

Although he'd lost his personal sense of awe and wonder years before, he had to admit he felt more than a few sparks now. The stones were his.

Finally.

His father's oldest brother had been part of the intelligence team that had kept record of the jewels. And it was his uncle who'd let it slip several years later that they were no longer on British soil. Even now, Richard's blood still burned at the mistaken idea something so rare and so prized had been dismissed with little more than a royal command.

The rubies were a treasure, presented to England as a diplomatic gift. And the ravages of wartime and some misguided belief in a curse had sent them merrily on their way with the Queen's jeweler.

The heavy honk of a truck's horn pulled him from his imaginings, and Richard moved to the side of the road, unaware he'd even drifted into the street. His knee burned with pain, and he ignored the damned horn, even if it had provided a ready reminder of what he needed to deal with.

St. Germain had seen him and knew his part in the stones' retrieval. Which meant he'd become collateral damage. One of his best, too. With a resigned sigh, Richard pulled his phone from his pocket. Might as well get things started.

St. Germain needed the tools MI5 could provide.

And those same tools would be his demise.

Death wish?

Knox wasn't sure he'd have stated it that way, but he could hardly argue with the sentiment. He'd chosen a dangerous profession and had deliberately volunteered for missions that veered toward the reckless end of the spectrum. And while he wasn't exactly anxious to die, he supposed he had accepted a long time ago that outcome was a distinct possibility.

No one gets out of here alive, anyway, boyo.

His father's words filled his thoughts, and he shook them off as quickly as they arrived. It didn't do to dwell, and memories of Marcus St. Germain inevitably led to a macabre sort of lingering. And the hard-won knowledge that no matter how safe and comfortable one believed themselves, it was all a mirage anyway.

"You do realize a death wish suggests I've got nothing to lose?"

One slim shoulder lifted in an attempted shrug. "If that's how you want to live your life, who am I to stop you?"

He pushed off the door frame and took a few steps toward her. "A man who has nothing to lose is a dangerous sort."

"You won't hurt me."

He took a few more steps, the edge of the kitchen table at his hip. "You seem pretty sure of that."

Gabriella shrugged again, but he saw the frayed edges of her nerves in the hard clench of her fists at her sides. "If you were going to hurt me, I presume you'd have done it by now."

"You presume too much."

"Do I?"

Knox had to admit he was reluctantly impressed. He'd moved close enough to see her pulse once again fluttering in her throat, but she stood her ground.

"Brave words."

"Or foolish. My family's accused me of both more than a time or two."

"They care for you."

"As I do them."

"So why are you helping me?" He knew he'd backed her into a corner when he'd arrived at her business, but her ready abandonment of her brother and seeming determination to help him had come as a shock.

"Because you need it."

For reasons he wasn't quite prepared to address, her words stopped him. He focused instead on what they implied.

From the first, Knox had sensed her family caused her any number of challenging moments, from over-protection to frustrated expectations. The knowledge came through in small ways—especially when they'd spoken of her cousin's party—and he'd have bet his life on the accuracy of his thoughts.

What he hadn't quite understood was the flip side of those very same emotions. Deep-seated devotion. Knowledge and awareness of one another. A kinship and willingness to look out for one another.

And woven all through and around was a love that she wore like an unconscious badge.

Her simple comment humbled him, and in that moment Knox knew the deepest sense of remorse. He should never have come to her tonight, no matter the strange lure that had pulled him to her door.

But now that he had, he was honor-bound to care for her and keep her safe.

Bright light streamed through lacy curtains, and Knox rolled onto his side to bury his head into the pillow. Pain radiated from his shoulder into his chest and back so quickly he saw stars behind his eyes, and he sat straight up in bed at the raw agony that consumed him.

Where the hell?

He squinted into the bright sunlight before taking in his surroundings, sleep subsiding in favor of ready alertness. He never slept that hard on a job.

Never.

So why couldn't he remember where he was?

Blinking a few times, he continued his steady catalog of the room. The pale, lacy curtains he'd noticed on opening his eyes lay against walls painted a deep shade of green. The mate of the twin bed he lay on was separated by the width of the window, and a dresser took up nearly the entire length of the opposite wall. The distinct whirl of air-conditioning hummed a steady tune, a counterpoint to the bright sun that already threatened another blisteringly hot Texas day.

He was in Gabriella's house, he remembered. Or her grandmother's, to be more precise. The life-affirming scent of coffee added to his catalog of his surroundings, and he pushed at the sheet that covered his naked ass.

Damn, but he'd slept hard.

He reached toward the floor for his pants, his hand coming up empty from the spot where he'd tossed them. Another glance around the room showed them neatly folded on a small chair beside the dresser. His soiled T-shirt was nowhere in evidence and instead a fresh black one lay folded on top of his cargoes.

She'd slipped into his room and he hadn't even been aware of it?

Knox wasn't sure what was the greater affront—the fact he'd slept through an intrusion or that he'd missed out on a beautiful woman folding his clothes while he lay bare-ass naked on a bed. He slapped a hand on his hip, rewarded with the sure knowledge he'd slipped out of his underwear as well the night before. Another glance at the pile of clothes confirmed a small peak of gray edging out under the T-shirt.

Damn, the woman had folded his Skivvies, too.

Blaming the subtle tightening of his body on the early morning hour, he pushed himself out of bed and got dressed. The night before filled out in his mind as sleep receded, and he was pleased to see that his satellite phone as well as the clutch piece he kept strapped to his calf were both where he'd placed them, in the top drawer of the dresser.

The lethal piece and his ticket out of Dallas lay on a stack of tablecloths, and he stilled to trace the elaborate pattern woven into the top cloth.

Family. Domesticity. A place to belong.

The odd thoughts made no sense and he quickly grabbed his things and closed the drawer, unwilling to dwell on the strange impressions that formed in his mind, Gabriella at their center.

With the delicacy of his mission and the suspicions about Moray—a well-respected leader within the Security Service—few even knew he was in Dallas. He owed his team lead a ring, but he was still processing the loss of the rubies and wasn't quite ready to call that one in.

Focused on playing it cool, Knox dialed a friend in the service and hoped he could tap dance well enough to keep suspicions low while digging for intel. He'd like nothing better than to track Moray and get the rubies back before anyone was the wiser.

Knox considered few people friends, but Sam Langston was one of them. The man answered on the first ring, the cultured notes of his voice belying his elite upbringing and status in the extended line of succession to the throne. Whether it was the distance from that vaulted position or the man's all-around decency, Knox wasn't sure, but they'd become fast friends all the same.

"Sam."

"Where are you?"

"Finishing up a job that's gone a bit sideways."

"That's not like you. You've got the coolest head in the Security Service."

Knox hated lying to his friend, but he wasn't in a

position to shatter any illusions at the moment. "Yeah, well, it looks like my luck is out. This job's been a mess from the start."

"What do you need?"

Sam's ready acceptance and offer to help were proof he'd called the right ally, and Knox laid out what he needed, including safe house access and a ticket out of the country for one of his aliases. His friend promised to set him up, and Knox let the conversation play out naturally before he lobbied his last volley. "Moray in a good mood this week? I need to report in on this, and I'm not looking forward to the old man's disapproval."

"Then consider it your lucky week. He's been out for a few days, his office dark."

"That's a relief."

"I heard someone mention he's taken a few weeks to spend up at his country home. Must be nice."

"This from a man with his own estate in Cornwall."

"It's a small one, mate. And since it houses my mother, I can promise you it will never be big enough."

"So you tell me."

The joke was an old one, and Knox sunk into the familiarity, satisfied he'd gotten the confirmation he needed on Moray. The man had conveniently laid the groundwork to be out of town, which also meant he needed to put his commander's large estate on his list of places to check for the rubies when he returned to England. He mentally added it to Moray's flat in London.

Knox ended the call after a few more good-natured insults and headed out of the room to find coffee. The halls he'd walked in an exhausted stupor a few hours earlier were now filled with warm morning light, filtering in through several open doors. He counted two more bedrooms and wondered where Gabriella had slept, the answer to the puzzle not readily apparent as both had well-made beds. Shrugging off where she slept as a mystery better left unsolved, he headed downstairs toward the kitchen and the promise of hot coffee.

And promptly slammed into a brick wall of lusty desire as he took in Gabriella standing before the stove, her long legs on display in a pair of sleep shorts. The thick mass of her hair was piled on top of her head, and her bum wiggled to some tune only she could hear as she pulled something from the stove.

"You're awfully bright-eyed on three hours' sleep."

"Can't help it." She gave one final wiggle before pulling a glass dish from the oven, settling it on a cooling rack. "I'm a morning person."

It briefly crossed his mind to call Sam back and ask for backup in the form of a priest willing to exorcise whatever morning demon had crawled up her ass, but then he reconsidered.

It was a damn fine ass, and acting like a grumpy jerk would likely limit his opportunity to continue staring at it like a randy schoolboy.

He'd been so focused on said rear that it took him a minute to key into the incredible smell that filled the kitchen.

"What did you make?"

"A breakfast casserole."

"It smells like pancakes, bacon and eggs all rolled into one."

"It basically is."

Knox snapped his mouth closed, suddenly unsure if his tongue was hanging out over her body or her baking.

Can't it be both?

"Mugs are next to the coffeemaker. Pour yourself a

better attitude, and please refill my mug while you're at it."

"What do you want in yours?"

"Just the coffee. I take it black."

He ignored the subtle tingle at the back of his neck at the cozy domestic moment and took a seat at the kitchen table, reluctantly impressed at her ability to drink her coffee at high-test while he dumped several spoonfuls of sugar into his mug. He was even more impressed by her early morning burst of activity. In addition to making coffee and breakfast, Gabriella had cleaned up the makeshift medical station from the prior night, and he almost wondered if he'd dreamed the quiet moments.

Her words suggested otherwise.

"How's your shoulder?"

"Fine."

"And your temper?"

"Improving."

"This should help."

She set a steaming plate of food in front of him. As the rich scent of bacon wafted toward him, his stomach let out a hard rumble, a reminder of how little he'd eaten over the past two days.

He'd nearly tucked into his breakfast when something glinted against the window, pulling his attention from his plate.

But it was the bright red dot square on Gabriella's forehead that had him in motion. Their bodies hit the kitchen floor as the window shattered into a million pieces.

Chapter 6

One minute, she was standing upright and the next she was cradled in Knox's arms, the floor rushing up to meet them both. Gabby reached out her hands to break their fall, but Knox shifted at the last minute, absorbing their combined weight before rolling them toward the cabinets.

Four more bullets flew through the window in rapid succession and Knox kept the back of his arm spread across her shoulders holding her still. "Put your back against the cabinets and don't move."

She nodded, unsure if she should speak. When he added a press of his finger to his own lips, Gabby was pleased she'd said nothing and settled back as he'd told her.

He had a gun out, pulled from a holster at his ankle. He whispered instructions. "Don't move unless I tell you or if I get shot. If either happens, get yourself out of here."

"I can't leave you."

"You'll do as I say."

The grumpy, tired soul who'd poured coffee was nowhere in evidence, replaced by a man in control of the situation and his role in it. Staying low to the ground, he crab walked to the window, his focus on whatever threat lurked outside. After what seemed like an eternity, he leaped up, gun forward, and shot off several rounds into the yard. A loud curse suggested he'd missed, and in moments he was back beside her.

"Is it that man?"

"Moray?" Knox checked his ammunition. "Yes. And the dodgy bastard is still out there."

"How'd he find us?"

Knox stilled at her question, the movements almost exaggerated in the sudden quiet. "Intel. Basic research. Or he played a hunch even your brother didn't think of."

"But he didn't follow us. I'd have known."

"No." Again, that preternatural stillness greeted her in his stance. "But there are resources. Databases."

"On me?"

"On everyone."

He stood up with resolute finality, extending his hand and dragging her to her feet. "We need to get out of here."

"The car?"

"The motorcycle. Give me the keys."

"You're not leaving me."

The liquid blue of his eyes settled on hers. Urgent. Penetrating. "I'm not leaving you. And I won't. You have my word."

She hesitated, not sure if she should believe him. He'd attempted an escape last night, and she didn't doubt her presence was the proverbial albatross around his neck.

Knox grabbed her hand, those long fingers enveloping hers. That small measure of comfort was just the trick to stop the waffling in her mind. "Gabriella. I promise."

With a quick shake of her head, she pointed toward the door. "I've already packed a bag."

"Where is it?"

"On the bike."

"You packed a bag? With what?"

"Supplies. Clothes. Things we might need."

Where she expected censure or at minimum a laugh, she never expected the tight hold as he dragged her flush against his body, his mouth crushing hers. The kiss was hard and fast, and it screamed of promise and power.

"I take back every nasty thought I had this morning."

"About what?"

"About you and the demon who crawled up your delectable bum spouting sunshine and merriment."

"Oh."

"Let's go."

She followed him, stopping for the briefest moment at the door frame, her gaze taking in the kitchen where she'd spent so many happy hours of her life. The hours she'd spent with her family—her grandmother in particular—and where she'd learned her life's work.

"Gabriella. We need to go."

"I know."

With a sigh she turned her back on the familiar scene and followed him to the garage, sure in the knowledge she might never see this house again.

* * *

The heavy roar of the hog's engine lit up the confines of the garage. He'd have preferred a quieter ride, but he knew the raw power would go a long way toward the notice he was giving Moray.

How did he find them so quickly?

Knox had done his homework in advance of the op, and once he'd met Gabriella Sanchez, he'd looked into her, as well. Her grandmother's family home had never even popped on his radar, let alone come up in any of his databases.

So how did Moray know?

Knox snapped on a helmet and cycled through the previous night, trying to figure out Moray's source of intel. The man was on foot, so even if he had found a car, there was no way he could have followed them after the tussle with the rubies. Gabriella had ignored outreach from her family, so no tracing there.

Or had she?

She was strapped onto his back, her own helmet firmly in place. She had the garage door opener in hand, ready to lift the door at his signal. They'd run out of time, and he wasn't going to waste more questioning her, but he would when they stopped.

"Now!"

A spray of bullets lit up the ground the moment he met asphalt, and Knox revved the bike as he screamed out orders. "Hang on!"

Gabriella's arms tightened around his waist. He trusted she had a firm grip, his sole focus on the road. They needed distance, and he put them at greater risk of a crash if he didn't keep his attention on getting them away.

The time between Moray's assault on the kitchen

and their race away on the bike had given the man a chance to retrieve his car, and a squeal of tires lit up the early morning air as a large SUV bore down on them. Another spray of bullets littered the road, and Knox swerved hard to avoid losing a tire or ending up stuck to the car's grill. Moray's ultimate goal might be to kill them, and his current approach seemed focused on disabling their getaway vehicle.

"Knox—faster! He's gaining on us! Quick. Take the right between those houses."

He didn't question her, just followed the orders, and the bike moved over a smooth stretch of grass before he threaded them through a narrow path between two fenced backyards.

"Hurry!" The hard press of Gabriella's chest against his back spurred him on, and he flew from the fenced pathway to a paved alley. "Left!"

He took the turn as directed, a busier main road visible in the distance. "When you hit the street up ahead, go right!"

True to her word, she'd promised to get him out. Going over a pothole, they took the last turn out of her grandmother's neighborhood. The press of her body lessened, and he sensed her keeping watch behind them before she turned back to give more orders. In less than a minute, they were on the last straightaway toward the interstate.

Knox had no illusions Moray wasn't following them—the man was now focused on cleaning up loose ends—and Gabriella was in even more danger.

He'd made a promise to her that he wouldn't leave her behind and he meant it. The stunt he'd attempted the night before with the bike was in bad form, and he wouldn't do that to her again. But bugger it all if he wasn't still trying to figure out how to keep her safe.

A flash lit up his side mirror and he saw Moray's SUV wending and weaving its way down the highway, drawing closer.

"Knox!" Gabriella tightened her arms around his waist as a heavy shot echoed behind them, unmistakable, even with the hard whistle of wind streaming past them.

Horns honked and tires squealed as the other drivers on the road recognized there was a problem. Gabriella screamed once more over the rush of air. "The upcoming turn! Take it at the last possible minute."

Knox understood her meaning and quickly squeezed one of the hands at his waist. He kept an eye on his mirror while focusing on the exit and took the ramp at the very last possible moment.

The ploy worked. Moray couldn't shift as quickly and at the last moment Knox saw the SUV veer wildly as additional traffic pressed in on it from both sides. A light at the end of their exit ramp stayed green for them and he flew through the intersection, determined to put as much space between themselves and the highway.

Gabriella hollered another set of instructions for an upcoming turn, then directed him as he wended his way through East Dallas. His pulse slowed as the traffic vanished and the threat of Moray following them failed to materialize. The streets grew residential once more, intermittent large homes in between smaller bungalows. Gabby's friend Cassidy Tate lived here with her fiancé, Tucker, and their big dog.

"The fifth house down on the right." Gabriella's arms relaxed and she pointed to a small shed in the back as he pulled into the driveway. "It will be crowded, but you should fit in there."

He stopped, the hard-pumping adrenaline fading at the evidence they'd reached their first milestone. Gabriella unwound herself from the back of the bike and opened the shed door. She was right on the narrow space, but he had the room he needed to stow the bike and hide it with a firm snap of the shed door.

"Are you okay? You weren't hit at all?"

She shook her head. "I'm fine. Your driving took about three years off my life, but—"

He cut her off. "Tell me why we're here again."

"Because we need help."

Gabriella grabbed the large duffel she'd prepacked off the back of the bike, but he intercepted her, taking the heavy canvas firmly in hand. "Buchanan's not going to like this."

"He'll be fine."

"I wouldn't be fine if I were him."

She patted his lower back before reaching up to rap on the back door. "You're surly and sneaky—Tucker Buchanan isn't. He'll understand."

Knox wasn't so sure when the door opened a few minutes later to reveal the long, lean form and scowling features of Tucker Buchanan. Once again, Knox went over what he knew of the man. Tucker was former Army Corps of Engineers and now owned an architectural firm with his partner, Max Baldwin. He'd been engaged to Cassidy Tate for a few weeks, whom he had met after he discovered her standing in front of her business the morning of a break-in.

The break-in that had put everything with the Renaissance Stones in motion.

The discovery of the gems in the floor of Elegance

and Lace. The hidden threat in the form of successful businessman Tripp Lange. The kidnapping of Violet Richardson.

And then that final showdown in the park downtown.

Knox couldn't fight the shot of remorse that MI5 hadn't tried to act sooner.

Or let people know they were at risk.

One glance at the stoic form of Tucker Buchanan, and Knox knew the man was equally dissatisfied with the events of the past few weeks.

Cassidy hollered from over Tucker's shoulder. "Let them in and stop staring Knox down, Tucker."

He could more than take care of himself, but it was funny to see the byplay between the petite seamstress and her beau. He also didn't miss the way Tucker's gaze softened as he turned toward his love. "I'm not staring. I'm withholding judgment."

"So do it inside. Besides, it's a billion degrees already this morning."

Tucker reluctantly opened the door and gave Gabriella a warm hug. "Two of your brothers have already called Cassidy."

"I'm sorry for that. Really, I am." Gabriella rushed to Cassidy for another tight hug. "But it can't be helped."

"They're worried about you."

"I will call them. But they can't know what's going on."

Cassidy's tone held sympathy, but it belied the hard edge to her words. "We tried that, too, Gabs. Hiding what we were doing from the police. They found out anyway."

"And you uncovered a layer of corruption even Reed didn't know about as a well-respected detective in the PD." Gabriella shook her head. "We need to tread carefully with the police. And since I know my brothers and cousins aren't dirty, I can't put them in more danger. We shouldn't even be here with you."

"I'm very glad you are. We're in this to the end. And Tucker's already taken precautions." Cassidy let the word hang there for a moment. "We're good here."

Knox glanced at Tucker. "You're sure about that."

"I know how to plan an op, and I excel at explosives."

Knox nodded, well aware of the man's history and reputation. He'd already figured the three women had been fortunate to ally with Buchanan and Baldwin, but this made Knox's estimation of the mild-mannered architect ratchet up a few more notches.

"Gabby?" An elderly woman stood at the entrance to the kitchen, her arms outstretched from her pale form. "Is that you?"

"Mrs. B!" Gabriella was already up out of her chair, wrapping her arms around the woman before she led her to the seat she'd just vacated. "I didn't know you were here. Come. Sit down."

"Are you okay?"

Gabriella patted her arm. "We're fine. How are you? How'd you come to spend the night at Cassidy's?"

"Everyone insisted I get looked at in the ER after last night, but I pitched a fit at the doctors and told them I wanted to sleep in a real bed after all that excitement in the park."

A quick wave of silent communication arced between Gabby and Cassidy before Cassidy added the confirmation they all sought. "When Tucker and I promised to keep a vigilant eye and offered a warm, cozy bed, we were able to sway the docs in Mrs. B's favor. She's headed back later today for a follow-up appointment with her own doctor."

"And since I'm here and fine, you can all stop worrying about me."

The affection between the women and the landlady of Elegance and Lace was a living, breathing thing, and if Knox didn't know everyone's history, he'd have believed them related by blood. Instead, they were a group of friends who watched out for one another and cared for each other deeply.

"Is Mr. Baldwin here?" Gabriella asked.

"He's still sleeping." Tucker provided context. "He and Max stayed up late discussing what happened at the park last night. I think grandfather and grandson were just happy to have the time together."

"Not to mention a joyous reunion once Max Junior told Senior he and Violet were engaged." Cassidy said.

Gabriella clapped her hands. "I hadn't heard yet."

Cassidy, Gabriella and the landlady all began talking at once until Tucker brought the conversation back around. "I think the two Maxes were surprised by what happened. Especially once the rubies disappeared."

Again, Knox had to give Buchanan credit. The man was respectful of Mrs. Beauregard, but he wasn't about to let it slide that he knew Knox's role.

Gabby's eyes widened and darted toward his before she patted Mrs. B's arm. "I think you should talk to Mr. St. Germain. Tell him what you know."

"Who are you?" Bright green eyes assessed him thoroughly, and Knox had the abstract thought that Mrs. Josephine Beauregard could have been a screener for the Security Service.

"I'm a member of Britain's Security Service."

"MI5?"

"If you prefer the nickname, then yes." Knox took the seat as he was ordered, pleasantly surprised when a fresh mug of coffee materialized at his elbow just before Gabriella pushed the sugar bowl in his direction.

"How are you involved, dear? Or perhaps a better question is why? I wasn't aware anyone had contacted the British government. And even if they had, my father communicated with MI6, the foreign intelligence service, all those years ago."

"The jurisdiction shifted on this one. When the stones were moved off British soil, they were an international matter. Getting them back has become a matter for the domestic security agency, MI5." *Along with someone who shouldn't have an interest in the gems.* It was on the tip of his tongue to implicate Moray, but something held him back.

Standard protocol had been drilled into Knox's head that he should keep his own counsel on an assignment. While he understood the required secrecy, he experienced yet another wave of raw anger at Moray.

How could one of the service's best betray them in this way?

Greed dated back to the dawn of man, but even such base emotions still didn't answer all the whys. Richard Moray held a position of respect, and he came from a family who'd commanded the same. Add on that he was wealthy in his own right, a sizable inheritance from his mother's family setting him up in style, and his choices made even less sense.

Unless rumors of a curse had some merit.

Knox brushed off the fanciful notion and focused his attention on Mrs. Josephine Beauregard. "I appreciate you telling me what you know."

"I just want this over." Josephine shot a furtive glance toward Cassidy and Tucker before it skipped on toward the living room. "Too many have suffered over these stones, and people have been hurt."

"I want this over, too, Mrs. Beauregard. So maybe you can fill in the gaps for me. While the government has kept records on the stones, including your father's removal of the gems from British soil, we don't fully understand the urgency around his departure."

"He and my mother wanted a new life. A fresh start, as Mother always called it."

"So they chose Texas." Cassidy's voice was gentle. "I'm so glad they did."

Mrs. B smiled at that, memories sparking deep in her gaze. "I think my mother would have settled anywhere just to leave England. My parents were so devastated by the destruction during the war. They had small children and wanted a place that was far, far away from war and midnight air raids." She stared deeply into her mug, the years vanishing from her features as if they'd never been. "Then my father heard about this town called Dallas, so we came to Texas. A great big adventure underneath great big skies."

What Knox wasn't quite steady on was how the stones had ended up in the floor of the warehouse building that had become Elegance and Lace. "It sounds like your father was handpicked for the job. If that's the case, they were basically given to him. Why did you feel the need to bury the stones?"

"He'd made every effort to start a new life, but occasionally he'd remember all the reasons they left England. He built a reputation for himself in a new place, but I think a part of him always felt dragged down by the past. After he died, I couldn't help thinking about what a piece of history we had, locked up in a firebox in the house. I just felt—" She broke off, a small tremor shaking her lips. "Max Senior and I decided the stones did no good lying around. But it also felt like a betrayal to simply give them away to a museum or sell them into a private collection."

"Why?"

"My father was trusted with those gems. And he knew how the Queen felt about them. She believed them cursed."

And there it was again. That odd, steady murmur that suggested the stones held some sort of otherworldly power.

Which he was not about to fall for.

Claims of a curse or some supernatural power suggested responsibility didn't really lie with those in pursuit of the gems. Assigning the rubies some sort of innate power meant the leader he'd believed incorruptible was simply a stupid rube, in thrall to a few gemstones, instead of a calculating bastard bent on destroying anyone who got in his way.

Knox had learned at the knee of his father that people were responsible for their own actions. And he was bloody well sure Richard Moray was responsible for his.

"They're just shiny rocks, Mum. Beautiful and valuable, of course, but nothing more."

"You believe that?"

Once again, that quick, penetrating gaze skewered him, and Knox knew the woman saw far more than she let on. "To believe anything else diminishes the good people who've done right in trying to keep them out of the wrong hands."

"Yes, well, there's a fair point." Whether he'd simply placated her or perhaps answered a question Josephine Beauregard pondered on her own, he wasn't sure. But his comment seemed enough to reimmerse her in her story. "I'm not sure it matters any longer, anyway. But all those years ago, we thought it was a good idea to bury the jewels. So we put them somewhere we could forget about them."

"And you and Max never told anyone?"

"We were discreet." Mrs. B frowned, the years quickly returning to her tissue-thin skin. "Or we thought we were. Until recently."

"You're not to blame, Mrs. B." Cassidy's support was ironclad. "Tripp Lange was a bad man."

"But I still don't understand how he found out!" The outburst was a surprise, even more so than the line of tears that ran over her cheeks. "He's ruined so many lives. His poor wife. The people he killed. All the families he's harmed. All done for a few stones."

"Shh." Cassidy moved into mother hen mode once more, and Knox accepted he'd discover no more this morning. Josephine Beauregard had been through an ordeal. And, while he refused to give any further attention to the nonsense about a curse, Knox couldn't deny the stones had wreaked immeasurable havoc on this small group of people.

And now he'd gone and made it worse.

He'd played the past few days over and over in his mind, and no matter how he twisted things, the answer kept coming out the same. Gabriella Sanchez had been only peripherally involved in the mess with the stones, supporting her friends as they dealt with something far bigger than them.

He was the one to blame for bringing her into the sick and twisted game the retrieval of the rubies had become.

So why had he done it?

She was beautiful, sure. But he'd met a lot of beautiful women through the years and had never had the bloody urge to drag them into his work. In fact, he'd deliberately avoided sharing any details of his work with anyone.

A glance toward Gabriella only gave him more questions. He was attracted to her, but surely he hadn't lost so much perspective he'd pull her into something so dangerous.

Yet that was exactly what he'd done.

He'd always avoided regret, believing it a useless emotion. Decisions were made. Results happened. Dwelling on the outcome offered little benefit.

Yet here he was, smack in the middle of a dangerous mess.

And he had no one to blame but himself.

Other than refilling coffee, which gave her something to do with her hands, Gabby had remained quiet throughout Knox's discussion with Mrs. Beauregard. Despite the harrowing few weeks she'd just survived, the woman's memory was sharp, her green eyes even sharper.

Until the reality of what had happened simply grew too large to take in.

Cassidy's gentle, soothing words restored the calm, but there were no words to fully eliminate the roiling emotions Knox had churned up. She only hoped he'd gotten the information he needed to fill in whatever gaps he hadn't closed on his own.

Not that it mattered all that much.

She questioned Knox's method for retrieving the stones to get them back on home soil—all his cleverness had really done was put the rubies out in the open once more. And while she believed his promise he wasn't going to simply ditch her, she knew she didn't belong in the middle of a government investigation.

Knox St. Germain was a highly trained government operative. There was absolutely nothing she could bring to this situation that was additive.

Yet he'd come to her shop. He'd sought haven with her. And he'd protected her with his body when Moray had come after them.

She knew it was only a matter of time before he stuffed her with someone else or shoved her in a safe house. He might think it was a good solution, but how could she stay put? She was far too deeply involved now to back away. The attack this morning had only reaffirmed it. Surely hiding out and waiting for things to blow over—*if* they blew over—put her family in an equal amount of danger.

An image of Ricardo's stiff form, a gun pressed to his temple, filled her mind's eye once more. The sight hadn't been far from her thoughts and had kept her from sleeping at all the night before.

Which was why she'd made her decision in the first place to stay busy while she left Knox to his much-needed rest.

She'd added gas to the bike from a canister in the garage and packed their overnight bags. She'd sent a few emails from her work account to her family, offering assurances that she was fine. And she'd borrowed her grandmother's US cell phone that always stayed in the top drawer of the dining room hutch when her *abuela* was back home in Mexico.

Her decision was made. Now it was just a matter of forcing Knox to let her see it through.

She'd already proven herself an ally. And she had

no desire to be hidden away in a hole while this mess blew over.

She did not believe Knox had all the answers, despite the endless bravado he wore like a suit of armor. His questions for Mrs. B were simple and straightforward, and while it could have been a ploy, she'd been surprised more by what he didn't know than what he did.

Which only made the question of his involvement that much more curious.

If the British government wanted the stones back, surely it knew how they'd arrived in the United States so many years before. And surely it would have communicated at some point with Mrs. B's father if it ultimately intended to retrieve them at some later date.

Yet it hadn't done that. In fact, the British government's lack of *action* suggested it had no interest in the stones at all.

So why now?

Gabby let her gaze wander once more around the room. Tucker stood guard at the counter near Cassidy's side, his boxer, Bailey, stretched out at his feet. Mrs. Beauregard sat quietly sipping her coffee, peppering Knox with questions about London. The agent solicitously answered her questions, even as his gaze kept a steady progression around the room.

When he looked at her, their eyes locking across the small space, Gabby was forced to ask herself the question that battered her in her quiet moments.

What was Knox's endgame? Was it truly the restoration of the Renaissance Stones?

Or possession?

And why did the mere idea he was after the stones cause a spear of sadness to settle beneath her heart?

Gabby was smart enough to know the two of them

had no future. Moreover, she had no business even allowing her thoughts to drift in that direction over a man she'd known for a handful of days.

Yet drift, they did.

And in those quiet moments she could admit to herself the truth.

With her whole heart, she wanted to believe in Knox St. Germain.

Chapter 7

Tucker Buchanan was a quiet man. He wasn't prone to outbursts or making a fuss, and he wasn't the type of guy to pick a fight and ask questions later. He left choices like that to his partner, Max.

But ever since Knox walked into his fiancée's bridal boutique a few days before, Tucker had fought the insatiable urge to deck the guy.

He wasn't sure if it was the suave veneer or the cheeky accent, but St. Germain had an answer for every question they'd thrown at him. And Tucker suspected very little of it was the truth.

Or at least not the full truth.

His early morning arrival with Gabriella in tow only added to Tucker's sense of mistrust and misgiving, and barring tying Gabby up and physically expelling St. Germain from the house, he wasn't quite sure what to do with the cocky bastard.

So he'd waited until everyone had moved out of the kitchen and into the living room, and then did his level best to get something out of the man he didn't already know.

The only thing in the Brit's favor was that Bailey liked him. The two had become fast friends, and Bailey already had his long legs in the air, his belly exposed for rubs in his favorite spot just beneath his ribs.

Even his beloved boxer was enamored with the Brit. *Traitor.*

"You want to tell me what you were really doing in the park last night?" Although Tucker had planned on a more subtle opener, the resignation that covered Knox's face was worth the gaff.

"You don't want to know."

"You took the rubies."

"I did."

"Why?"

"Classified, mate."

Tucker had done his fair share of deeds that fell into that category, but he couldn't summon much sympathy for Knox's position.

"Where are they now?"

"They're in play." With a swift pat on Bailey's rump, Knox stood, his piercing-blue gaze at Tucker's eye level.

"Where?"

"That one's classified, too. But rest assured—I will get them back."

"Why'd you drag Gabby into this mess?"

"And you didn't?"

The answer was flippant—like the man—and just fast enough Tucker thought he might reconsider his first impression after all. "She's a friend of Cassidy, Lilah and Violet's. She'd have been involved, no matter how hard they'd have tried to hide a dug-up floor full of three priceless gems."

"That's a rather comfortable excuse."

Tucker shrugged. "Cassidy and her friends didn't go to Gabby's shop with a pocket full of gemstones. You did."

Years in the military had honed his instincts to a razor-sharp point, and they didn't disappoint. The shadowy remorse Tucker sensed when he brought up Gabriella's name bore fruit.

"It was the wrong choice. The wrong bloody choice."

"So what are you going to do about it?"

"Fix it."

Knox recognized Buchanan's concern for what it was—affection for Gabriella—but he didn't need those too-sharp eyes assessing him for weak spots. Especially when the biggest weak spot he'd ever encountered sat a room away.

"You seem damn sure of yourself if you think you can fix the mess you're in, find the stones and keep Gabby safe."

"I won't let anything happen to her."

"You should leave her here."

The thought of leaving her behind—out of his sight—hit him with a swift punch to the gut. Even though that had been his very plan the night before, Moray's actions that morning were proof he intended to be relentless in his pursuit.

And Gabriella wasn't safe.

"I'd consider it if I thought she'd stay."

"She can stay with us. I know what I'm doing, and I don't intend to let anyone hurt Cassidy. That goes for the people she loves, too."

"I gave her my word I wasn't going to leave her. I mean to keep it."

He had given his word, but Knox knew it was more than that. Somewhere in the past twenty-four hours, Gabriella had become his responsibility. Self-inflicted, no doubt, but now that she was in his purview he was hesitant to relinquish his hold.

Bailey's sprawl on the kitchen floor morphed in an instant from casual to lethal. A low growl rumbled in his throat as he positioned his large, square body between Tucker and Knox.

Tucker placed a hand on the dog's head. "What is it, boy?"

With a glance to the living room and the bright sounds of laughter that spilled into the kitchen, Knox edged toward the door while Buchanan moved into sentry position at the living room entrance. Knox slipped his gun from the top pocket of his cargoes when a hard knock echoed off the back door.

"Buck! Let me in."

"It's Baldwin." Buchanan waved a hand before moving to stand next to the dog. "Let him in."

Knox stowed his gun and opened the door. Max Baldwin held the door, allowing Violet Richardson entry first, before following her inside. Gabby had made mention of the sparks that flew between the two of them, but he didn't need sparks to see the sheer affection and attentive body language between Max and Violet.

Another win for the mysterious Renaissance Stones, or something deeper?

Unbidden, thoughts of Gabriella filled his mind's eye, and he shook off the haunting thoughts.

"What's he doing here?" Max pointed at Knox before he closed the door.

"Charming as always, Baldwin."

"Intrusive and unwelcome as always, St. Germain."

Violet laid a hand on Max's shoulder before she turned the full attention of her blazing-green eyes in Knox's direction. "We weren't sure what happened to you last night."

Buchanan's voice rang out, the distinct notes of tattling lighting up each word. "He stole the rubies and hid out at Gabby's."

In his first meeting with Violet, Knox had seen the woman at what he'd assumed was her lowest. She'd just survived a kidnapping by Tripp Lange and his henchman, a long car ride home and a continued threat against her life. Even then, she didn't look nearly as shell-shocked as she did in that moment.

"You took the rubies? You've got them?" Shock gave way to eagerness and she moved closer. "We can finally put this behind us? All the way behind us."

Their small group might be ready to put the Renaissance Stones firmly behind them, but he wasn't in quite so fortunate a position. "I retrieved the gems last night. I no longer have them at this time."

Had it really been only last night? Time had either sped or stretched on previous jobs, depending on what was going on, but he felt as if he'd lived a lifetime since departing the night before for Klyde Warren Park and the arranged meet with Tripp Lange.

A lifetime since he'd come face-to-face with the truth about his boss.

"I don't understand." Violet glanced toward Max. "Where'd they go?"

"I think what our new friend here is trying to tell you," Max interrupted before Knox could answer, "is that the assets are in the wind."

Although coming to see Gabriella's friends had been a necessity, both to understand what they knew and to get the valuable help they could provide, Knox was done with the inquisition. He was well aware of his role in the prior night's drama and even more well aware of the implications of his actions.

But having his nose rubbed in it chafed.

Gabriella chose that moment to enter the kitchen, a broad, welcoming smile for Violet and Max suffusing her face. She extended her arms toward her friend. "You're okay."

Violet slipped into the hug, then giggled at something Gabriella whispered to her. "Yes, things did work out."

With one final squeeze, Gabriella stepped from the hug, a satisfied smile on her face. "Well, I, for one, am glad you two finally came to your senses."

"No one ever accused me of taking the easy road."

"Me either, *chica*. That must be why we're friends."

Violet kept an arm around Gabriella, the two a perfect image of good friends who cared for and supported each other.

Had he ever had that?

The thought was as unexpected as the memories— or lack of—behind them.

He supposed he had a few chums from school that he'd have called friends, but it had been so long since he'd seen them he wasn't sure they quite counted any longer. He was friendly with a few folks at the Security office, Sam chief among them. And he had the occasional conversation with an older neighbor down the hall whom he could talk to in a pinch.

But he had no one intimately involved with his life.

The image of Moray's face, twisted into a cold mask of greed and indifference, filled his mind.

Richard had been a calculating bastard even before his truer nature had come to light. He expected total involvement from his team, and he had minimal tolerance for those who didn't fall into line. And up until the night before, Knox had believed in his leader. In the choices and personal sacrifices he'd made in service to queen and country.

So why did his life and his career suddenly feel so empty?

"Knox?" Gabriella's dark gaze narrowed, the rich dark chocolate color of her eyes filled with both question and concern.

"I need a minute."

Without waiting for a response, he slammed the back door behind him.

A hard shot of empathy lit up her system, her spine tingling in awareness. Gabby had always prided herself on being a good, intuitive friend, and she'd thought to give Violet comfort and a bit of a tease over finally giving in to her feelings for Max.

But the raw pain that settled in the angles and planes of Knox's face had an answering response centering itself just below her heart. Gabby gave Violet's waist a quick squeeze before dropping her arm. "Would you excuse me for a minute?"

Curiosity ran high in her friend's gaze, but she simply nodded her assent. "Of course."

As Gabby left the house, a blast of hot, muggy August heat slapped her in the face. The yard was small, and a quick check indicated Knox was nowhere in sight, so she marched toward the shed where they'd parked the bike. The old wooden door still quivered slightly and she tugged it open, unsurprised to find her quarry leaning against the seat of the motorcycle.

"You okay?"

She asked the question, unsurprised when he ignored the root of her query. "Of course. I simply figured you needed a bit of privacy with your friends."

His voice was formal—deliberately so—and Gabby marveled at yet another facet of his personality. He even used the cultured tones of his homeland to manipulate a situation.

"That accent's a great weapon. I never realized it before, but you wield it well."

His eyebrows shot up over the piercing blue of his eyes, a not-so-subtle reminder the man wasn't easily toyed with. "Excuse me?"

"The whole upper-crust thing. You can pull it on and off when you need to. The endearments, too. A well-placed 'love' or even calling Mrs. B 'Mum' when you wanted information. It's effective."

Wickedly so.

"If you say so."

She ran a finger over a set of gardening tools, tracing their shape as an image of Cassidy's flower beds in full spring bloom popped to mind. "I do."

"Why does it even matter?"

"Why are you here, Knox? I mean, really here."

The shovel and small hoe were hard beneath her fingers, yet she knew what they could create out of those unyielding surfaces. Had seen herself the fruits of their labors in the swell of colors that painted the beds around Cassidy's front door.

"You first."

Expectation hummed in his words, and Gabby toyed

with a small trowel, the worn handle smooth to the touch.

"It all matters. The things that happen to us. That shape us. That create us. They matter."

"Sometimes things happen to people and they shouldn't."

"That's life."

"No, it's irresponsible." His gaze shifted from a point along the wall to her face. "*I've* been irresponsible. With you."

Although the shed had no interior light source, sunlight filtered in through the various cracks and crevices in the walls. Enough so that she could see him—could see the battle he waged with himself. A battle she'd somehow become the center of.

"You didn't do what's happened here. You didn't shoot at us this morning."

"No, but I took the rubies. I came to your business. And I led a killer to your door."

The darkened interior and his hard rush of words—of taking responsibility—gave Gabby the oddest sense of confession. Those private moments of unburdening her soul had always given her a sense of peace.

But she saw no peace in the man before her.

"Where else did you have to go?"

"There were other choices."

"I don't think so. Were you going to go to your hotel, covered in blood? Or walk into a drugstore to buy supplies to stitch yourself up? Those places are trained to address problems like that."

"I'd have found a way."

She mentally shook her head. *Damned foolish man.* "You stumbled through my front door and practically passed out on me. How much farther do you think you'd have gotten?"

"I failed in my job and put you in danger. There is no excuse for my actions."

Recognizing there were no words that would penetrate whatever mental argument he'd sunk into, Gabby went with instinct instead.

The tight space gave her the opportunity she needed. She reached out and wrapped an arm around Knox's neck, pulling him close. She remembered his shoulder at the last possible second, arcing her elbow so she wouldn't put pressure on the wound.

And then she took.

She pressed her lips to his, pleased when he opened for her without question. Whatever self-argument he waged with himself over his choices, the heat that flowed between them seemed to be something he accepted.

It's something we both accept, she marveled, as his tongue slipped lazily against hers.

A wash of need speared through her, sensitizing her nerve endings and adding a tremble to her knees that she'd never felt before.

Not once.

She'd kissed men before, of course. Had dated several and had even shared herself within the confines of several solid relationships. But none of those men had ever made her feel like Knox St. Germain did.

He'd crawled underneath her defenses in a matter of hours, and she had no idea what to do about it.

Realizing there would be plenty of time to worry about it later—it wasn't as if they were building something permanent—Gabby focused on the moment.

On the man.

And on the way he made her feel.

The dim lighting and sultry air seemed to wrap them in a sensual cocoon, where nothing lay beyond the two of them. No rubies. No bad guys. Not even her friends and family.

Just them.

The accent she'd accused him of wielding whispered against her lips. "You make a rather persuasive argument, Miss Sanchez."

She smiled. "I'm just getting warmed up."

The tease quickly gave way to more urgent needs, and his arms tightened around her as he took control of the kiss. Long, sure strokes of his tongue pressed against hers. His hands settled against her back, his clever fingers tracing a soft path over her lower spine.

Gabby pressed into him, the muscles of his chest hard against her fingertips. He was a big man—solid—but with an elegant grace like a sleek cat. She pictured the bare chest she'd seen earlier and traced the remembered image with her fingertips. Muscle and sinew, bone and tissue—she explored it all beneath her hands, like an artist refining a marble statue.

She committed him to memory, willing his touch and hers to imprint themselves in her mind, preparing her for the day when he'd be gone.

Because he would be gone.

She just had to hope she could help him before he decided to leave again.

During his training for the Security Service, Knox had spent several harrowing minutes in a raging waterfall, desperate to catch his breath. He'd bob and weave, hitting the surface only to be pulled under again before he could fully prepare himself for the next stretch of airless struggle.

Raw panic had assailed him during the initial exercise. After it was done, he knew his reaction was unacceptable. So he'd forced himself back, day after day, until he'd conquered the need to panic. Until he'd rid himself of the fear and the terror that the water brought.

He'd beaten the task through sheer, mindless will.

So how odd was it that he struggled with that same panic as he kissed Gabriella?

He wouldn't tell her—a woman wouldn't care to be compared to a drowning exercise—but try as he might, all he could think about was his first day under the waterfall.

Only the cold rapids weren't nearly as enticing, his conscience not taunted then as it was when he pressed his lips once more to the delectable Gabriella.

Her body was magnificent, and he reveled in the opportunity to explore every feminine dip, curve and secret. He dug his fingers into her hips, delighted as they gave way to a lush bottom. Continuing his exploration, he once again pressed his fingers low against her spine, pleased when he felt her curve into his hand in answer.

She was beautiful and sensual, responsive and as into the moment as he was, and all he could think about was drowning.

Stupid, buggering idiot.

The heat that had felt oppressive when he'd stomped into the shed now added to the moment; the air coating them only added to the hard, driving need that built between them.

He lifted his hands from her lower back, drifting his fingertips over her slender rib cage before the flesh gave way to the sides of her breasts. He flicked a thumb beneath one of those heavy globes and was rewarded with a hard sigh. Pleased with the result, he repeated the action on her other breast and felt himself going under the driving power of that waterfall once more.

Another wave of panic gave way to desire, and he let himself enjoy the moment. Drifting with the power instead of fighting it. Allowing the undertow to pull him beneath the surface, into the welcoming silence.

Into Gabriella.

Alarm bells went off as Knox realized he could gladly stay in the quiet welcome of her body forever.

And just as years before, he let the panic win. Struggling to surface, he channeled that terror and forced himself to focus on reality.

What was he going to do about her?

He had no doubt Buchanan would keep an eye on her. But he had equal certainty Moray would make another play for her. She might not know who she was dealing with, but he did, and now that Moray had made his move he wasn't going to leave any dangling threads behind.

He lifted his head and nearly returned straight back to her lips at the sensual look in her gaze and delicate pink tinge that suffused her cheeks. Her warm brown eyes were large, the pupils wide with need and the darkened light in the shed. Her hair, lush and wavy, grabbed his attention, and he followed the path of one lone curl, fascinated by its twisty trail down her back.

"Who are you?" Her voice was quiet and thick with need.

When he didn't answer, she pressed him again, more urgently this time. "Who are you? Tell me. *Please.*"

"I don't know anymore." The words were out before

he could censor them. Knox puzzled through the abstract thought. Who was he?

He'd believed in his choices for so long, it was more than a little unnerving to realize they didn't fulfill him any longer. Especially since he'd wrapped his entire life in his career. In being the badass member of MI5 who took on the jobs that needed to get done. He did the hard things. Willingly.

And suddenly all that time, effort and energy seemed like a horrible waste.

"Maybe that's why you're here."

Gabby's words were spoken so softly he wasn't sure he'd heard them. "What's that?"

"I don't know who I am anymore, either. Maybe that's why you're here. Maybe I'll finally find out."

Knox had sensed something about her from the first moment they'd met. He'd arrived at Elegance and Lace to interview Cassidy, Lilah and Violet, and Gabriella had been there instead, cooking a mountain of food as she waited for them to get back to the shop.

He'd later learned they were all out retrieving Violet and Max from her kidnapping and rescue, and Gabby was making a welcome-home meal. But at the time, all he'd seen were her curves, her welcoming smile and the five-inch heels that made his mouth water.

He'd teased her a bit, unwilling to give her the upper hand, but he had been humbled knowing she'd held the control all along as his hands had shaken all the way to his car. Hell, he'd considered it a victory he'd kept his tongue in his mouth.

While she wasn't the first beautiful woman he'd encountered, she was more than a pretty picture. It had taken him the entire drive back to his hotel to finally work through the mystery that was Gabriella Sanchez and what had nagged him during their first conversation.

And what he'd discovered, puzzling through that beautiful, cryptic veneer, was that the pretty picture that was Gabriella housed a sharp mind and an equally sharp awareness of others. It also housed a subtle sadness that was hard to see unless you really looked. And, oh, how he'd looked.

And in doing so, he'd recognized a kindred spirit beneath the dazzling surface that he figured most never got past.

Perhaps she struggled as much as he did on that eternal quest to figure out what made up a life. Goals and ambition were important—and they carried a person far—but were they everything? Could they be everything?

Or was that asking far too much of the things in life that couldn't love you back?

He'd put distance a long time ago between himself and those who were supposed to love him. He'd buried the heartache and the betrayal, accepted their shortcomings and had moved on with his life, refusing to look back.

But he'd also closed himself off to feelings and needs and the basic comfort that came from making a life with others.

"We should probably get back inside. Cassidy will send out a search party."

The comment pulled him from his musings with an abrupt start. They were inside a toolshed, facing down an extraordinarily well-connected foe, and he'd allowed his mind to wander down paths better left grown over.

Since they weren't more than ten yards from the house, Knox figured that was a stretch. A few moments spent away from watchful eyes—especially since Gabriella was the person he'd passed the time with—was welcome. "Her watchdogs know where we are."

Gabriella stilled at that, her hand steady on his good shoulder. "You don't like Tucker and Max?"

"I like them fine. I don't think that's reciprocal."

"They don't trust you."

"I wouldn't trust me, either."

"They're good guys. You can tell them what's going on. Give them some details to help you."

"It's like I told Buchanan. It's classified."

She slipped from his arms and placed her back against the shed door. "Is that why you haven't told me anything? Why I don't know who that man is who has the rubies or why you took them in the first place?"

"Don't ask me for things I can't give you."

"You don't do me any favors, keeping me in the dark."

"You can ask all you want, but I can't tell you. I've already put my mission in jeopardy and added a civilian into the mix. You're safer not knowing."

"That's a cop-out."

A mulish expression settled over her features, making her even more beautiful, if that were possible.

How could stubborn be so damned sexy?

Knox almost shook his head, but he stopped at the last minute, refusing to let her see his frustration. "It's the truth."

"I—"

Her words were cut off by a heavy burst of fire and splintered wood that exploded at her back as gunshots penetrated the small shed.

Chapter 8

For the second time in barely an hour, Gabby found herself flat on her back, Knox St. Germain pressed intimately against her. Her body was still overheated from their intense make-out session, and she desperately tried to ground her thoughts in reality.

They were being shot at.

When another spray of gunfire lit up the door behind their prone bodies, her hazy, languid thoughts firmly vanished in the need to do something—*anything*—to get to safety.

"Are you okay?" Knox whispered against her ear, his body firmly planted on top of hers. "You're not hit?"

"No." She ran her hands over his back, more instinct than sensual exploration. "Are you?"

"I'm good."

They might be untouched, but she'd hardly classify their situation as *good*. "We're sitting ducks in a toolshed."

"And those watchdogs I mentioned are holed up across the yard. We've got backup this time around."

Although Gabby knew Tucker and Max weren't strangers to violence, the idea they had a ready supply of ammo loaded up in Cassidy's house took some adjusting to. "You think they'll shoot?"

"I'm counting on it, especially since I'm not moving and giving you any room to get hit."

The warm, intimate moments that had vanished at the reality of being shot at flooded her once more at Knox's words. He'd made a human shield over her.

He was *protecting* her and keeping her safe.

Unbidden, a hard wash of tears pricked the backs of her eyes. "You don't have to—"

"Shhh." He pressed his lips to her ears. "It's okay."

The muted sound of gunfire was audible through the shed walls, loud but not targeted at the flimsy structure, and Gabby let out a small sigh that Max and Tucker had lived up to expectations.

"Buchanan and Baldwin save the day," Knox muttered before he ran a hand over her hair, smoothing the curls as he went.

"I'm so glad—" Three more shots splintered the wood, effectively ending her statement before the loud roar of an engine gunned from the direction of Cassidy's driveway. "Is he leaving?"

The shed door swung open with a hard thud against the outside wall. Gabby glanced up from her position beneath Knox's shoulder. Tucker stood over them both with a wicked-looking shotgun. The roar of Max's truck screamed from the driveway as he pulled out in a squeal of tires.

"Stop him!" She tried to scramble out from beneath Knox but couldn't dislodge his weight.

"No one stops Mad Max, Gabs. You know that."

"But he—"

"What are you two doing out here?"

Knox put his weight on his forearms and pushed up. She didn't miss his wince of pain as the movement registered in his injured shoulder. If it bothered him beyond more than a grimace, he didn't show it. He pulled himself to his feet before reaching down to help her up.

"Wanted a spot of fresh air. The kitchen had grown a bit close, mate."

Tucker's eyes narrowed. "Your friend's a damn good shot."

"He's paid to be."

Raw surprise registered itself in the small O of Tucker's lips, but Gabby beat him to the punch. "Paid to be? Who is that man?"

"My boss."

Moray ignored the GPS and the incessant throbbing in his knee as he took turn after turn, willing himself out of the shabby little neighborhood. He'd planned an ambush and damn near got his ass handed to him for his troubles. He took a hard left, cursing as the street took him toward another row of small homes instead of the exit to the neighborhood.

He scanned the road ahead, debating between turning around and trying a fresh course or just seeing where this one took him, when the heavy roar of an engine idled behind him. A monstrous truck was visible in the rearview mirror, and he made it out as the same one Baldwin had just pulled up in a few minutes earlier.

Damn—he couldn't catch a freaking break. And he'd been so close.

The prep work he'd done in advance on the women

who owned Elegance and Lace had provided some indication of where Knox had disappeared to, and he'd taken a shot steeped in a well-educated guess. There weren't that many possible places for them to go between their original hideout and the point he'd lost them on the highway; his speed far outpaced whatever they could have managed on the bike.

As soon as he realized they were gone, he'd turned around, calculating where they had to have exited the highway and then, by default, where St. Germain was headed.

He wasn't the best damn tracker in the Security Service for nothing, even if it had been far too many years since he'd put the skill to good use. He knew maps. He knew terrain. And he knew how to navigate an environment, be it cityscape or out in the wild.

He was a hunter, by damn. And he was the best.

But it had all blown to hell when backup had arrived at the house. The dog was the first distraction, his mad barking the first hurdle. Richard figured he could have gunned down the dog, then taken Knox and Buchanan on his own until the damned partner had shown up.

He'd barely made it into a hiding spot behind the house next door, the pain in his knee slowing him down to a near crawl, when Max Baldwin and Violet Richardson trooped into the house.

Too many people.

The truck drew even closer, undeterred by the narrow street, and Richard made a decision. A four-way stop held an opening up ahead, his last place to take the shot.

With a hard turn on the wheel, he spun the car in a tight arc, wheels screaming on pavement as he executed a 180-degree turn. The truck sped past him, moving too fast to slow down and narrowly avoiding a clip.

Richard didn't wait for the man to catch up. A glance at the map displayed on the GPS showed the main road was off a street that ran parallel, and he bore down, refusing to slow.

In moments, he was back on the highway, racing toward the gleaming towers that made up Dallas's downtown skyline, willing his racing pulse to calm.

He needed to deal with loose ends, but he also needed to get the hell out of town. Knox was far from an amateur, and the men who'd swooped in to help out the owners of Elegance and Lace were far more adept than he'd ever given them credit for.

No. He had to get out of Dallas and get the gems to safety. Once he was on his home soil, he could finish this up. The fence he was moving the rubies through was standing by for a view of the gems. His housekeeper had his house ready and waiting for him in Surrey. And once he was home and had access to all his tools, he could bait his trap.

Richard Moray didn't leave loose ends.

But he knew damn well when he needed to go to ground and rebuild his plans.

Knox paced the living room, six pairs of eyes tracking his movements in unison, seven if you counted the dog. Cassidy sat next to Mrs. B, her hand firmly wrapped around the older woman's in a show of comfort and solidarity. Max Senior and Violet took turns grousing about the idiotic move of hiding out in the shed. Tucker stayed quiet, standing staunchly against the entrance to the living room, Bailey playing sentinel at his side.

And then there was Gabriella.

She hadn't said anything since they'd walked back into the house; instead she sat in a small wingback chair next to the couch, her gaze intent upon him.

Moray's bullets had missed her by millimeters. And he might be bloody well overestimating at that.

The heavy idle of an engine pulled his attention, and he saw Baldwin swerve into the driveway. The man was out of the large vehicle in moments, his long strides eating up the front lawn.

Violet rushed to Max's side before he could get out anything more than a swift curse, her hands flying over his face and shoulders. "Are you all right?"

"I'm fine." He pulled her close in a tight hug, before his unerring gaze landed exactly where Knox expected it to.

On him.

"Who in the hell was that?"

"Another Brit," Tucker offered up. He added drily, "His boss, as a matter of fact."

The information was enough to get everyone talking at once, and Knox waited out the storm. He used the chaotic moment to watch Gabriella. She stayed still, her stare straight and level.

The feel of her underneath his body was imprinted on his skin. The seconds when he'd waited to determine if she'd been shot through the door of the shed coated his stomach with a raw, acidic fear. Jittery waves of adrenaline chopped through his bloodstream, and it was only through sheer force of will that he kept his hands at his sides.

Why didn't he plan on Moray circling back around for them?

Knox knew they weren't followed off the exit ramp—

he'd kept watch himself and had done another check before they went into Cassidy's house. But he knew well and good his boss was damn near psychic in his ability to track and retrieve.

And of course there were files on the women of Elegance and Lace. A home address wasn't that hard to find.

Amidst the internal rebuke, another thought stopped Knox cold.

Was it possible Sam had shared his whereabouts? Did Richard's corruption extend that far?

Questions without answers. Worse, the risk of paranoia grew with each passing moment. He'd taken this job because he'd believed in what he was doing. If there was corruption in the Security Service, he wanted to be the one to root it out.

But did it go deeper?

And was he the rube being set up to take the fall?

Early morning light filtered into the room, and a small swath of bright, incandescent yellow washed over Gabriella's features through a split in the curtains. The light formed a partial halo, and he found himself caught, his endless questions stilled in the simple moment.

He already thought her beautiful, but the play of warm light over her dark hair brought out a range of highlights that had him itching to move closer to touch. To look his fill. To assure himself that she still took breaths in and out, could still smile and laugh and *feel*.

The chaotic chorus of questions and curses filling the room faded away as he took in the thick brown mass of curls, an endless bounty of colors and tones threaded through the waves. Rich brown gave way to strands of sable and chocolate, auburn and—if he looked hard enough—fiery red. Those strands—that special shade of red—caught the sun like divining rods for the morning light.

And he was caught. Utterly and completely captivated by her.

The spell snapped as Baldwin's voice rang out.

"That man's your boss?" Max kept an arm around Violet, but his attention had shifted toward Knox. "What gives, St. Germain? What the hell kind of stunt are you running?"

Telling a room full of civilians—not even British citizens, at that—about the ins and outs of his mission was the absolute last thing he needed to do. But Gabriella was already in way over her head, and Baldwin and Buchanan—for all their bluster—had put themselves on the line in a big way.

He owed them.

"The man who just shot at us was Richard Moray. He's my boss and a senior-level leader inside the Security Service."

"Why's he shooting at anybody?" Mrs. B asked.

Knox turned toward her, determined to give the woman at the center of all this the truth as he knew it. And if he could glean some additional information in return, all the better.

Anxiety narrowed the tissue-thin skin around her eyes, tightening her lips and stiffening her frail body. Something hard caught in his throat, squeezing his vocal chords with a wickedly tight fist, as his thoughts ambushed him with another day in another time. The day he'd stood before his grandmother and told her of his father's choices.

The day he'd told her his father was leaving.

She'd asked questions then, too, the weight of living and seeing the worst in others filling her eyes with a sort of resigned sorrow. Her disbelief that her own son—a man who'd seemingly loved his family—could trade it all in for a newer model. A fresh start.

Ignoring the memory, he fought to keep his focus on the here and now. On Josephine Beauregard.

"There's been suspicion for some time that Moray's gone rogue. People didn't look his way early on because of his reputation. He's multigenerational. His father was part of the service after the war."

"No pride," Max Senior muttered, and Knox thought it more than fitting. He'd already consigned any number of poor terms to Moray's behavior, but at its core, the elder Baldwin was absolutely right.

"No, sir. He doesn't. He also has no remorse for his actions, something he's proven repeatedly since I met him in the park last night."

"What flagged him to MI5?" Tucker asked.

"Suspicions finally jingled loud enough on a job he handled late last year. That's where I come in."

"So you're the inside man?" Tucker phrased it like a question, but Knox knew the comment for the statement it was.

"Yes."

"But none of this explains how this man, Moray, came to know about the gems or why he's here now," Violet said. "They were buried in our floor up until a few weeks ago. Suddenly the man goes rogue and finds a way to come after them?"

Since meeting up with the individuals caught up in this mess, Knox had known them for a bright and capable bunch. Each had a ready set of skills and an appropriate ability to reason out whatever came at them.

But in his limited interactions, Violet had proven

herself the most adept at putting the pieces together quickly.

In for a penny, Knox thought with a resigned sigh.

"The Security Service has known about the rubies for a long time. We didn't know the hiding place, but we knew of their existence and knew there was underground attention on them, whispered about in certain circles. Gems that high profile don't fully disappear, no matter how deeply someone wishes to bury them." Knox offered up a stiff smile, pleased when Mrs. B rewarded him with a small, tremulous one in return.

"Charlie." Cassidy murmured her late brother-in-law's name, the man who'd instigated the theft that had started the whole mess in the first place.

Knox nodded. "Charlie McCallum was the linchpin. He made the connections and moved the information to the right buyer, Tripp Lange. We've kept tabs on the gems, as I said, and we monitor for chatter. Charlie conducted his business via email and mobile. It's not that hard to track."

"So where does Moray fit?" Tucker moved to sit next to Cassidy, his arm tight around her as he pulled her close. "He just found this information in a file?"

"Moray's multigenerational in the Security Service, but his uncle worked for MI6 during the war. He knew about the stones and was the agent assigned to the paperwork on Joseph Brown, Mrs. B's father."

"I remember him." Josephine spoke up, her voice strong and clear. "Edward Moray. He came to our home in London before we left for Texas. My father spoke of what a great man he was. How heroic."

Knox knew the files—had committed them to memory several times over—but it was something else to be confronted with someone who had actual knowledge.

"He was all that. He was also decorated several times over and was knighted by the Queen for his service."

"And his nephew is a rat bastard who has decided to soil all he worked for." Max beat his grandfather to the punch on that one, his growl effectively punctuating what they all thought.

"I'm afraid so." Knox glanced at Gabriella, who'd remained silent. "He's also a rat bastard with a stellar reputation, impeccable connections and the services of the British government at his disposal."

Sunlight flowed through the curtain, forming that haze of light around Gabriella's head. Despite the warmth, her eyes were dark liquid pools.

Knox couldn't look away, nor could he disagree when Gabriella finally spoke.

"He's unstoppable."

Rogue government agents?

Gabriella felt as if she'd descended into the middle of a spy novel. She'd imagined any number of scenarios about the man who'd held her brother at gunpoint, stolen the rubies and come after her and Knox, but she'd never imagined he was part of Britain's premiere government agency.

When Knox didn't contradict her comment, she pressed for more details. "Who else knows besides you?"

"It's been kept quiet. A deputy leader to Moray initially informed me of the situation, and I know he's got backup from one other agent."

"Do they know Moray's in the wind?" Max asked, his normally dour expression tinged with a decided darkness. "Are they sending you reinforcements?"

"I can't tell them, Baldwin," Knox said. "Not now."

"Why the hell not?"

"I have no idea how deep the corruption goes or how much Moray knows. For all I know, I'm the one being set up."

Violet's gaze darted between Knox and Max before landing back on Knox. "A handy fall guy."

"Exactly."

Gabby knew her judgment was somewhat impaired when it came to Knox St. Germain. The man did things to her, and she struggled to be calm and rational where he was concerned. But with this latest information, she had to admit he was well and truly stuck. He'd come to Dallas to deal with a problem inside his organization, and he now faced the fact that he might have been betrayed by the people he trusted.

Moray's duplicity would have been bad enough, but the people who assigned him to manage the problem? Unthinkable.

For the past twelve hours, she'd questioned why she was there. Why she'd put herself at risk to help Knox.

And yet now it all seemed so simple.

"I'll help you."

"Gabriella—" Knox hesitated, his vivid blue eyes clouded with frustration. "You can't do that."

"We'll all help you." Cries of "What?" "Why?" and "Are you crazy?" rang out through the room before Cassidy spoke once again, her normally quiet voice loud. "We *will* help you."

"Cass." Tucker never dropped his arm from her shoulders, but he did turn to her in clear surprise. "This isn't our issue."

"It started with us. It should end with us."

"St. Germain is a member of Britain's Security Service. Think the FBI here in the States. We're not equipped to help an agent of the British government deal with his problem. We shouldn't even know an agent of the British government *has* a problem."

Gabby adored Tucker and had seen enough of the man in action to know he didn't run from danger. But she couldn't stand by and let him use logic to deal with a situation that was rapidly veering into wildly illogical and flat-out instinctual.

"You don't have to. I already said I will."

"You can't help me. You're not even—"

Knox was cut off by an unlikely source: Max Senior. "We'll all help you. And don't underestimate Gabby. That girl has more can-do in her little finger than most of us have in our whole bodies. If she says she can help, I'd suggest you take her up on it."

Touched by the show of support, Gabby fought the hard knot in her throat and crossed to Max Senior. She bent to kiss his cheek, inhaling the sweet scent of cherry cough drops he seemed addicted to.

Max Senior had been one of her staunchest supporters, visiting her in her business's earliest days and ordering trays of enchiladas to bring to his buddies down at the community center for lunch. The gesture had been simple, but it had meant so much to have that support when her family was so intent on making her feel bad for following her dream.

Although he'd never admitted it, she suspected he'd also put her name in for a few events around town that had been enough to get her some follow-up gigs, and she'd always be grateful for his willingness to put kindness into action.

"Thank you."

Knox moved through the room, pacing back and forth in the small space that made up Cassidy's living room. "You can't help me. Regardless of my doubts, I can't simply bring you into my problems."

The dark clouds had lifted from Max's eyes, replaced with a definitive hint of mischief and excitement sparking in their place. "So you use us for intel only. Buck and I aren't exactly amateurs. And we'll pull Reed in and see what he can snag out of his resources at the Dallas PD."

Knox shook his head, his shoulders hunched as he marched out of the room. "It's nice of you and all, but it's not your problem, mate."

Chapter 9

Moray's recent attack was too fresh to risk another jaunt outside, but Knox needed to get out of the living room. Needed to get away from the attention and the stares and the bloody offers of help.

Help? Who did that?

Gabriella, he understood. She'd already proven herself, giving aid simply because it was needed. In support of her friends as they dealt with Tripp Lange. Rolling five trays of enchiladas in the middle of the night for her family. Even to him, her touch firm as she stitched up his shoulder.

The woman gave of herself so freely—so easily—he wondered how she kept anything for herself.

But the others? What was their game—their angle?

People didn't just *help*.

It didn't work like that. He'd spent his life well aware of that simple fact. It's why he'd entered the Security

Service in the first place. The work was physically hard and mentally demanding, but the outcome was shockingly simple and extraordinarily satisfying. Bad guys got caught. Criminal rings were torn apart. Bastards who betrayed their country were brought to justice.

No *help* required. Just a job and a mission and loads of well-funded intelligence to see it all through.

The house was small, and with a short walk down the hallway off the living room Knox found himself inside one of the bungalow's bedrooms. A daybed ran along the wall and several dress forms lined the wall, many draped in rich, silky fabric.

Cassidy's wedding dress creations.

He ran a lone finger in an abstract line over the delicate silk before dropping down onto the daybed.

Gabriella was a helper, and there was no way he could continue taking advantage of her.

"Don't sit too close to the dresses. They give a man ideas." Gabriella moved into the room, then closed the door behind her with a soft click.

"About what?"

"Forever."

"Women wear them, not men."

"Yes, but women wear them so men's eyes will pop at the opposite end of the aisle." She moved around the room, her focus on the dresses. Just as he had, she ran a finger over the fabric before crossing to a large drafting table Cassidy had set up in the far corner. Several tiaras rested on the slanted surface, and Gabriella lifted one, nestling it in her hair.

With a satisfied sigh, she turned toward him. "There."

"There what?"

"I'm now properly British. You can tell me what you need to tell me."

A hard bark of laughter clogged in his throat at the image she made. "British women don't wear tiaras."

"The ones I read about in magazines do. So now I'm properly British. Talk to me. Tell me what you need to tell me. Without six other people watching."

"Seven. Don't forget the dog."

"He doesn't judge."

"Those big eyes looked sort of judgy."

Gabriella sauntered toward the bed, her gaze flicking to the closed door before coming to rest back on his. "He's easily swayed. I happen to know Cassidy keeps bones in the canister on the far end of the counter."

"I'll keep that in mind. Maybe toss him one before I leave."

"You mean when we leave."

"Gabriella—"

"You promised."

He reached for her hand, her skin soft beneath his touch. With gentle motions, he rubbed his thumb over the back of her hand, reveling in that softness. "I did promise. And I'm not just going to run off and leave you. But I do wish you'd consider staying here with Cassidy and Buchanan."

"They've offered you their help, as well."

"You can't help me. They can't, either! Why do you refuse to see that?"

"Why are you so quick to dismiss us? To dismiss me?"

"What can you do? Do you know how to monitor intelligence equipment? Bait a trap and hunt down your quarry? Shoot people? Because that's how this drama's going to play out, and last time I checked, caterers didn't walk around with those sorts of skills."

She snatched her hand from beneath his, her mouth set in mulish lines. "Don't belittle what I do."

"Then don't diminish what I do." He leaped off the bed, the momentary escape he'd hoped for vanishing as if it had never been.

Memories flooded his thoughts, dark and twisted images he carried, buried way down deep inside. He'd seen some of the darkest things human beings could throw at each other. Some he'd been a part of ending. And others he could only deal with the carnage left behind.

"When I was fourteen, I was selected to play on a traveling soccer team."

Gabriella's abrupt change in direction surprised him, and he stilled for a moment. "Soccer?"

"Yeah. Oh no, wait." She waved a hand. "Football. You Brits call it football."

"Footy if you're feeling frisky."

She lifted one perfectly sculpted eyebrow before continuing. "So. Traveling soccer. It's an honor to be chosen for a team like that. It means they think you've got some talent. But it also means a lot of weekends actually—"

He couldn't resist cutting her off. "Traveling?"

"Yes."

"Go on."

"So my mother was against it. She thought I spent too much time playing on the team and not enough focused on my schoolwork. She also thought I should begin thinking about my *quinceañera* and not running around on a field chasing a little ball."

"Couldn't you do both?"

Triumph flared in her gaze, and she raised her hand in a large, sweeping gesture that he took to mean agreement. "That's what I said!"

"So did she give in and let you play on the team?"

"No. She's as stubborn as I am. More so, actually."

"So you didn't play on the team."

"No, I played."

"So what's the point? She gave in because it was the right thing to do. You were interested, talented and it was a great way to stay healthy and in shape."

"No. Because I wore her down until she couldn't stand it any longer. And because I found an answer to every objection she raised and eventually dragged my grandmother in to shame her into letting me play. Oh, and to be my driver all over Texas and Oklahoma for games."

While he hadn't been sure where she was going when she'd launched into the footy story, he had to admit her hard left turn threw him for a loop. "So what are you saying? You're proposing to call your grandmother and drag her along to chase after Moray?"

"What I'm telling you is, I don't give up. And I keep pushing until I find the right solution. I'm going with you to chase after Moray."

Something hard and swift punched him low in the stomach, a rough punctuation to her comment. His first instinct was to scream "no," but even with the limited time they'd spent in each other's company, he was well aware that wasn't going to end well.

So he leaned back instead, determined to make her state her case.

"Does that mean you've found a way around the fact that you're not a British citizen or a professionally trained agent of the Security Service?"

"I don't need to be either. All you need to do is pretend I'm your new American girlfriend you're squiring around London. Tell everyone we're wildly crazy about each other and you need a few weeks off. Then you use me as your cover as you try to figure out who's working with Moray."

"I'd never take time off from work just to shag a new girlfriend."

"You would for me. Your fiery American girlfriend who you're crazy about. Besides—" she pulled off the tiara to inspect the faux stones embedded in the embellishments "—I'll have you know I'm a damn fine shag. The story's quite plausible."

The lighthearted teasing, so desperately needed after the tense morning and the two run-ins with Moray, vanished as if it had never been. Instead, all he could see were images of him and Gabriella, tangled up in the sheets of his king-size bed, glorying in each other in the midst of that damn fine shag.

Gabriella, her hair splayed across his pillow where she lay wrapped in his arms, asleep after making love all night.

Gabriella, her legs wrapped around his hips, pulling him deep inside her as the sun rose over London, the eastern sky flooding his bedroom with morning light.

He saw it all in exquisite detail, and the power of those images nearly took his knees out from underneath him.

He was raw with need and some strange insanity that had taken root the first moment he met her, and Gabriella's offer lured him in. The woman was Eve in the garden to his easily swayed Adam. All he could think about was devouring the apple she offered.

She was temptation.

Original sin in its purest form.

But if he played the situation right, she just might be his salvation.

* * *

Gabriella held perfectly still, unwilling to upset the delicate balance that had descended since she'd launched into her dopey story about soccer. She had no idea where that had even come from, but somehow—some way—it felt as though she'd gotten through.

I'll have you know I'm a damn fine shag.

Now where had *that* come from?

If the soccer story was a long-buried memory, the shag reference was pure heat of the moment. The words had tripped off her tongue with gleeful abandon, and she was still warm from the haze that had filled his sky-blue eyes at her suggestive promise.

"You want to go to London?"

His words shook her out of her stupor. She nodded. "Yes."

"With me?"

"No, with Tucker. Of course with you."

"There's no way I can get back into my hotel to get my things. And you don't have a passport, either."

"Sure I do. It's in the bag I packed that's still on the back of the bike."

"How the hell long have you been planning this?"

"You slept last night. I didn't. I had time to plan."

He shook his head. She could have sworn she saw a brief glance heavenward before he took himself in hand. "Why don't you look more tired?"

"Because I'm not. I sleep when I need it. I guess I don't need it yet."

"I have several coworkers who'd kill for that skill." His gaze narrowed. "Actually, I might kill for that skill."

"I'm quite useful. You should consider keeping me around a bit longer."

"So you keep telling me."

She pointed toward the door. "Max or Tucker can go to your hotel and retrieve your things."

"Just like that."

"Yes, just like that. They offered to help. Take them up on it."

"So fine, they go to my hotel. How do you propose we get out of the country?"

"You think Moray can pivot fast enough to know you're booking an international flight and take you down?"

"He found us here. I'm not putting an airport full of people in danger."

"Then feel lucky you know Reed Graystone. He's quite rich. Or his mother is, after being married to that slimeball Lange. We'll get her to charter us a private plane."

"You really have thought of everything."

"I have."

With a sigh that held more resignation than a disgraced politician, Knox nodded. "I guess we're going to London."

Her flip remark about not needing sleep finally caught up with her, and Gabby flopped down on the daybed in Cassidy's spare room/workroom. Knox had disappeared to take a shower. She'd admonished him to be careful with his shoulder; his grumpy request to leave him alone still lingered in the air.

"Stubborn ass," she muttered to herself.

Whoever said British men were more suave, subtle and graceful than Americans had rich fantasy lives. Knox St. Germain was as stubborn and mulish as the rest of the men in her life.

And if she read the signs right, he was also scared.

He'd done well with the cocky attitude all night at her shop and after they'd headed to her grandmother's. Even their initial arrival at Cassidy's had still held several notes of bravado and control.

But the dustup in the shed had shaken him.

It had shaken her, too.

She'd managed to put it out of her mind, but now that she had a few moments to herself, those tense moments came back in shocking clarity.

The horrible sound of exploding wood, the splinters flying through the air.

The scent of gunpowder, thick and cloying in her lungs in the hot, clammy air of the shed.

And the feel of his body, pressed to hers, putting himself in the line of a firestorm to keep her out of harm's way.

He'd done that for her.

She'd heard the term "take a bullet" her whole life and had always thought it a heroic notion. Romantic even, given the proper circumstances.

But to be the recipient of such attention was…unnerving.

Shaking it off, Gabby glanced at her phone, which was charging on Cassidy's desk. Her mother had already left three messages that morning and each of her brothers had left one at minimum, with Ricardo matching her mother in volume and tenacity.

She wanted to call her mother. The woman made her crazy-mad and ripe for Bedlam, but she loved Elena Sanchez with all her heart.

But she couldn't draw her mother into this.

Tenacity and sheer stubborn will were her mother's stock-in-trade, and there was no way she'd accept a quick call with no further explanation than "Oh, Mom, I'm headed to Europe for a few days."

So she'd taken the coward's way out by sending a text that she was fine, just busy. And then she'd negotiated free meals for a month with Cassidy in exchange for her friend's help in slaying the mom-beast that was Elena. As soon as she and Knox were airborne, Cassidy would call Elena and confirm she was totally fine.

"I still say you got off too cheap with one month of meals." Lilah Castle's voice preceded her as she and Cassidy walked into the bedroom.

"A month's a long time, Lilah. I'm doing her a favor, not putting Gabs into indentured servitude."

"The woman makes food for events that feed hundreds of people at a time. I still say she can do you better than a month's worth. Or you could have at least gotten me a few meals out of it, too."

"I'll make you a tray, too—quit your bitching." Gabby stood up and pulled Lilah into a tight hug, glad her friend had arrived to complete their increasing party. Lilah's soft blond hair with the long pink stripe was soft against her cheek, and Gabby squeezed harder, suddenly aware of what she might lose in taking on this adventure.

"You okay?" Lilah pulled away but didn't break contact. "You thinking of backing out?"

"No."

"So you want to run by me once more why you're even doing this? I mean, the Brit's hot and all, but he's trouble."

"I'm not doing it because he's hot. He needs help, and his boss already has designs on killing me anyway. I figure I'm safer with Knox than without him and way safer to my family five thousand miles away."

"Gabs." Few things ruffled Lilah, but her face fell at the frank words. "You can't be that nonchalant about this. The man's being hunted by a professional operative. You're not safer with Knox."

"Of course I am."

Somewhere between her rash decision the night before to become his guardian and chauffeur and the shoot-out at the shed, Gabby had come to an understanding. She'd put herself in harm's way and, by default, everyone she loved. Her brother wasn't her only family member in the Dallas PD. All it would take was a search party headed up by Ricardo to put any number of people in Moray's direct line of fire.

The same applied to her friends. While she didn't doubt the protective skills of Max, Tucker and Reed, they just got themselves out of danger, putting down the threat that was Tripp Lange. She didn't need to risk them any further because of a rash decision.

So she'd go with Knox and pray his skills were honed enough to capture his quarry and get this done.

"Would you talk some sense into her, Cass?" Lilah's sympathy edged over to frustrated. "She's clearly not thinking straight."

"We spent an hour this morning after she announced her plans. Our Gabby is an immovable object on this."

Gabby valued their opinions and knew their pushback came from a place of love, friendship and support. But she'd made her decision, and hashing it and rehashing it was pointless. "And I'm not changing my mind, so I need you both to help me before we head to the airport."

"You don't want us to call any other pushy family members, do you?" Lilah asked, her voice rife with suspicion.

"My mother's more than enough on that front. No. What I need you both to do is help me with a few outfits. I packed light last night and realize I need a bit more flash."

"Honey, you could put on a few dish towels and you'd scream flash. Nobody misses you when you walk into a room."

"This coming from a woman who believes pink Crocs are high fashion." Gabby shook her head. "Cassidy, would you please talk some sense into her?"

"You want the best buttercream in the Northern Hemisphere, you go to Lilah Castle. You want an outfit to rock a man's world, you come to me." Cassidy moved closer, her attention fully focused now as her gaze traveled over Gabby from head to toe and back to head again. "Give me a sec. I have an idea."

Cassidy disappeared into a small closet at the opposite end of the room. An occasional grunt floated out of a sea of taffeta, lace, silk and satin before she let out a triumphant whoop. "I do have it here."

A long swath of material draped over Cassidy's arm when she finally resurfaced from the closet.

"Where'd you get that?" Lilah asked. "You make wedding dresses."

"I make clothing. Wedding gowns just happen to be my specialty. It doesn't mean I don't know good fabric when I see it." Cassidy pointed a finger. "Strip for me."

Gabby did as Cassidy asked, then slipped into the material her friend held out.

"Oh, wow. I can already tell that's gorgeous and you're only halfway into it." Lilah moved closer. "It's totally seventies."

"It should be. This baby apparently spent time inside Studio 54." Cassidy moved closer, a pincushion in hand.

"Your gorgeous legs fill the jumpsuit out to perfection, but I need to take in the waist."

"Bitch," Lilah muttered.

"Just for that, I'm not making you any enchiladas," Gabby shot back before pulling up the bodice. She slipped her arms through the sleeveless top, the one-piece ensemble closing over her breasts in a low-cut V. The flowing material draped her in a mix of sexy elegance, sparkly sequins and raw sexuality, and she felt her temperature rise a few degrees as her hasty words once again haunted her.

I'll have you know I'm a damn fine shag.

Cassidy must have seen the waves of doubt that suddenly had her waffling because she rushed forward. "Don't get cold feet on me now."

"I look like a tramp."

"You look like a sexy, confident woman who knows what she wants." Cassidy reached for the waist, the waving pin in her hand effectively rooting Gabby in place before she ended up impaled on it.

"Or who she wants," Lilah added, her face alight in mischief.

Knox.

The man hadn't been far from her mind for days, his heavy-handed ways and cocky demeanor on a permanent loop through her thoughts. "I'm not. And, I mean, we're not—"

"You are," Cassidy said from the vicinity of her waist.

"And you will," Lilah added in a singsong voice. "Especially since you're rockin' that *American Hustle* look even better than Amy Adams."

"You're both being ridiculous. And Amy Adams is gorgeous."

"So are you, my friend." Before Gabby knew the intent, Lilah leaned forward and planted a big smacking kiss on her cheek. "So are you. And Knox St. Germain, international man of mystery, isn't going to be able to keep his eyes off you."

Cassidy stood up and moved back a few steps, her hands on her hips. "This is perfect."

"Where did you get it, anyway?" Gabby smoothed her hands over the material and tried to forget the fact she felt more naked than the day she was born.

"I found it in a vintage shop and couldn't pass it by. I'm too short for the outfit, but figured I could do something with the material at some point. But I could never bear to cut it up." Cassidy ran a hand over the fabric, her gaze lost in an image only she could see. "Clearly it was waiting for you. Just as it is."

"You want me to wear this in London."

"Yep." Cassidy leaned forward and fiddled with something at the waist.

While Cassidy continued to fuss over the outfit, Lilah played cheerleader. "It's the perfect cover. You'll have Knox's attention *and* the attention of whoever is trying to set him up. And while the bad guys are looking at you, Knox can find what he needs."

"Do you really think he's being set up?" Gabby had hesitated pushing her thoughts in that direction. From what she understood and from some research Reed had done on his own a few days before, Knox was legit. A well-respected member of MI5. Was there really someone in his organization trying to set him up to take the fall for the Moray situation?

Although she resented Knox's implication earlier that her life was tame and simple compared with his, he wasn't far off the mark. The worst things she dealt with in her job were clients arguing the bill or a shipment of bad supplies. No one shot at her or plotted against her or tried to double-cross her. Hell, she didn't even have anyone in town with whom she competed for business like some sort of strange arch nemesis. Dallas was on fire with business and industry, and there was plenty of work to go around.

So what would it be like to question everyone you trusted professionally?

"Take it off. I want to make a few quick alterations so you can take this with you."

Cassidy's order pulled Gabby out of her reverie and she obediently stripped out of the outfit. She'd wanted something sexy and attractive, a fit for what she needed to accomplish as Knox's cover in London. She hadn't quite bargained for a skintight jumpsuit that showed off enough cleavage that she could sit on the prow of a ship like a buxom mermaid.

But she couldn't deny she wanted to wear that outfit for Knox.

And maybe—just maybe—she'd protested a bit too much when Lilah had insinuated it was only a matter of time before she and Knox would sleep together.

A girl had to keep her illusions, after all.

Didn't she?

Chapter 10

Knox had to hand it to Gabriella; the woman knew how to make things happen. Max and his grandfather had been dispatched to the hotel to collect Knox's things, Violet and Mrs. B began compiling a list of everything the older woman could remember about the rubies from her father, and Tucker and Reed worked out a flight strategy.

In the end, it had made more sense to fly commercial; the risks were minimal enough to get him home without dragging a private pilot into the mix. Sam had come through with the ticket for one of Knox's aliases, and it was quick work to get Gabriella on the same flight.

And if that small spot at the back of his neck itched, he'd live with it until they landed at Heathrow and finished the last few kilometers to his flat.

He flipped off the shower taps and reached for a

towel. How had he been talked into this? He knew his training, and he knew his responsibilities.

But he needed help.

It was a bugger of a feeling, but that didn't make it any less true.

Buchanan and Baldwin had enough training and skills to feel familiar. They didn't need to share the missions they'd gone on to convey the more obvious fact they had the experience. Graystone was all cop and, from everything Knox had seen, a damn fine one. The man had been shaken by his stepfather's betrayal, but he was good stock.

And then there was Gabriella.

Fierce, proud, beautiful Gabriella.

She'd disappeared into the workroom/bedroom with Lilah and Cassidy, leaving him to take a long, hot shower and figure out where the hell his life had gone off the rails. It had also given him a few moments by himself to question why he couldn't stop thinking about her.

She'd surprised him before, with the soccer story. He'd braced himself for a fight—had even attempted to tease one to life with the snide remark about her job— when she flipped the tables on him. A folksy story from her childhood and the not-so-subtle message that she wasn't going anywhere, and in a matter of minutes she had him dancing to her tune.

And going along with her crazy plan.

He rubbed the steam off the bathroom mirror and leaned forward, inspecting his shoulder. "The madwoman even knows how to stitch up an injury," he muttered to himself before quickly toweling off his hair.

The steam in the bathroom lingered in a heavy wave and Knox opened the door into Cassidy's bedroom to air it out. Padding over the aged hardwoods to the fresh set of clothes she'd laid out on the bed, he saw a small note.

Figured you'd like something that didn't belong to anyone else. These are spares I keep for nervous grooms and drunk groomsmen who end up needing a change of clothes.

Once again, the sheer ingenuity and thoughtfulness of these women struck him. Gabriella's friends were as efficient as she was, their ability to shift gears and pivot to something new as effortless as breathing.

What made a person like that? Was it freedom from experiencing circumstances so horrible they broke you? Or was it personality that determined if you were breakable or unbreakable?

A long-forgotten conversation with his sister, Daphne, filled his thoughts, and Knox fisted the cotton shirt in his hands at the remembered frustration and lack of understanding.

"You're leaving again?" She'd chased him out the front door and down to the street. *He'd weeded that footpath just the day before, painted the house two weeks ago and fixed the furnace the prior weekend. He refused to leave the house in poor repair before he left, and didn't want his mother or sister giving any of it another thought.*

That counted for something, didn't it?

"I have a job to do, Daph. I need to get to it."

"Running to it is more like it."

Why the hell wouldn't he want to run away? Everyone had crawled up his damned arse since his turd of a father left town. It had been almost two years now,

and his mother still could barely get through the day.
"So what if I am?"

"And leaving me here to deal with Mum."

Guilt swamped him, growing over his rib cage
in thick bands. Unlike the weeds on the footpath, he
couldn't dislodge or cut away the remorse that his
choice limited his sister from having any.

But they needed money, and other than a small
amount his mother had tucked away over all the years
of her marriage, pound by stupid pound, they had noth-
ing.

"The recruiter says I'm good."

"Of course you're good. We all know how bloody
smart you are and how clever you are with a problem.
They're lucky to have you."

He pinked up at the compliment and knew she meant
it as such. But the mention of his brain put him into
uncomfortable territory. Everyone had such high ex-
pectations for him, and Daphne's favorite tease was
"rocket scientist" every time he made a comment she
didn't fully understand.

"It's not just the recruiter. This guy, Richard Moray,
he's a big deal there, and he told me I can be someone.
Make something of myself. I need to see this through."

"You are someone. You're a son. A brother. A bloody
person who should stay and do what's right here. You
already got that fancy scholarship to university. Why
are you messing around with some weird recruitment
project?"

"I want this, Daph."

She turned, her gaze roving over the small home
they'd spent their lives in. "I want something, too.
Something bigger than tears and fights and mourn-
ful wailing in the middle of the night for the bastard."

"It will get better. She's gotten better."

Daphne laughed, the blue eyes so like his own dull and listless. "Whatever helps you sleep at night, little brother."

"Daph—" She turned on her heel, marching toward the door. "Daph!"

The door swung open on her hard tug, and he tried once more, more forceful this time. "Daphne!"

But she didn't turn and he stood stock-still, rooted to the spot.

He should go after her and try to work something out. The recruiter didn't give him a sense of timing on his initial requirements, but surely he'd get time to come home after he went through his first round of training. He'd relieve Daphne then, sending her off on a leisurely spa weekend for some time to herself.

He would take care of her.

He would.

Knox snapped from the memory, the long-buried remorse landing in his stomach like a falling weight. He did take care of Daphne and their mother, too. Each paycheck was carefully sent home, payment for his escape from the hellish life he'd fled at the first opportunity.

But he'd never counted on just how broken his mother was. Nor how vast and deep his sister's anger and pain were, until she'd taken hellish to an entirely new level.

And he'd never gone home again.

"You don't look very excited." Gabby buckled into her seat, the plush leather in first class cradling her as if she were a baby in a car seat.

"Why should I be excited?"

"Um, because we're sitting in first class and London's on the other side of the trip."

"So's Moray."

He'd kept his voice low, the comment about his boss for her ears only. Gabby knew there was danger, but a small part of her wanted to resent him for the wet-blanket routine.

Until she stopped and considered it from his position.

She was on an adventure. An ill-considered one, no doubt, but one all the same. He, on the other hand, was facing the reality of a boss gone rogue and a broader organization behind him possibly hiding additional corruption and dishonesty.

"Perspective, Gabriella. Consider where others come from before making a rash decision. Before your tongue becomes as sharp as your mother's."

Her grandmother's remembered words, from one long-ago day, rose up to swat at her. She'd been working on her college applications and had had yet another wicked fight with her mother over the decision to even go. She'd fled to her grandmother's house, desperate for a willing ally in her fight, and got scolded instead.

"You say she angers you, yet you don't even listen or consider her opinion. Consider her side. Hear her out. Give her an opportunity to speak." Her grandmother winked. *"Then do what you want to do."*

The lesson had been hard-won and it had taken a few more years for the broader message to sink in. Eventually her stubborn streak had given way to an understanding of her mother's words and actions.

And a deeper understanding that they were motivated by fear. Fear for her daughter to strike out on a path that didn't—on the surface—appear to have built-in security.

"Are you afraid to fly?"

The question interrupted her memories of that day

in the kitchen, and Gabby turned toward Knox. "No. Why?"

"You look upset."

"No, I'm not—" She stopped and reconsidered. "I'm sorry I can't tell my mother where I'm going. And I'm even sorrier Cassidy's going to bear the brunt of the conversation."

"Why not have it yourself?"

"She's not very understanding. She likes things her way."

His gaze traveled over her face. The consideration she saw there was part evaluation, part question. "You don't know what comes next. And you don't know what we're facing. She deserves to talk to you. And you to her."

Gabby glanced down at the phone in her hand. He had a point, both in what he said and what he didn't. She didn't know what they were facing, but she was stupid to think she wasn't playing with her life.

Unwilling to give her thoughts any further time to betray her heart, she hit her mother's preprogrammed number, her heart leaping when she heard Elena's voice on the other side. "Gabby, love. Where are you?"

"I'm on a plane, Mama. On an adventure to London."

"Ricardo's here. He's worried. We're all worried."

Her mother's voice vacillated between a mix of Spanish and English as she recounted Ricardo's experiences of the night before. "He's a bad man, Gabriella."

"Which is why we must stop him."

"No, the man you're with. He's a bad man."

"He's not." Gabby briefly toyed with switching to Spanish to outline all the reasons why Knox was far from it, but she knew he'd translate.

Besides, he didn't need to know her innermost thoughts.

"He's not, Mama. He's going to keep me safe."

"You can't go."

Her mother's voice remained hard, but Gabby heard the tears beneath the quivering words. "Mama. *Mama*. Listen to me, please. Whether I like it or not, I am a part of this. And someone needs help. *My* help."

"It's not your fight."

"It is now. I don't expect you to understand, but I called so you know how much I love you."

"I love you, too."

"And I'll bring you something wonderful back from London. Papa, too. I'm only going for a few days." *I hope.*

Gabby ignored the crushing weight of her heart as it descended into her stomach. "The plane is taking off soon, so I need to go. Give Maria my best and my apologies I'll miss the engagement party."

"Be careful, baby girl."

"I will, Mama. I love you."

"I love you, too."

Gabby hung up and switched her phone into airplane mode. She wasn't going to dwell on the conversation or focus on the fear beneath her mother's words. Cassidy had loaned her a large tote and filled it with some additional necessities, including a few fashion magazines for the trip. Tucking the phone into the side pocket, she pulled one out.

She'd done the right thing and called her mother.

Now all she could do was continue to pray Knox knew exactly how to slay the monster that waited in the wings.

* * *

Gabby awoke with a start, her neck screaming in pain at the odd angle she'd lain against the window. Rubbing her nape, she glanced over at Knox. He fiddled on a computer, the wire frames he'd worn the first time she'd met him propped on the bridge of his nose.

He seemed absorbed, but she didn't doubt for a minute he knew she was awake.

So *stop staring,* chica. *He's not a piece of meat.*

Which was the problem, wasn't it?

The magazine she'd flipped through earlier tilted against her thigh, and she caught a glimpse of a male model on the back page, oiled and glistening to perfection. The perfect two-dimensional image.

She'd wanted to paint Knox with the same brush, but no matter how hard she tried, she kept coming back to the three-dimensional man. He was gorgeous, yes. Distractingly so. But it was something more.

He had a chivalrous streak that layered over a steely core of responsibility. She knew it pained him to have her along—to drag her into his current situation—but once he'd accepted her presence, he shifted his entire focus to keeping her safe. Even in the hour they'd spent waiting to board their flight, she'd observed his constant vigilance. He'd sat with her in one of the terminal's restaurants, their backs to the wall in a dark corner, his gaze never veering far from the entrance.

Knox St. Germain was a protector. A haunted one, at that.

It was none of her business, but she wanted to know why there were shadows behind his eyes that never quite faded. She wanted to know why he marched so stoically toward his goals, even though they seemed like leaden weights around his ankles. She wanted to know why he was nearly maniacal in his focus.

But most of all she wanted to know about the shadows.

"Do you need me to let you up?" He turned toward her, the shock of that direct blue stare as potent as electricity. More so, she amended, when it was amplified through those crazy-sexy glasses.

"I'm good."

"We've got about four more hours. It's good you slept."

"Did you?"

"Now I'm the one who's not tired."

Her distracted train of thoughts coalesced into something more tangible and whether it was the dark, cocoon-like feeling of their seats or simple curiosity she didn't know. "Will you see your family now that you're back in London?"

"No."

"Do you ever see your family?"

"No."

"Why?"

"There's no one to see."

That news should not have been a surprise. She'd suspected all along he had secrets—something that had made him willing and able to do his chosen profession. And while she'd not directly asked him, in passing conversation most people mentioned their families. The people in their lives.

And he mentioned no one.

And isn't that rich?

She had so many family members you practically needed a roll-call list to keep up, and he had no one. The stark reality hit her with a swift punch. What if no one was ever there? There to celebrate the good times. The bad times. The holidays. The average days. The boring afternoons when you wanted to drag someone along to a movie or a lunch date.

What if no one was there?

"I'm sorry, Knox."

He stilled for a moment before removing his glasses. The lack of filter seemed to make his eyes bluer, if that were even possible, and the shadows even more stark. "Don't you want to know why?"

"Do you want to tell me?"

"Not particularly."

"Then, no, I don't want to know." She laid a hand on his arm, unable to sit by and not touch him. Not attempt to make some sort of physical contact. "When you want to tell me, you will. Until then, know I'm here."

When you want to tell me, you will.

When, not if.

Knox remained in his seat, unable to tear his gaze away from Gabriella. Where had she come from? This woman who continued to show facet after facet, each one more rich and beautiful than the next.

She was intuitive and perceptive, caring and instinctively compassionate. In short, she was amazing.

And her simple kindness unnerved him more than he could have ever imagined.

When.

He actively avoided thinking of his family. He'd learned long ago there was nothing to be gained by dwelling on the past, and he focused on the here and now.

Always.

Even his future seemed like a dim, distant idea,

pointless to focus on if he failed on a mission or didn't give his current priorities his full attention. But in the rush of living in the moment, it was humbling to realize he'd lost any sense of wonder or excitement about things still to come.

"You're an unusual woman."

"Thanks. I think." The cabin lights were off except for the overhead that illuminated his seat. The beams scattered, highlighting a portion of Gabriella's face while keeping the rest in shadow.

"I mean it as a compliment."

"Then I'll take it as one. Thank you."

When she said nothing, just continued staring at him, he pressed on. "You have your own mind. And you live according to no one's rules but your own."

"I lived under someone else's for so long, when I finally got to make my own decisions, I decided to do things my way."

"You're fiercely loyal to your family, yet perfectly willing to go against them."

"Which ties into my choices and decisions. I love my family, but they're the ones who tried holding me back. I won't live that way."

He reached out and ran a hand over her cheek before tracing the curve of her neck. "No, you wouldn't. You're your own person, through and through."

He wanted her. He'd known it from the start, but the time spent with her only reinforced his desire. Yet it was something more than that.

Simple lust would be easy to define. Something he could put in a box, just like his past and his future. He could take his pleasure with her, classify the time as a few fleeting, ephemeral moments and go on about his life.

Only he had the increasing suspicion things with Gabriella wouldn't be quite so simple. Nor would she be all that easy to get out of his system, should he be lucky enough to share a few of those fleeting moments with her.

"I want you." The longing spilled from his lips before he could censor his words. He'd wanted women before—had known need and desire and sexual intent in equal measure.

But in his entire life, he'd never ached for another person. It humbled him.

Humbled and strengthened in equal measure. And it made him deeply, unbearably vulnerable.

Knox knew the feeling for the sheer irony that it was. He fought the biggest battle of his life—Moray wasn't simply a threat to his profession, but to his very existence—and he'd finally gone and found a woman who held his interest for longer than an evening.

While he'd never been crass enough or so blindly dedicated to his job that he accepted the concept of collateral damage, he ran the very real risk that Moray could—and would—harm Gabriella as a path to get to him.

His carefree, unattached lifestyle had caught up with him. All the things that made him an outstanding agent—namely, lack of emotion and connections to others—had changed in a matter of days.

Gabriella Sanchez had crawled inside him somehow, her long legs and her warm brown eyes and her intense loyalty to those she loved a beacon of hope that pulsed in him.

Transformed him.

And there was nothing he wouldn't do to keep her safe.

Chapter 11

Bright sunlight flooded the concourse as they stepped through the doors at Heathrow. Knox had worked some magic in Customs—clearly his job had a few perks—and in moments Gabriella was following him past the guards and toward the exit to baggage claim. They both traveled light and had cleared the airport not even fifteen minutes after getting off the plane.

She'd wanted to take in the sights, even if it was just an airport terminal, but Knox's words continued to play over and over in her mind. They were so powerful they'd managed to obscure her vision as the memory of their quiet moments on the plane filled her thoughts.

You're your own person, through and through.

She'd understood her attraction to him. He was a powerful man, with an equally powerful—and attractive—physical form. But it was humbling and awesome to realize that he saw her.

That he listened to her.

And that the very things she'd worked so hard to accomplish weren't seen as barriers.

"Sam booked us a car."

"Oh?" She surfaced from her thoughts. "Your co-worker?"

"Yes." Knox kept a hand on her lower back, his body positioned like a shield as he displayed the same vigilance she'd seen at the Dallas airport.

A man with a sign spotted them and raised it higher, St. Germain written on a small placard he carried with him, and Gabby pointed. "I see one down there."

"What's the number on the car?"

Gabby read him the numbers off the corner of the driver's placard, and, after checking his phone, Knox seemed satisfied. "He's ours. Let's go."

"Mr. St. Germain?" the driver inquired. "I'm Hugh and will take you and your lovely friend here into the city. To the office, sir?"

"No, Miss Sanchez would like to freshen up. We'll head to my flat." Knox gave a set of directions that sounded incredibly foreign to Gabby but seemed perfectly normal to Hugh.

"Excellent, sir."

Hugh took their bags, and Knox helped her into the car. The black luxury car was understated, but definitely top of the line, and she had the sudden impression of falling down the rabbit hole.

When Hugh pulled into traffic on the wrong side of the street, Gabby knew she was well and truly in a foreign land.

"You look surprised," Knox murmured in her ear, the slight bump of his lips against the outer shell when

Hugh took a sharp turn out of the airport sending shock waves through her.

"I look like a rube, staring at the big city."

"I'd hardly call Dallas small."

He was right, and Gabby recognized size and space was dependent on what you knew and loved and where you felt comfortable. She toggled between Dallas and her visits to her grandmother in Mexico with ease and didn't think twice about being in another country.

But something about *here*. The accents. The sights through her window. The driving on the other side of the road. It all felt so foreign.

Yet to Knox it was home. They were truly from different worlds.

"No, Dallas isn't small. Or certainly not any longer. But that doesn't change the fact I was sitting in my grandmother's kitchen less than twenty-four hours ago, just like I have for over thirty years. And all that time, this was here. A world away."

"It's been here a lot longer than that. As much as I love seeing the world and all of mankind's ingenuity, I love coming home to my city that's thousands of years old. She still feels like she's getting warmed up."

"That she is, sir." Hugh's gaze was visible in the rearview mirror. "I'll take the M4?"

Knox nodded. "Of course."

Gabby sensed something in the exchange, yet couldn't put her finger on what or why. But as Hugh got onto the on-ramp for the motorway, seemingly going the wrong way, her stomach cratered once more with the reality of where she was.

Five thousand miles from home with a stranger.

What was she thinking?

Flashes of memory and a series of simple impressions hit her all at once. The first time she met Knox when he knocked on the back door of Lilah's kitchen at Elegance and Lace. His injured form, bleeding as he fell through her front door. The warmth of his touch on the plane, his hand tracing soft, tender lines over her cheek.

She remembered each and every one so clearly it was almost visceral. Gabby couldn't stop the wave of panic at the reality of her situation.

What the hell was she doing there?

Traffic was heavy, but Hugh traversed it with expert grace and economy of motion, slipping between cars and generally moving them along faster than the rest of the drivers on the road.

And once again, she sensed something beneath the surface, just like the man's quick discussion of routes with Knox.

With a furtive stare, she shifted her attention forward and took in the back of Hugh's head. He'd seemed innocent enough, his slender frame and soft brown hair tinged with gray making him appear just as he was—a well-heeled driver.

But there was something in his movements, the clean press through traffic like a shark beneath the water.

"Knox?" She leaned toward him, her voice purposely low, veering toward sultry to keep up their appearances as hot new love interests. She pressed one hand to his thigh, while with the other she traced a path down his cheek, then on down toward his chest.

Those blue eyes she swore would haunt her until the end of her days widened before filling with an answering response that spoke of long, fevered nights in bed. Recognizing she may have overplayed her hand, she tightened her grip on his thigh and dropped her voice one more notch. *"Knox."*

Husky need and raw impatience blended into a near growl. "What?"

"I think our driver's a problem."

His eyes darted toward Hugh before returning toward her. "He's fine."

"He's—"

Gabby stopped, willing her thoughts to calm. Why was she so convinced something was up with Hugh? Because getting into this car was a sudden reminder she wasn't home anymore. Or because he was a nice, aging British man who'd spent his life driving a car and who knew how to navigate the heavy traffic on the wrong side of the road.

"He's *fine*, Gabriella."

Again, some strange tableau seemed to spread out before her, but no matter how hard she searched, she couldn't quite make sense of the players or what was really going on beneath the surface.

When a hard pop hit the glass behind their heads, exploding into an intricate pockmark pattern, Gabby realized her instincts had been spot-on all along.

Knox grabbed Gabriella, pulling her across his body and hollering out orders. "Hugh!"

"On it, sir."

The car swerved, and Knox held Gabriella tight against his body to minimize the jerking movement of the car. It might be a top-of-the-line luxury vehicle with bulletproof glass, but Hugh was going nearly a hundred kilometers an hour, and no amount of luxury could displace the basic laws of physics.

He'd worked with Hugh before—the Security Service's best wheelman knew what he was doing. But damn if he'd been lulled into a false sense of security anyway.

Knox toyed with leaving their seat belts on and keeping them at such an odd angle or unbuckling so they could move into the seat wells when Hugh took another swerve, this time to the right side of the highway.

"What's going on?" Gabriella's gaze was wide, her voice choked with fear.

"Our problem seems to have followed us home to London."

"How'd he get here so fast?"

"He likely has help, love." Hugh's voice echoed from the front seat, his teeth gritted as he took another expert dive around traffic.

"Can't we get off the highway?" Her voice was tremulous, but the core of her—the strength and solid focus that was Gabriella—came through loud and clear. "We can't expose all these people to our problem. Someone's going to get killed."

Knox trusted Hugh with their lives, but he knew if they got off the highway, they put themselves in far greater danger. And it wasn't as if the London suburbs were empty of humanity. A firefight on a residential street was as dangerous, if not more so, than taking their chances on the M4.

"Hugh knows what he's doing."

"Not my first rodeo, ma'am." The Texan colloquialism, uttered in such cultured tones, seemed to do the trick, and Gabriella relaxed slightly beneath his touch.

Signs for the Central Business District were visible from his perch on the backseat and Knox reconsidered his position on the suburbs. If they were at risk on the highway, they'd become sitting ducks on the crowded streets of London, along with every pedestrian in a block's radius.

"We need to get rid of them."

"Here, sir." Hugh handed back a wicked-looking Glock. "Fully loaded. Perhaps you can be my eyes and line up a few shots of your own?"

Knox patted Gabriella's back, willing her to stay as calm and unmoving as possible. Hugh had some serious skills, and he didn't doubt the man's well-honed reflexes went a long way toward keeping them moving forward, but they had to deal with the threat from behind or risk the dangers in upcoming traffic no amount of skills could work around.

"Sunroof."

The subtle release of air as the sunroof popped was proof Hugh had heard him, and Knox unbuckled his seat belt to climb up. "Stay down, Gabriella. Sit between the seat and Hugh if you can."

She did as he asked, folding herself into the small space without complaint.

When he moved up into the open rooftop, he felt her hands grip his waist. He glanced back down in surprise, but she only shot out orders as she lifted up onto her knees. "You need as much stability as you can get, and Hugh can't focus on you. I'll hold you as steady as I can."

Whatever attraction or fascination or even plain old lust he'd held inside coalesced into something else in that moment, and Knox could have sworn he heard his heart crack wide-open. The woman was amazing.

Mind-numbingly, soul-shatteringly amazing.

"Knox! Go!"

He did as she asked, pushing himself through the sunroof. He was careful to keep his chest below the roofline as he worked to get a bead on their shooter. He followed the flow of traffic, the waving arms and silently mouthed screams of several drivers on the road more than evident.

"So bloody, buggering exit the damn road!" he hollered at a few, waving his gun for added effect.

One by one, he followed the cars, seeking his quarry. Hugh's maniacal focus on threading them through any available traffic hold knocked him sideways a few times, but Gabriella kept her hands firmly at his waist and back and he righted himself quickly.

"Your ten o'clock, sir!" The shout echoed up through the window and the direction was just enough to give him what he needed. Two men in dark suits fit the profile, but it was the flash of a gun that matched his own that had Knox lining up his sights.

He fired off two shots. The first hit the metal edge of the car's windshield, easily deflecting. The second went wide, missing his target and thankfully anyone else in close proximity. An answering shot flew into the already impacted glass of the back windshield, and Knox renewed his efforts, aiming for the shooter while the man was distracted by taking his own shot.

Although he missed his physical target, he hit the windshield; the glass cracked instantly. It didn't shatter, but it was enough to slow his opponents slightly as they managed the physical impact of the hit.

Hugh veered once again, and Knox slid sideways. A hard push from Gabriella at his waist and his buttocks kept his ribs from slamming into the side of the sunroof opening. He couldn't resist sending down a small tease. "You feeling up my arse, Sanchez?"

A retort shot back up at him before he could blink.

"It's a damn fine arse, and I'd like to keep it in one piece."

"The lady's right, St. Germain. It's a damn fine arse and a rather valuable one at that!" Hugh's voice floated up through the opening in the roof. "Come back down before I execute my boldest move yet."

Although none of them were quite ready to laugh, Knox appreciated the attempts at humor in the midst of the firefight. He slid back through the hole, Gabriella's hands moving over his body as she kept him steady, waist to ribs to chest.

"You missed?"

"I didn't miss." He stumbled, fighting the sheer affront of her statement. "Bastards have bulletproof glass, too."

She shrugged. "You can't blame them."

Hugh's voice was sharp, any layer of teasing vanishing in the moment. "Hold on tight."

Knox pulled Gabriella close, anchoring himself in the base of the floor as Hugh executed a neat 180 toward an open embankment. The move was something men in Hugh's position trained for, but it required precision and left no room for error.

The screech of tires echoed before the car seemed to shudder, coming up off the ground as they spun high in the air.

Her bones jarred against each other as the car slammed to the ground with a heavy thud before bouncing several more times. Gabby clung tightly to Knox, well aware they at least had a port in the storm, while Hugh only had a seat belt.

"Nicely done, mate," Knox hollered over his shoulder before scrambling up onto the backseat. He reached for her hand, gently pulling her up when a heavy shout echoed from the front seat.

"Company!"

Another gun appeared as the window next to Hugh rolled down. Gabby watched—half-awed, half-appalled— as Hugh fired through the open window.

"I've got your—"

Whatever Knox was going to say vanished in the loud crack of a gunshot and the blood that exploded over the interior of the car.

"Hugh!" she screamed, not even aware the sound was coming from her lips as she climbed over the seat, trying to hold on to the man who'd been so full of life only moments before.

"Gabriella! Back!"

The moments slowed to a near standstill, and Gabby watched as if unattached to herself. Knox scrambled over the front seat, holding the wheel steady as he attempted to move over Hugh to take control of the car. Gabby tried to keep her grip on Hugh, willing her hands to somehow provide a barrier for the blood that poured from a hole in his forehead.

"The seat, Gabriella! Move the seat."

"I can't…I can't let go of him."

"The seat! Now!"

The words snapped her out of her stupor and she fumbled against the side of the driver's seat, her hand finding the button that moved the seat back. She slipped, the slick wash of blood on her hands making her slide over the button until she stopped and focused. With trembling fingers, she pressed on the lever.

The luxurious leather slid on the electronic command, and Knox climbed over Hugh's body, positioning himself at the wheel to keep them moving forward. She continued pressing on the button after the seat stopped moving, willing more space and distance between Knox and Hugh, even as she knew there was no way they could help the man.

No way they could bring him back.

"How can I help?"

"I need you to take the gun and keep an eye on the road. Anyone looks suspicious, you need to shoot at the tires."

"Not at them?"

He shot a quick glance over his shoulder, his blue eyes warm like a summer's ocean. "Focus on the tires, love. That's all I need."

His endearment added a layer of calm, and she reached through the space between the driver's and passenger's sides for the gun still in Hugh's hand. The grip was firm, but she carefully pried open his fingers, struggling against the reality of his still-warm flesh. He was just here. Alive. Triumphantly racing them back to London.

And now he was gone.

The London streets were a haze of motion outside her window, but Gabriella saw none of it. Knox had stopped just outside the city, once he was sure they'd shaken their murderous tail, and repositioned Hugh's body across the backseat. He'd then pulled her out of the car, buckling her into the front passenger seat for the rest of the drive.

A protective veil shrouded her emotions, and she kept looking back, feeling the need to keep watch over Hugh.

"Don't look, Gabriella."

"I need to. I need to see him. To remind myself he

died keeping me safe. If I don't, then his efforts were in vain."

Her voice cracked, but she couldn't find any tears. It was like her eyes had gone desert dry and nothing could erase the stark, cold reality of what she saw when she looked at Hugh's lifeless body. She'd known from the first that she was playing with fire. That her decision to help Knox was the start of a dangerous adventure that put her at risk.

But it wasn't until the ride from the airport that she truly understood the stakes. That the reality of what and who she was dealing with had sunk in.

Richard Moray had deep pockets and nearly inexhaustible resources.

He was also determined, insane and completely without any moral compass. He'd wanted the Renaissance Stones, and he'd set out on a campaign to secure them. Anyone who stood in his way was an enemy to be destroyed, as ruthlessly and efficiently as possible.

What power did those damned stones hold? Violet had filled her in on all the research she'd found on the rubies, and she'd done plenty of her own.

And now it seemed as if poor Hugh was their latest victim.

"I'm going to take you to my flat, and then I need to call in help to manage Hugh."

"Manage?"

"Yes, I—" He stopped and reaching for her hand, wrapped it in his own. "Hugh will be well cared for, his service to Britain properly acknowledged. And he will have a proper burial, as well. But we still don't know who within MI5 is possibly working with Moray, if anyone. We need to manage the news flow, and we need to make sure his body is handled properly."

That fall-down-the-rabbit-hole feeling struck once more, and Gabriella struggled to understand Knox's meaning. "How could his body be mishandled?"

"If Moray does have his tentacles deep inside MI5, I don't want any evidence planted on him between us bringing him back and his autopsy. I need my friend Sam's help to escort the body."

"Oh."

Once again, the reality of Knox's life struck her as something out of a movie. The man worked for the British government, managing a royal secret that dated back more than six decades. While he'd chafe at the moniker, the man was as good as a royal spy, working to save the monarchy's reputation all while rooting out corruption and madness in his organization.

She'd never considered herself naive—she was well aware the world was full of some seriously bad people who had no issue with harming others to get what they wanted. She'd seen Ricardo and several of her cousins live with that reality as members of the Dallas PD. She also accepted that crime was crime and being the victim of one was equally horrible if the perpetrator was some street-corner thug or a well-heeled government operative.

So why did it *feel* so different?

No matter how she sliced it in her mind, the end result was the same. One was faceless and random, even as it was a horrifically sad indictment of humanity.

But the other…

How did someone build relationships and a career in a position, only to throw it all away for an object? How did one spend a life working with others—training them, mentoring them, leading them—and then become the very thing he'd worked to root out?

Was it about power? Greed? Corruption? Or did the rot on Moray's soul go deeper than that?

Knox's thumb rubbed over the back of her hand in a gesture of reassurance. "So like I said, I'm going to take you to my flat and set you up. The security is top-of-the-line, with enhancements I've made on my own. You'll be safe there while Sam and I care for Hugh."

"Okay."

"You can't go out."

"I understand."

"I'm sorry for that. More than you can ever know."

"Of course."

Gabby turned her head and looked at Hugh once more. Even with the windows cracked and Knox's earlier attempts to wipe up as much as he could, the car held the coppery smell of blood. She hadn't yet become accustomed to it and was glad of it.

As long as she could smell the blood, she could feel for Hugh. Could summon the proper layer of anger and fury and the need for raw, cold-blooded vengeance.

And as long as she felt for him, she'd work tirelessly to find his killer, both the one who'd delivered the final shot and the one who'd ordered it from the shadows.

She would do everything in her power—use every tactic at her disposal—to help Knox bring Richard Moray to justice.

The man deserved to pay. And she was ready and more than willing to dispense the toll.

Chapter 12

Knox rode the elevator up to his flat, glad to finally escape the basement parking in his building. He'd left Gabriella hours before, while Sam and two other men from the Security Service came to help him with Hugh.

The hours together had been at times somber and raucous, each remembering their friend in different ways. Hugh's role in MI5 had gone back more than three decades, and each of them had stories and memories in equal measure.

He was a stellar colleague and a good friend, so they'd all done the job and protected Hugh's mission. Knox had told them what he needed as they worked, and they carefully pulled, catalogued and filmed essential evidence to ensure there couldn't be any manipulation posthumously.

Sam had put them all in peals of laughter, remembering a mission with Hugh in the suburbs. Late-night boredom on a stakeout had finally gotten to Hugh, and he'd jaunted into a nearby backyard with clothes drying on the line. He'd nicked a rather large pair of knickers, then donned them to pass the time, making up a ribald story about their owner.

"Cheeky bastard even sent me a love note after the ginormous knickers event," Sam had sputtered out through his laugher as the rest of them doubled over.

Knox had his own memories, still so vivid and tangible even though several had been in his earliest days in the Security Service. No one knew how to maneuver a moving vehicle better than Hugh Tolliver.

And no one had loved his job more.

"Cheeky bastard," Knox muttered to himself as he stepped off the elevator.

A knot the size of a fist lodged in his throat as he accepted the inevitable. He'd never see his old friend again.

The scent of food wafted toward him across his flat, and he stared in shock at Gabriella, who stood before his stove. "What are you doing?"

"Cooking you a meal. You must be exhausted."

"Likewise."

She shrugged. "It's not so bad. And I lose track of time when I cook."

He'd done the same, only to find now that his endless day had given way to early evening. Soft light filtered through the two large windows that bookended the exterior wall of his living room.

This particular flat had been his home for the past four years, and he could count on one hand the number of times he'd used the stove. While he'd occasionally get a good whiff coming out of the microwave, he'd yet to have such a homey scent greet him upon arrival.

"Where'd you get the food?"

"I ordered from an online grocer and asked the door-man you introduced me to earlier to bring it up. I know you didn't want me going out, but I figured that sort of help was sanctioned."

"Quite right." He moved into the kitchen, the fist in his throat receding as the soothing scents of a pot roast filled the room. "This is an amazing spread."

"There's nothing more comforting than a pot roast, potatoes and vegetables."

"I'm not going to argue. Though I am a bit surprised. I thought enchiladas are your specialty."

"A fan favorite, no doubt, but I'm pretty good with a variety of dishes. You know, being a caterer and all."

She winked at him, the sassy move not doing much to cover the slightly haunted look still visible in her eyes.

"I also made an investigation of your wine rack. You've got some nice bottles for a Brit who probably likes to knock back a few pints."

"Can't I like both?"

"Fair point."

"Besides, I might not cook worth a damn, but I'm a civilized man and I like my wine." He glanced to the end of the counter. "Looks like you picked out a few."

"I figured the cabernet would work with the roast, but we could also do a rosé if you prefer."

He wasn't sure if it was her or Hugh or the simple power of the moment, but Knox didn't care any longer about wine. Or food. Or anything outside the apartment.

He only cared about Gabriella.

She turned from the counter, setting one of the bottles back after an inspection of the label. "What's wrong?"

"Nothing. Everything."

She moved closer—not more than a few steps, really—but it was enough.

Without bothering to check himself or quell the urge, he pulled her close and took. Took comfort. Took an opportunity to slake his thirst. And took her.

Her arms wrapped around his neck, immediate acquiescence in the moment as they joined together. Lips, mouths, tongues, all melded—merged, really—into something more.

Something greater.

The fear and anguish, grief and deep, deep pain receded. He'd cared for his old friend too much for any of those feelings to fully vanish, but in Gabriella's arms the pain faded, replaced with need and with desire and with *life*.

The high heels she perpetually wore were nowhere in evidence, and he found he liked her height in bare feet. She was still tall but now short enough he had to bend his head to kiss her. He liked the eye to eye—and would never argue with what the heels did to her legs—but it was refreshing to pull her close and bend into their kiss.

She'd showered earlier, and he could smell the scent of his soap and shampoo on her. The masculine brand he preferred had blended with her skin, reflecting back an enticing scent that was 100 percent feminine.

And wildly sexy.

He'd taken a quick shower upon their return himself and had used the wash purely for function, but now he knew he'd never smell that scent the same way again.

Hell, there was little he'd ever see the same way again, and he damn well knew it.

And it was all because of Gabriella.

He wanted to keep her safe and whole. He wanted to see the smile and light and laughter return to her eyes.

And he wanted her. It was madness, this wanting, but no matter how hard he tried to rid her from his thoughts, deftly ignoring the way she managed to creep in anyway, she was still there.

She was a risk, this woman with the witchy smile and the siren's hair and the glorious body. She made him want things he swore he'd never have because he'd never deserve them.

And he'd never deserve her.

But, oh, how he wanted her. Ached for her. And yearned for the promises behind her dark chocolate eyes.

"Knox." His name was a whisper on her lips, pressed against his own.

"Shhh."

"I need—"

He cut her off, his lips again crushing hers, his tongue sweeping in to mate with hers. The hands he'd settled at her waist when he'd pulled her close grew restless, and he drew his fingers over her body. Soft curves—so different from the harder angles of his body—tempted and tantalized as he ranged over her hips, then up her torso. He trailed a finger from her rib cage over her stomach, tracing a soft line around her bellybutton that had her shuddering against him.

"Ticklish?"

"Very."

"Then I'll have to do it again." He teased her once more, then continued his exploration. His hand drifted up, reaching the heavy fullness of the underside of her breast, and he stopped there, relishing the feel of it against the back of his hand.

She pressed against him, pushing closer, silently asking him to touch her. Unwilling to deny himself any longer, he turned his hand, cupping the weight of one breast, adding his other hand to cup the other. She filled him, the enticing feel of her body enough to make his legs tremble with the force of his desire.

He pressed his thumb against one sensitive nipple, never breaking the contact of their mouths as he explored. Instead, he gloried in the dual response of her lips and tongue urgent against his own while she pressed herself into his hand, her nipple growing harder beneath his touch.

She was so responsive—so *with* him in the moment—and he knew she would spoil him for anyone else, ever again.

And he didn't care. He just stood there, the fading color of evening streaming through his windows, a beautiful woman taking her pleasure in his arms.

Gabriella gasped as Knox swept his fingers over her nipple once more. She'd always considered foreplay a fun step, but one that didn't last all that long. Knox St. Germain had practically turned making out into an art form.

He'd pulled her close with that odd light in his eyes—one that spoke of grief and unbearable pain and a desperate, fervent hope—and she was lost. Lost to him and the way he made her feel.

But nothing had prepared her for the sheer joy and pleasure of being in his arms.

Although she loved working in her kitchen, she couldn't honestly say she'd ever found it a particularly sexy space. Sensual, yes. Food was always sensual, the taste, texture, color and scent mixing into an experience that transcended simply eating. Especially as someone who prepared food, she'd always appreciated the raw beauty to be found in the art of cooking.

With Knox, the kitchen became a wonderland of sexy moments. The hard counter at her back was cool and unyielding as he pressed against her body, effectively caging her in with his strength and heat. She loved the mix of sensations and how safe and secure she felt with him. Only after he'd thoroughly explored her body, from lips to cheeks to neck and on down over her breasts and stomach, did he flip her around, positioning her so she faced the counter.

His hands did wicked things, trailing over sensitive nerve endings while he maintained steady contact with his mouth.

For the vaguest moment, she thought to protest—they'd known each other for a matter of days—yet the thought of moving away from him was actually painful. She didn't want to walk away—not from Knox or from the opportunity to finally, gloriously feel what it was like to be with a man who made her come alive.

Long fingers roamed over her breasts, again teasing her sensitive flesh into hard peaks. She cried out at the sensual play of his hands over her body and practically melted as he ran his lips and tongue over the sensitive skin of her neck. She pressed her bottom into his groin, the ready evidence of his erection fitting against her. She craved those final moments when they'd join their bodies together.

"You are so beautiful." The words were whispered against her ear, his lips pressed to the lobe before he took the sensitive flesh between his teeth.

She'd been told that before—many times, in fact—and she'd always chalked the sentiment up to the crazy quirk of fate that had given her large breasts, a flat stomach and a long mane of hair. With Knox, the compliment felt different, as if he viewed her as beautiful because of what he truly saw. Her heart. Her mind. Her determination.

She knew it was silly to dream, but when Knox St. Germain looked at her she felt beautiful from the inside out.

"Thank you."

He turned her around to face him once again. "While I'd like nothing more than the gorgeous memory of you naked in my kitchen, I think we should move this to the bedroom."

"Why can't we do both?"

Their shirts had come off in their well-choreographed make-out session and Gabby finished the deed with a quick flick of the back hooks on her bra. Wiggling out of the straps, she stood proudly before him. The appreciative look in his eyes added to the sensual moment.

The blue of his eyes had turned a rich sapphire, and Gabby focused on those gorgeous depths as she reached for the button on her jeans. Impatience had her hands trembling, but she continued on, peeling down the zipper and gripping the small swath of silk underneath. Knox reached out for her, but she danced away, enjoying her role as temptress too much to stop.

Her jeans and panties pooled at her feet, and Gabby stepped out of each leg. She'd turned on the air-conditioning earlier while cooking, and the cool breeze swirled around her shoulders but did nothing to quell the flush that covered her skin.

"Come here. Please."

"Not until you're as naked as I am."

For the briefest moment, she thought he was going to sneak forward and pull her close, but instead he shucked his jeans and briefs in the same move she'd done. Whatever imagining she'd had about him naked—and she'd had several fantasies over the past four days—nothing matched Knox St. Germain in the flesh.

The man was gorgeous. Long, lean lines roped his body in corded muscle. She'd already seen those muscles in his chest and was delighted to realize that muscle tone covered his entire body. Hard ridges sculpted his stomach, descending into a trail of hair that expanded into the most intimate part of him. Her mouth dried at the image he made, but it was the thick erection, flush against his body, that drew her closer.

He was magnificent and only one word echoed in her mind over and over.

Mine.

Their time together might not be permanent, but for this moment—this point in time—he was hers. And she was going to take every moment of beauty and joy and pleasure she could possibly wring from it.

Knox struggled against the demands of his body as Gabriella's gaze roamed over his naked form. He'd always loved foreplay and the exploration stage of sex, but he hadn't ever been all that in tune with the making love part of the equation.

Until now.

The thought humbled him as it empowered, and he tried to keep a mix of dry, boring thoughts in his head to keep his body from going off like a bottle rocket. But if she kept looking at him like that...

"Vixen. Come here."

"That's awfully demanding."

"I seem to have developed an awfully demanding problem."

She smiled at that, the knowledge of a million years reflecting back in her eyes. The witch knew what she did to him, her liquid gaze heating his body as effectively as her touch.

"I believe I promised you the bedroom."

"Then we'd best get to it. Although, give me a minute." She danced away from him toward the stove, flipping the dial to Off. "That'll keep now without risking a call to the fire department."

"We may do that on our own."

She smiled before slipping into his arms and lifting her lips to his. "Then it will be a needed intervention and not an unnecessary interruption."

"I like how you think."

He wrapped his arms around her waist; the full-bodied press of flesh made him see stars once more. His body had moved past the point of arousal to near-painful need, and he wanted to move them to the bedroom.

He attempted to walk them backward, but when he hit his hip on a hard corner of the counter, so wrapped up in Gabriella he couldn't even manage a straight line, he opted for expedience. In moments, he had her swung up in his arms.

"Knox! I'm too heavy."

"You're perfect."

"I'm—" He shut off her protests with a hot kiss and moved with long strides toward the bedroom.

"But your shoulder."

"It's fine."

She could protest all she wanted; as far as he was concerned, she was perfect. And he wasn't sure he'd ever felt anything quite as good as having her in his arms. There was no way in hell he was letting a flesh wound intrude on the moment.

His flat was large by London standards, but it was still the work of a few feet to get to his bedroom. He hit the light switch with his elbow, and the small bedside lamp he had connected to the outlet glowed to life. His large bed dominated the room. It was humbling to realize just how much had changed since he'd last slept here.

The discovery of the rubies. Moray's betrayal. And Gabriella.

She was the good that had come out of his mission, even if the stark reality was that she should never be here in the first place.

"What's that frown for?"

She edged his jawline with the tips of her fingers, her touch a gentle counterpoint to the raw passion and wild attraction that hummed between them. It was quite amazing, really, to realize they could manage both ends of emotion so effortlessly.

Knox set her on her feet beside the bed, and her arms wrapped around his neck without a moment's hesitation. He reached up and ran his fingers over her shoulders and down the firm muscles of her arms. "You shouldn't be here."

"I—" Her gaze clouded, and he anticipated her move before she made it, holding on to her arms before she could pull away.

"That has nothing to do with how badly I want you here. How awed I am to stand here and imagine making love with you in my bed. In my home."

The frustration in her eyes softened, then shifted into acknowledgment. "I finally understood that today. With Hugh."

She ducked her head, and he reached out to tip her chin up with a finger. "You understood what?"

"I started on this path without a full understanding of what I was getting into. Of the danger involved and the ruthless people playing at anything but a casual game."

"Yes."

"But, Knox." She didn't attempt to shift away, but he felt a clear wall between the sexual attraction they sought to fulfill and the realities of why they were in London together. "You have to trust me that I'll listen to you and that I can help you. You're not in this alone."

"You don't belong here."

"Yet for a variety of reasons I am here. We can make that work. We *will* make it work."

Knox knew her words for truth. He could curse himself any way he wanted, but Gabriella was here, and she was a part of things. Moray knew who she was, which meant until he was dealt with, Gabriella was in serious danger. He could continue lamenting that fact, or he could look at her as the bright, capable woman he knew her to be and leverage her help.

"Yes, we'll make it work."

She kissed him again, first with a small nip at his lower lip, then with something more potent as her tongue slid between his teeth. Helpless to resist her or the electricity that coursed through his veins at their coming together, he held on to her as he laid them down on the bed.

He reached for a condom in his end table drawer, then slipped the packet beneath the pillow. They'd get to that in due time. For now, he wanted to experience Gabriella, imprinting everything he thought and felt onto her skin.

The teasing moments from the kitchen returned, and

he reveled in the pure joy of the moment. He kissed his way down her body, surprised when she flipped him over as he began the journey over her chest.

"It's my turn, secret agent man."

"Secret agent man?"

"It has a nice ring to it." She grinned before plying a row of kisses across his chest, her tongue flicking over the sensitive skin of his nipple. "And it's a crazy-potent fantasy."

He fought the strangled moan at her touch and tried to focus on the moment. "Aren't fantasies for when you're asleep?"

"Then don't wake me up," she whispered the words against his rib cage before she slid down his body, slippery and elusive as smoke.

Knox willed himself to enjoy the moment, yet fought desperately not to unman himself as she plied her tongue and hands over him. Wet heat and the most inventive tongue he'd ever experienced drew him deeper and deeper into her orbit. The woman held him in her thrall, and he could barely remember his name, let alone where they were or what they were running from.

Here. Now. There was only Gabriella. Glorious, wonderful Gabriella.

His body tightened painfully, and he wanted to see her face—wanted to watch her—when they came together. "Gabriella." He thought to whisper her name, but those four syllables came out on a hard moan. With deft hands, he reached for her, pulling her toward him. "Come with me."

She pressed several more kisses over his stomach, then back over his chest on a return path before reaching beneath him and snagging the foil packet from beneath the pillow. "Allow me."

Knox had the fleeting panic he wasn't going to last through her ministrations, but she made quick work of the condom, then rose up over his body. The image she made—hair down and wild, her slim shoulders and chest that flowed into generous breasts, and then her hips, positioned over his own.

He'd normally shift the game at this point, but she seemed so in control—so confident and sure—and he was rendered mute by the sheer beauty of her pleasure. Reaching for her hips, he held tight as she seated herself over him. He clung helplessly to her when a wave of black misted his eyes in raw, mind-numbing pleasure.

Managing a few rounds of multiplication tables, color reformed in his vision, and Gabriella came to life once more before him.

And then she moved.

Knox held tight to her, helping her set a rhythm for the both of them as she moved over his body. Skin slicked and the light banter and teasing smiles vanished as they both sought that moment of completion.

He'd spent his entire life running from this sort of intimacy. From the wild, desperate craving for someone else's body *and* their soul.

He'd believed himself immune. Unconquerable. Yet as Gabriella moved, her dark, mysterious gaze locked on his, Knox had to admit to himself he didn't know anymore. He wanted her with a strange, befuddled madness that cut him off at the knees, yet made him ten feet tall, all at the same time.

His thoughts increasingly grew more and more abstract as the demands of his body grew more pronounced. He watched her, unwilling to break their connection, until her eyelids dropped, closing as she rode his body toward her own pleasure.

When he heard a small cry and felt the tightening of her around his body he finally let go. Let that buildup of pleasure grip him in a shuddering release.

And held her tight, desperate for a handhold in the storm.

Gabriella collapsed over his chest, and he pulled her even closer, humbled by the power of what they'd created. Her body continued eliciting small shock waves and he kept a soothing hand low on her back, holding her still as the enormity of the moment passed.

Knox drifted, the endorphins filling his body slowly giving way to something softer and lazier. The large hand on her back moved in large circles, and he felt himself floating in a sort of waking dream.

Gabriella. Pleasure. Satisfaction.

Those three thoughts seemed to center over him, wordless feelings that comforted in the midst of the roiling storm that was his life.

He had no idea how long he drifted, but he registered the movement of the lithe form beneath his fingers as she snuggled into him.

Opening his eyes slightly, he stared up at her, surprised when she had the ability to speak.

"See."

He shifted his head off the pillow to look at her. "See what?" he mumbled huskily.

"I told you I was a damn fine shag."

A hard rumble erupted in his chest, and Knox had no idea how he had the energy to even respond. But the laugh rumbled harder, taking on a life of its own when he couldn't hold back the carefree feeling. So he went with it, pulling her close again and wrapping her up in his arms.

He had no idea how she'd done it, but in the midst

of the most powerful moment of his life, Gabriella had made him laugh. As her own throaty giggles met his, he wondered if he'd ever felt so good.

Or how he'd survive when she went away.

Chapter 13

"This is a first."

Gabby glanced up from plating roasted potatoes to see Knox peering over her shoulder. "What's a first?"

"I don't think I've ever had a home-cooked meal after sex." He snatched a potato off the plate. "Of course, I rarely have home-cooked meals, so I guess the sex part is just a lucky addition."

A very lucky addition, but she wasn't about to say that. She was still trying to figure out how she felt about the soul-bending, mind-blowing experience she'd had barely an hour ago. She'd believed herself capable of handling a physical relationship with Knox, but now she wasn't so sure. Every sign was in place, telling her not to get attached, from their different lifestyles to the fact they lived five thousand miles apart.

Oh, and that one small, other tiny detail she seemed determined to forget. The man was a royal spy. Or an international one, at least.

They were completely incompatible.

Yet here she was, her heart falling rapidly toward a place she knew she'd never fully recover from.

Pasting on a bright smile, she fought for some level of equanimity. "Home-cooked meals are a Sanchez specialty. I don't think I even ate in a restaurant until I was about ten and out with a friend's family."

"Seriously?"

"Yep." She handed him his plate, then picked up her own. He had a small nook between his kitchen and living room with an old drop-leaf table nestled in the corner. "My mother felt it was a waste of money to buy someone else's food. She also thinks anything she makes is better, so between the ranting about the price and the embarrassment over her food criticism, I think my father always found it easier to eat at home."

"Your mother's not an easy woman."

"She'd give Attila the Hun a run for his money."

"Ouch."

Knox had already poured glasses of wine and had lit a few tapers that flickered soft light over their meal. "This is nice."

"I can pour wine with the best of them."

She lifted on her toes and pressed a kiss to his cheek, the light growth of his beard scratchy against her lips. "It's lovely."

He stilled for a moment, and Gabby could have sworn she saw something in his eyes—something heavy and full of promise—before he shut it down and offered up a cheeky smile instead. "Let's eat."

Despite the monumental moments they'd shared in his bed—or perhaps because of them—conversation flowed freely. Food was always an icebreaker, Gabby knew. Heck, she made her living making and serving food at large events. But even with that knowledge, the time she spent with Knox had been strangely freeing.

She was at ease with him.

It was a surprise, Gabby admitted to herself, to realize just how easy he was to talk to. Even her comments about her mother he managed to take in stride, no obvious judgment coloring his words. He had few preconceived notions about anything and seemed able to debate any topic she could come up with. He also listened, which was a far headier experience than she could have ever imagined.

Her family loved her, but they came to every discussion with a set of arguments.

Why invest in a business of your own?

Why work such long hours?

Why not work as hard on finding someone to settle down with as you do with your events?

The ongoing criticism had grown tiresome, and in the past few days with Knox, Gabby had begun to realize just how much she'd come to resent the constant haranguing.

"Everything okay?"

"Sure." Gabby stilled in the process of cutting her slice of roast. "Actually, no. I'm not sure."

"Want to tell me about it?"

Gabby took in the broad shoulders beneath worn gray cotton and the wire rims that he'd put on before coming into the kitchen. She knew he was more than an attractive picture, but the solid form and the sexy glasses still filled her with a powerful need that hadn't even been remotely sated by the time they'd spent together.

"You listen to me." The words spilled out before she could debate them any further. "I know it's an odd thing to say, but since meeting you I hadn't realized quite how much I missed that. Or even realized it was missing at all."

"You're fascinating to listen to."

"That's sweet."

"I'm serious." Knox set his fork down. "You're a fascinating woman. You're beautiful, which is the part that knocks me on my ass and takes my breath away, all at the same time. And then by the time I get it back, you're wowing people with mad cooking skills and bone-deep compassion and damn fine stitches."

The compliments hit her like unrelenting gunfire; only instead of wanting to run, she could feel herself preening in the glow of his words.

Unwilling to sit too long in the glare for fear of falling even harder for him, she latched on to the part of his conversation she could do something about. "How is your shoulder?"

"Fine. But for someone who likes being listened to, you're not listening very hard. I told you—my shoulder's got some seriously well-done stitches."

She laughed as he tossed her words back at her. "You really are a turkey."

"Another thing you were right about. Although I'd like to think I taste better."

She didn't miss the innuendo or the soft reminder of what they'd shared an hour before. The air grew thick, the gentle teasing morphing into something more urgent.

More *present.*

Her skin tingled, and a restlessness gripped her. Dinner had been going so well, their conversation easy, fluid and simple, and in a matter of seconds, attraction obliterated any sense of calm.

It really would be so easy to slide all the way in love with him.

The thought caught her so off guard she pressed a hand to the table, seeking some balance despite her seated position.

Love?

The thought was so foreign—not to mention impractical, ill conceived and impossible to pursue.

Yet there it was all the same.

She'd developed a thick skin over the years, well able to withstand disappointment, and she'd have to depend on that to see her through the next few days. Smart girls didn't go around falling for international spies. It wasn't done. Certainly not from her small neighborhood in Dallas.

Swallowing around the knot that had settled somewhere between her throat and chest, she pasted on a broad smile. "Are you hunting for a compliment?"

"Just stating a fact. I'd think someone equally tasty would understand."

Oh, my. She pressed her fingertips into the table, still struggling for purchase against the heady waves buffeting her like a storm at sea. The man was certifiably lethal, and the only defense she had—and it was a weak one at that—was humor.

"You, Knox St. Germain, sure know how to flatter a girl."

"First, you're a woman." He reached for his wine, his smile appreciative as his gaze moved over her face. "And, second, I don't flatter as a general rule."

The tinge of something serious stuck beneath the comment and she latched on to it, both out of curiosity and for some way to break the sensual heat that refused to recede between them. "Why not?"

"What's the point? People either know their worth or they don't. It's not my job to waste my time figuring out which camp they fall into because the ones who don't know won't believe me and the ones who do don't need me."

"Wow. That's awfully profound."

His eyebrows rose over the wire rims. "Now who's flattering?"

She lifted an eyebrow in return. "Why would I do that? It's a useless waste of time."

Silence descended once more between them, and Gabby accepted the next few days would be challenging. She wanted him—she'd already proven that to herself—and she saw no reason to avoid him or what was between them. Even now, memories of making love with Knox filled her with a languid grace and a most desperate craving to repeat the experience.

To repeat something that made her feel whole and real and alive.

So she'd simply have to protect herself against thinking too far ahead. The danger that had brought them to London hadn't simply evaporated, and she'd do well to take her enjoyment where she could find it.

Beyond that…

"I like listening to you, by the way."

"What?"

"Before. You said that not many people listen to you. I'm sorry for that."

"It's fine." When he only stared at her, that penetrating blue gaze unyielding, she hurried on. "It is fine. I learned a long time ago it's harder to be the one watching than doing. And I also accepted that I'd rather do. My mother wasn't born with that need, so she struggles to understand it in me."

"That's her loss."

"I'd say it's our loss. She doesn't understand, and I pull away. Even when I purposely try not to, it happens."

"Your family doesn't define you, Gabriella. You should be proud of that and proud of what you've created on your own."

Cassidy, Lilah and Violet had often said something similar, but it felt good to hear it from an outside source. She loved her family and counted them among her greatest blessings, but she struggled with the guilt of disappointing them. Since spending more time with her friends—all driven women in their own right—she'd finally come to see her life and her choices through a new lens.

"The girls say the same thing. Cassidy, Lilah and Violet are my biggest champions."

"Add me to the list."

"I will."

That steady gaze turned considering. "It's hard to break free. You're lucky to have friends who applaud the effort."

Break free?

The comment was unexpected, yet telling. And she'd been so focused on herself the past few days and the life-altering decisions she'd made about following Knox to the UK that she hadn't seen the signs.

Now that she did, there was no way to *un*see them.

The apartment had no mementos. He'd called no one save his work colleagues in the entire time she'd been with him. And he never spoke of a family.

"*Break free* is an interesting term. I'm not quite sure I see it the same way."

"You don't feel caged?"

"No, I don't. Underestimated at times, but not caged."

"That's good then."

She stilled, surprised to find herself hesitating. She'd shared her body with him, for goodness' sake. What was she afraid of? "You don't talk about your family much."

And in the span of a heartbeat, the easy moments vanished as if they'd never been.

"No, I don't."

"What do they think about what you do?"

"They don't think anything."

She shook her head, unable to imagine any scenario where family would stand idly by with no opinion at all. "I'm sure that's not true."

"I can assure you, it's quite true."

Stop pushing.

She cursed herself in equal measure for ruining a special, easygoing moment she couldn't get back and for her damnable curiosity that wouldn't allow her to stay silent.

"Why doesn't your family have an opinion about what you do?"

"Because they're all dead."

The comment landed with a thud, just as Knox expected it would, and he focused on the last two bites on his plate instead of on Gabriella's crestfallen features. Her dark eyes filled with sympathy, and the mouth that drove him to distraction turned down in a considering frown.

After stabbing the few remaining pieces of meat, he shoved them in and stood, still chewing, and walked his plate to the sink.

It didn't happen often, but people did ask him about his family from time to time. Casual comments at work or the few relationships he'd allowed to go farther than a few dates. He was typically able to shut it down with a quick comment and a change of subject.

Yet Gabriella had pushed. And now she was horrified.

"I'm sorry, Knox."

He was sorry, too. More than he cared to admit. "They've been gone a long time."

"But you don't have any memories of them. No photos to keep them fresh in your mind."

He couldn't imagine why he'd want to do that. Place strategic reminders of how idyllic his life was once upon a time?

Hell bloody no.

"Look. I've got some work to do. Feel free to leave the dishes in the sink. I've got housekeeping services, and they can take care of cleaning up."

Before she could say another word, he turned on his heel and left the kitchen.

Knox wasn't dumb enough to believe his movements weren't tracked by his employer, so he'd gone to considerable time, effort and expense to secure the slender silver laptop computer in his office.

A man needed his privacy.

From work and from prying women who saw far too much.

He worked his way through several layers of security in MI5's firewalls as he worked through the problem of Gabriella in his mind. He'd let her in. It was that simple. He'd allowed the intimacy of their time together and the danger they were both in to color his behavior.

And when she'd pressed him on his family, he'd panicked.

There were about a thousand ways he could have played that conversation, and he'd gone and selected the one answer that was going to stick in her gut and gnaw at her until she'd gotten him to give up all the reasons why he was alone in the world.

Why weren't human relationships as easy as hacking a few servers?

Although he took his commitments to the Security Service seriously, all in on the vow to protect queen and country, he wasn't immune to the need to get off the grid and have access to the world around him from time to time.

He also wasn't immune to the need for a backup plan. He trusted his employer—or had—but right now he didn't know what he was up against. And while he made it a firm personal policy not to abuse the knowledge of how to access inside information—he still considered himself ethical enough to dig only when necessary—he consoled himself that the current situation with Moray fit the bill.

Where he found absolutely no consolation was with Gabriella.

He'd dug there and hadn't anticipated the consequences. Neither his increasing attachment nor the fact that she'd ask questions of her own.

The familiar Security Service logo flashed on his screen, and he focused on his goal. Tapping on the keys, he followed the instructions he'd been given years ago, navigating the familiar pages as a ghost. A hacker friend had showed him how to keep his browsing activities truly anonymous, and he used this particular computer for special circumstances only. But he needed to be quick.

And shove thoughts of Gabriella into the neat, convenient compartment into which he put all his relationships.

The second laptop on the desk was his more obvious home computer, used for online banking, web surfing and sending emails. The British government could monitor that one to its heart's content. He couldn't care less if they kept an eye on his bank account—filled only by its own payments—or saw how often he monitored the performance of Manchester United or read the flirty emails he exchanged with prospective dates.

With quick fingers, he typed in his query on Richard Moray. Long-standing records filled the screen. He'd avoided taking this step in Dallas, only willing to risk the hack from his home computer.

And he was discouraged to realize that the face Richard Moray presented to the Security Service was damn near unimpeachable.

The guy had an impeccable record, the history of his family and his lineage, his service accomplishments and his comings and goings from op to op meticulously catalogued online.

A wife was mentioned in some of the earlier data, and Knox vaguely remembered mention of a woman years earlier when he'd started at MI5. He scanned the dossier. Earlier entries confirmed the relationship that had been over for more than a decade now.

The leader he knew publicly appeared to spend time with a series of attractive, age-appropriate companions. Knox had met several at state events, and each had a sort of vapid acceptability. They were attractive, quietly attentive and each blended into the background without leaving more than a base impression of cultured elegance.

Other rumors—ones Knox had been privy to from his colleagues—suggested the sophisticated series of companions were little more than they appeared.

Instead, Richard Moray was purported to enjoy a series of well-paid whores in his bedroom.

It was the prostitutes, Knox realized, that had given the initial tip-off to Moray's true nature. He and Sam had been out with a few workmates at the pub, and both men had groused about Moray's recent behavior.

"Moray's been a hard-ass lately. I got chewed for that op in Covent Garden last week."

"I spent time in the dumper for that sting in Newcastle. We caught the bastard, didn't we? Shut down the porn ring he had running, and still Moray wasn't happy. Hell, you'd think the bastard would be a bit cheerier for all the ass he's been shagging."

"Moray?" Knox set his beer down, images he could do without cluttering his thoughts. *"He's a monk."*

"Depends on your definition. The monk routine may be part of his public persona, but the man's more than willing to part with some solid British sterling to get his kink on."

Knox had given the news several days' time to settle, willing the warning bells to subside.

And then he'd begun digging.

While he had no doubt Moray had a rather slick setup in his own home office, able to hide from the system just as Knox was, the man wasn't fully a ghost. With painstaking study he captured in pages of notes, Knox constructed a pattern of Moray's behavior and comings and goings.

The late-night discovery of Moray's research activity on the Renaissance Stones had finally wrapped Knox's suspicions up in a neat bow.

Queries in the database on the stones. A request for archive files on his uncle's involvement with Josephine

Beauregard's father. And a flight to Dallas the previous spring.

Knox had used what he found and crafted his argument with all the rationale for why such a high-ranking member of the Security Service should be hunted down like an animal.

Richard Moray wasn't what he seemed, and he should be watched.

What Knox hadn't anticipated—or even considered—was Moray's arrival in the park the other night for the exchange of the rubies. He had been sanctioned for the mission by an elite member of the Security Service who was aware of the suspicions about Moray. Even with that support, it never dawned on Knox to anticipate the move.

If he had, he could have avoided the mess in the park and the even bigger mess of going to Gabriella's shop after he was shot. She would still be safe at home in Dallas, and he would be dealing with this internal blight on the Security Service all by himself.

Only she was here. And she was beautiful and generous and giving and they'd slept together.

Made love.

The words whispered against his thoughts, and for the first time in his life he had to admit the term fit.

Which only proved how far out of his head he was and why he needed to get his focus back. Richard Moray had focus. And resources. And no compunction whatsoever about using them to remove the two people he now saw as a threat.

A glance at the clock confirmed he had a few more minutes to dig before he needed to get out, so he hit a couple more keys and tunneled his way into office email. Moray's administrative assistant had the keys to Moray's schedule, and it was quick work to see what was on the agenda for the week.

A dinner tonight followed by an exhibit opening in Soho. Knox confirmed the time and calculated how quickly he could get himself to the event. A knock on his office door pulled his attention from the screen.

"Is everything okay?"

"Of course. I'm just doing a bit of work." The earlier tension still haunted him, and he was determined to regain some equilibrium. With a brazen smile for her benefit, he placed his tongue firmly in cheek. "Even besotted agents on two-week leave are expected to check in from time to time."

Gabriella's answering smile was tight and never reached her eyes. "Let me be more direct. Is everything okay from before?"

"Sure."

The smile faded along with any further questions. Instead, she moved into the room, her gaze trailing over his sparse furnishings. One lone bookcase held several rows of thrillers he'd enjoyed, and she ran a fingertip over the spines before she tapped one. "That was a good one."

"I thought so."

She continued on around the room, stopping at the edge of his desk. "I was thinking about what we should do next while I cleaned up."

"You didn't need to do that."

"It helps me think. And it was something to do."

A sinkhole opened in the bottom of his stomach and whatever quick, easy slide out of the apartment he'd envisioned for later that evening vanished. There was no way she'd stay behind. He'd gotten a pass earlier as he dealt with Hugh's body, but he wasn't going to get a second one.

"Don't keep me in suspense."

"You mentioned Moray's family. The multigenerational thing about his father and his uncle. I got the impression he was well connected."

"He is that."

"And wealthy?"

"Yes, that, too. He comes from family money, along with what he's made on his own."

"Whatever he's doing, he's got to have some secret place to hide it, right?" Gabriella asked. "I find it hard to believe he'd keep the rubies or whatever else he's into in a small London apartment."

"His flat isn't too shabby."

"But it's still an apartment." She glanced around the room as if punctuating her point. "Your apartment isn't shabby, either. But it's a far cry from a second home or an estate house. Besides, there's more people around. More people paying attention to your comings and goings."

"He does have an estate home. In Surrey." Which he knew for a fact—and reinforced—since he'd just reread the information in Richard's dossier.

"How far away is that?"

"Driving distance." He didn't want to encourage her, but he was intrigued by how her mind worked. "You don't think the rubies are in London?"

"No."

"The stones are easily hidden. They're large for gemstones but relatively small as items."

"He's still going to want a home base. A place to squirrel away his treasure. Or treasures, as the case may be."

"What are you suggesting?" Even as he asked the question, Knox had the sinking suspicion he knew what came next.

"Let's stake out Moray's house and steal the Renaissance Stones back."

Chapter 14

There matching rubies winked at him from the polished cherry of his dining room table, their bloodred facets catching the light before reflecting it back off their dark surfaces. Richard had tucked the rubies away in his safe upon his return from Texas, but they'd practically called to him as he lay down for a nap.

He'd avoided their siren song for about an hour before restless turning and repeated glances at his bedside clock had him getting out of bed.

Damned bloody jet lag.

He'd always been immune, but with age had come a fine-tuning of his circadian rhythms, and air travel was no longer the carefree breeze it had once been. Age had also reduced his pain tolerance, and the injury to his knee throbbed like the devil. He'd loaded up on painkillers before flying, consigning himself to an Atlantic crossing fast asleep, and had expected the time of rest would offer some restorative function to his knee. Eight hours at thirty-five thousand feet had done the opposite.

He adjusted the brace he'd put on before his attempted nap, then rubbed the muscle that connected to his thigh. He'd manage through this. He always did. But he had canceled Fiona's visit for that evening. He felt like boiled crap, and he wasn't about to add embarrassment to his list of ailments should he not be able to perform to expectations.

Not that the whore had any expectations beyond the sterling he lined her purse with, but a man had some pride, after all.

His gaze caught on a flash of red as the rubies winked at him, as if reinforcing his decision. Captivated, he lifted one and turned it over.

"Absolutely flawless. And far more elegant and entertaining company than a dirty whore."

He'd heard of the stones' beauty, but he hadn't believed they would truly be that magnificent until he'd held them in his hands and looked at them with his own eyes.

Knowing their history, he'd focused on the income they'd fetch. But since his trip to Dallas—since possessing the stones—he couldn't shake the need to keep them close. He could swear he felt a throbbing power each and every time he touched them, especially when he held them all at once.

A fierce lust stole over him, more powerful than any sexual experience and more potent than the strongest orgasm.

As individual stones, they were powerful. As three, they were beyond imagining. They were like a mirror into another time and place, their red facets born of an earlier age. A treasure that had lain dormant for millennia, just waiting to be discovered.

And now they were his.

The money he'd get for them increasingly seemed insignificant relative to ownership. To actual possession.

And to think they'd lain in the floor of an old warehouse for more than fifty years, buried by imbeciles who had no appreciation for what they possessed. For what had been entrusted to them.

He wouldn't make the same mistake.

Richard didn't know how long he'd sat there, but the light through his windows had faded to the golden hue of early evening when he looked up from the rubies in his hand. Vaguely, he remembered a commitment that evening and resigned himself to putting the stones back into the safe.

But later…

Later he'd possess them once more.

Gabby waited with bated breath for Knox's reaction. She suspected he wasn't going to be crazy about her idea, but it was the degree of reaction she didn't know how to anticipate.

"Richard's slated to attend a dinner tonight. We could check out his house then."

She exhaled on a hard breath. "You want to do this?"

"No."

Her spirits fell at the swift response. "Oh."

"More to the point, I don't want you to do this. But I've been overruled on that front since I stumbled into your shop."

"I can be your eyes and ears."

"So you say."

Just like that day so many years ago when she'd finally been given the go-ahead to join the traveling soccer team, a shot of triumph suffused her limbs. Where her fourteen-year-old self had known not to shoot her arms sky-high in a victory celebration to her mother, her thirty-two-year-old self had no compunction about doing the same to Knox. "Yes!"

"This is serious."

"I may not show it, but I do know that, Knox." The past few days had revealed the sizable mess they were in. Poor Hugh had paid for that reality with his life. "Even knowing that, I hate inaction. And this will give us a chance to get the upper hand."

"Maybe."

The hard set of his jaw didn't show the slightest trace of a smile. "Are you always so negative?"

"I'm cautious."

"Then let's map out our plan of attack. He got the jump on us at the airport, and Hugh paid for it. If for no other reason, we owe it to Hugh to see this through."

"That we do." He rubbed his eyes beneath the rims of his glasses before offering a terse nod. "Let's get started."

The small Fiat zipped through the roads, the starry night surrounding them in blackness as they drove farther away from London. The bright swell of the city had given way to less congested roads before the landscape had changed once again as they moved from thick outer-city sprawl firmly into the suburbs.

Gabby took it all in, less surprised this time by driving on the opposite side of the road. "I never pegged you for a small car like this."

"I resisted having a car at all for the longest time. But it's more practical to have something."

"No car? At all?"

"Sure. London's far easier on foot or via the Tube. A car's more trouble than it's worth." He gave her a quick glance. "And what's wrong with the Fiat?"

"You realize I come from Texas. People take pride in driving seriously huge cars and trucks."

"My bollocks are plenty big, thank you very much. I don't need a car as a stand-in."

Gabby was suddenly grateful for the darkened interior as a blush stole over her face. She'd seen *all* his parts, and there was no question Knox St. Germain's endowments were more than appropriately proportioned.

Since their time together hadn't been far from her thoughts—or when they might be together again—she latched on to another topic to try and keep her hormones at bay. "How many servants do you think he has?"

"I ran his tax returns, and, based on what he declared as income paid out, there should be four people at most. A cook, a housekeeper, a butler and a live-in maid."

"That seems intrusive. Especially if he's hiding things."

"It's an estate house. We should be grateful that's all he has." He tapped the steering wheel. "But you make a good point. I'll check later if that number's gone down over the past few years."

"You think that's when he started doing bad things?"

"I think he's always been opportunistic, but I think opportunity morphed into serious ambition in the last two years or so."

"Why?"

"I have no idea."

"How'd you get put on this case?"

"My suspicions. My case."

Gabby had no idea how a government organization

worked, especially one with as broad a remit as MI5. As with the FBI and the CIA in the United States, she suspected what was profiled on TV or elaborated on in movies had little to do with real life. But even without any working knowledge, she could imagine what his job entailed. Terrorism. Crime. Guns and Drugs. Far too many humans had unfathomable depths of depravity fueling their souls.

"It's a serious accusation. What tipped you off?"

"Richard Moray has a borderline addiction to ladies of the night. It wasn't a huge leap to think he might be willing to bend the law in other ways, as well."

"That said, it's still a pretty big leap from sex addict to killer."

"True."

"So what made you leap?"

He glanced at her again, this time holding her gaze a few heartbeats longer before turning back to the road. "You're incredibly perceptive."

"I like to watch people. And in my job, I do that more often than you think. When I cater a job. When I give classes or tastings at my shop. People fascinate me."

Just like you do.

The thought was as natural as breathing, and Gabby knew her crush had moved past basic attraction—even past the heavier feelings that could come from having sex with someone—straight into a deep infatuation.

She was helpless to resist him.

"We had a case about a year ago. Big drug bust in an outlying suburb that turned into an even bigger bust when we realized the drug lord was running guns and funding terrorists."

"Talk about a leap."

"Exactly. We worked for months getting everything

set up. The sting operation, the right operatives, everything. We had a big team from the Security Service. And once we closed in, the guns vanished."

"But how?"

"That's the problem. Every person on the team was questioned. The case was examined top to bottom. No one came up as questionable."

"Except Moray?"

"There weren't any questions about him, either. But he was the lead on the op, and something about how he stayed under the radar, avoiding certain meetings and discussions during the internal investigation, left a bad taste."

Shortly after they started their business, Violet, Cassidy and Lilah had hired a few extra helping hands for one of their larger weddings. It was an important event, and they all agreed they needed the extra attention for the day.

As the day was wrapping up, Violet discovered one of the women they'd hired had been rifling through evening bags of guests attending the wedding. Violet handled the matter quickly and managed to avoid any serious damage, but she'd been upset with the betrayal of trust.

How much worse must that betrayal be from a boss?

"Whether it was that job or another that tipped the scales, I've seen firsthand what he's capable of, Knox. Your instincts have been spot-on from the first."

"Trust that everything is being documented, too. I may be deep in this, but I will present a full report when it's over. Hugh's death will have serious weight, too."

"That's why you were so careful on how you handled the body."

"Yes."

Conversation had flowed easily for the ride from London, but at the mention of Hugh they both quieted. They passed several miles before Knox spoke again. "I'm sorry for earlier."

Lost in her own thoughts, Gabby thought he referred to sleeping together, and a wholly frustrated anger welled up. However when she ultimately remembered this event in her life, she wouldn't remember sleeping with Knox St. Germain with any sense of regret. When he added, "About my family," she calmed down. "I don't discuss them."

"You have a right to your privacy."

The urge to apologize in return was strong, but Gabby left off any further comment. He *did* have a right to his privacy, but she couldn't change the fact she was hurt by his reaction. She harbored no delusions they were going to go out into the world after the situation with Moray was over and live happily ever after. But they had slept together, and it stung to know she put more weight on that intimacy than he did.

"Yes, I do."

"I won't bring it up again."

"Good."

Silence returned, and Gabby tried wrapping herself up in it. She couldn't make someone talk to her. She was well aware she tended to be an open book when it came to her own life. She didn't *need* to know something so private and personal. Especially if the other person found it intrusive and interrogative.

Even if that person was Knox. A man she'd slept with. Shared her body with. Something she damn well planned on doing again.

"My father left us when I was nearing the end of secondary school. He'd given no signs he was even unhappy and we had been a rather close family up until that time."

Anger lined each and every word as a tremulous sense of vulnerability filled the space between them.

"My mother wasn't able to handle things and over time became increasingly difficult to live with and manage."

"Many people lash out when that sort of abrupt grief hits them. Losing him like that would have the same impact as if he'd died."

"Worse." His jaw was rigid, and she could see the mental control he tried to exert over the discussion. "Death often isn't a choice. Leaving is. He chose to walk away from us, and my mother couldn't handle it."

For all her family made her crazy, Gabby knew how lucky she was to have parents who were still married to each other. Still committed to each other and to their family unit.

"You said they had all passed away. Did you keep in touch with your father at all?"

"We were informed after he was killed in a car accident. He'd been drinking and driving and killed himself and another passenger in the car. A woman he was in a relationship with."

"I'm sorry."

His eyes never left the road, but his hands gripped the steering wheel, his arms stiff. When he said nothing, just continued to stare ahead, she pressed a bit harder. The wound might be raw, but leaving it to fester was what he'd done for far too long. "And your mother? How did she pass?"

"She and my sister had a fight one night shortly after he died. My sister resented how helpless my mother had become. The police report suggested they fought over a gun and my mother's attempts to kill herself."

"Knox—"

A sharp glance quelled the urge to say anything else. "They both ended up dead."

The reality of his life—and the complete and total loss of his family—struck with incomparable force. With the need to comfort came a layer of shock she had no idea how to work past.

"Do you see now why I don't want to talk about this? Why my family's fouled-up problems aren't something I want to pull out, polish off and discuss?"

"I never—"

"You never what? Weren't curious? Weren't waiting for the right time to ask me again?"

"I told you I respect your privacy."

And she did. He had put up a wall earlier. While that frustrated her, she wasn't immune to the pain he must have experienced. Or the sense of loss that would have to be pervasive, no matter how many years passed. Grief was grief, and it didn't simply vanish. It might lessen, but it never fully went away.

"If you don't want to discuss this, then we won't discuss it."

"For how long? You're a woman. And we had sex. It's only a matter of time before that little voice inside nags and nags at you to ask again."

Gabby twisted in her seat, any sense of calm vanishing at the insult. Yes, she'd had a similar thought and had been disappointed to find their physical intimacy didn't extend to the emotional. But she'd be damned if she'd sit by and be berated for having feelings for him. Or caring about what brought him to this place and time.

"I don't know who the hell you think you are or why you've suddenly decided to lash out at me, so let's get this straight. Your life is your business."

"It is."

"Then have at it. I don't want any part of it."

"Damn you!" Knox pulled over, the tires screeching on gravel as he maneuvered them to the side of the road. When he finally got the car in Park, he turned toward her, his eyes blazing, that vivid blue visible even in the darkened interior. "Damn you and your bloody willingness to understand."

The look in his eye was half-wild, half-terrified, and Gabby suddenly understood what it might be like to stand in the middle of a cage with a tiger. "Excuse me?"

"You weren't supposed to understand."

Before she could say another word, he had his hands on her shoulders, pulling her close as he crushed his mouth against hers.

One moment anger churned in his veins so deep he thought he'd never see past the years of fury and sorrow and agonizing pain. The next, his mouth was on Gabriella's, and his hands roamed over her shoulders, back and breasts as they kissed like two ravenous teenagers after a school dance.

Had he ever needed anyone so much?

Where did it come from? This all-encompassing desire for a person that was both physical and emotional. He wanted her, his body aching for the satisfaction to be found in her arms. Yet even in the need, he found himself opening to her, all the thoughts that had haunted him for years flying free as if of their own volition. Demons that had haunted him for almost fifteen years—the ghosts of his father, mother and sister—all demanded pieces of his mental energy he no longer had the strength to give.

They'd betrayed him—each of them in their own way—and now Moray had done the same. The man he'd looked up to. Respected. Was willing to be led by. He'd been loyal to the Security Service. Had found solace in the organizational structure and the belief he was doing good. Protecting others. Serving his country and fellow countrymen.

And he'd believed in Richard Moray.

Had clung to the idea of a multigenerational leader who lived every ideal MI5 espoused. The man held respect and admiration from all.

If people only knew.

A small mewl escaped Gabriella's lips, and he caught it with his mouth, deepening the kiss. Each long, sure stroke of his tongue was met with an erotic enthusiasm that numbed his brain and drove him closer and closer to madness.

She understood him.

How or why, he had no idea. Their lives epitomized the idea of opposites attracting. Yet they worked. On some odd, unfathomable level, they just fit together.

Her hands splayed against his chest, and he slowly keyed into the press of her fingers. "Knox." His name was a husky whisper on her lips. "Knox."

A fluorescent glow filtered in from the lights that lined the highway, and he took in the high cheekbones and dark eyes and the long flow of hair that floated around her head in curling waves. She was a stunning woman, deeply beautiful with a mysterious sensuality that pulled him in closer and closer.

But it was her heart and her warm, generous sense of spirit that seemed to light her up from the inside out.

She was all that was good and right about the world, and it killed him to think he was taking her into such a dark, dangerous corner of it.

If he thought he could put her somewhere and leave her where Moray could never find her, he'd do it without question. They'd agreed ahead of time this was a recon mission and nothing more. Promise or no promise in Dallas, his goal was to keep her safe and whole. But he'd yet to come up with a place that she would truly be safe from the man's influence.

So until he figured out a solution or someone he could trust without reservation, she stayed with him. He'd die for her, of that he had no question.

All he did question was if he was brave enough for something more when they finally put this entire mess behind them.

Chapter 15

A large gate loomed high into the darkened night sky as Knox drove past the Moray estate. Something creepy fluttered over her skin, and Gabby took several deep breaths to shake off the strange sense of foreboding that had settled over her as they drove closer and closer to Richard Moray's family home.

They could do this. They *would* find a way to bring the man to justice. She believed that.

Even when all the reasons she should leave Knox alone to do his job swirled through her mind like wildfire.

Had she made a mistake in coming here? She'd left Dallas for many reasons—keeping her family safe chief on the list—but she had to accept she might have overestimated her ability to be an asset to Knox. He was a highly trained operative, and she was good with garlic and olive oil.

Not exactly a match designed to take down killers.

"Have you been here before?"

"No. I've heard about the place, and Sam attended an event here years ago. All he could talk about was the size of the house and the estate. He drew me a quick map earlier of what he remembered."

"It's like something out of a movie." She twisted in her seat, staring out the back window as he drove past the estate to get a feel for the area.

And, while he hadn't said it, their escape route, should that be necessary.

"Why would someone who has all this want more? Especially when more isn't his right to have?"

"Why do people do anything?"

She supposed Knox was right—people did horrible things—but even with that knowledge, Gabby wasn't so sure. She'd expected Moray's home to be large. Stately even. But the monstrosity Knox just drove past was beyond her imaginings.

Why jeopardize this life? He already had what most people dreamed of. Yet Moray had done so willingly.

She saw the man's face as he held a gun to Ricardo's head. Greed and some perverse need to possess had lived in his eyes, a fire-breathing entity that demanded all light and goodness to stoke the flame.

She'd also seen fear.

And the very real knowledge that he now lived on borrowed time.

Richard smiled at the assembled dinner guests, his mind still filled with the glittering, gleaming facets of the rubies. He'd nearly brought one with him, thinking to carry it in his pocket so he could reach in and touch it whenever he wanted, but he had held back.

The trio deserved to stay together. Separating one from the others seemed unkind, somehow, and very wrong. So he'd locked them up and left them in his bedroom safe.

But he'd thought of little else.

Conversation tinkled around him, light and vapid. There was a time once that he'd have found the company engaging. Especially when the discussion inevitably floated to the latest gossip that hovered around the small cadre of beautiful people who were affiliated in some way with the British monarchy.

He'd gloried in being one of those privileged souls.

His wife had never understood that need. She'd contented herself with endless hours in their garden and a mad focus on getting pregnant. She'd never shown any interest in the things he cared for or the status that came with his position, and the day they parted had been one of the happiest of his life.

The thought of an heir had intrigued him briefly, but he'd ultimately decided against it and had taken proper precautions to ensure there was never a baby. Saddling himself to a life with Elizabeth had proven unsatisfactory—he had no interest in prolonging their association with progeny.

His fingers itched in his lap, the image of his ex-wife vanishing as the Renaissance Stones filled his mind's eye once more.

To think they'd been lost to England for so long. Worse, to consider they'd been thrust aside like a poisoned apple, the Queen so insistent to have them off British soil. He'd done his research. The stones had been a diplomatic gift—nothing more or less. How they'd come to symbolize, in her mind, the war and the devastation thrust upon London by the endless bombing of the Axis powers was ridiculous.

Yet her husband had indulged her, and Joseph Brown had carried out his sovereign's wishes and taken the stones to Texas.

A small dessert plate was set in front of him, jarring him from his thoughts. He'd agreed to come, and he needed to rejoin the conversation lest he miss something—*anything*—that would make this evening something other than a tawdry bore.

His phone buzzed from his breast pocket, and he toyed with pulling it out. His hostess hated any use of technology at her table, but if he hadn't ignored her for half the night he'd risk her wrath to check.

But he'd play the game. Finish his dessert and then make his excuses to leave. On his drive home, he could work through his plan to deal with St. Germain. The man was a vexing problem and one that he couldn't leave out in the open for long.

Had his knee been in top form, he'd have found a way to end this all in Texas. But even with that miss, it was good to be back on British soil. He was in his element here.

He was home.

And with access to St. Germain's comings and goings via his government-issued technology equipment, Richard knew Knox was home, as well.

Tomorrow would be soon enough. He'd eliminate the threat once and for all.

Knox cut the engine and turned to face Gabriella. "You have the gun?"

"No, Knox, I left it on your kitchen counter. Of

course I have the gun, along with the very nice leather holster you gave me before we left."

"And you're comfortable using it?"

"I know how to handle one."

They'd been over this before. He knew she was well versed on how to use the weaponry, especially since she kept a gun in a drawer in her kitchen. Even with the personal knowledge, he'd made her load and reload the clip and had been more than a little surprised at how easily she could handle herself.

"Remember. You don't have to kill him. His knee's already vulnerable. Just do what you need to."

"The man held a gun on my brother, shot at both of us and arranged for us to be killed, along with Hugh. I'm not out for his blood, but I'm not afraid to do what needs to be done."

"He's still a well-respected agent for the government. Why don't you try to avoid the *Terminator* routine if you can help it?"

She leaned over the seat and placed her lips against his. Where he'd expected something quick and placating, her lips were soft and warm, the kiss slow and sweet like honey. She lingered for a few more moments before lifting her head. "I'm not afraid of a little paperwork. But I will be careful."

"True to form, Miss Sanchez. You don't ever really agree. You just sort of give a general nod and then go off and do things your own way."

"A skill I've been honing since I was about three. It's just the way I'm made."

Knox did a bit of lingering of his own, his gaze roving over her features.

He'd spent more time with her over the past two days than he had with anyone in a very long time. Since the

loss of his family, he'd kept others at bay, willing to
trade off the personal contact for his privacy. Even his
affairs had remained simple and uncomplicated, women
coming and going in his life in an attractive blur.

But Gabriella had managed to linger. In his thoughts.
In his life. And, increasingly, in his heart.

Pulling away, he snagged the small black leather
pack he'd stowed in the back earlier and pulled it into
his lap. He'd already strapped a gun to his ankle and he
wanted his favorite side piece in his hand as they made
their way around Moray's property. He'd also packed
several rolls of duct tape, several meters of rope and a
wicked stiletto should he need backup.

He caught a whiff of the last item packed. "We're
going to attract every dog in Surrey with this stash."

Gabriella had suggested some meat should they un-
expectedly encounter guard dogs, and the scent wafted
from the open bag. "You'll thank me later if we run
into issues."

She'd tucked a few aspirin with sleep agents in them
into the meat to help sweeten the deal.

"A real guard dog wouldn't be tempted by strangers tossing meat."

"I don't care how well trained they are. You really
think a dog's not going to respond to a load of fresh
hamburger? Besides, all we need is enough time to distract them and get away. We're not making friends."

"No, we're not." His dry agreement vanished in the
air as she climbed out of the car. He watched the long
lines of her body, clad all in black, before giving himself
one extra moment to stare at her perfectly rounded arse.

He'd nearly shaken himself from his momentary stupor when her head peeked back in the door, a broad

smile painting those lips. "Stop staring at my ass and let's get this over with."

"Aye, aye, Captain."

She gave him a cheeky salute. "That's more like it."

Knox had already given her a spare set of keys to the Fiat, should she need to make a quick getaway. "You have the keys."

"In my pocket."

"And you're comfortable driving the car if you need to get out of here."

"I still say you drive on the wrong side of the road, but I think I can figure it out if our lives are on the line."

"Or if your life is on the line. You need to leave and get help."

"We've been over this."

They had been over this, and, once again, her lack of agreement was deliberate. "Yes, we have. And I need to know you'll be safe. I need to know you'll go for help instead of trying to help me."

He came around the car, his hand on her arm. "Please. I need to know this. No matter what, I need to believe I can trust you to take care of yourself."

Her gaze was militant, but the acknowledgment in her eyes was real. When she gave him a soft yes, he finally relaxed.

Knox locked the car, then took her hand. He'd parked at the northeast corner of the estate, and they had agreed to walk over the property rather than trying to approach through the front. The walk was shorter, but the security was likely tighter and had fewer gaps between cameras if they started on the street side.

While he had no doubt there were cameras strategically positioned all over Moray's property, the man wasn't omnipotent. And the dense countryside that made up the majority of the land offered some cover, allowing them to move like wraiths through the vast area.

Gabriella's grip was tight in his, belying her jaunty step. She kept alert to her surroundings, her gaze roaming half the property while he kept watch on the other. A few times she had him stop, her finger poised at her lips when she scanned the land, only to nod after finding nothing.

Bright property lights were visible in the distance and Knox stilled, keeping her hand tight in his. "There will likely be cameras on us soon."

"Then we move in like we planned. This is a quick stakeout to get the lay of the land, and then we head back to London. You know as well as I do Moray hasn't left the stones out in the open."

"No, he hasn't." Knox kept watch on the perimeter, ducking a few times and tugging her hand so they fell out of range. The stakeout wasn't neat or elegant, but it was effective, and in minutes they stood alongside the east wall of the house.

They kept their backs to the cool brick, and Knox visually measured off how far they were from the front of the house. When they began to move forward, a loud bang echoed through the night air from about twenty yards away.

"What was that?" Gabriella's wide-eyed stare darted toward the back of the house.

"Sam's map indicated the kitchen was on this corner wall." His map had also indicated the estate's technological nerve center might be nearby, but his colleague wasn't entirely sure. Sam's visit to the home had been brief, and Moray certainly hadn't given a tour of his security system while hosting a dinner party.

"We need to brace ourselves. It may be security. Or

a few more goons like the ones we dealt with coming out of Heathrow." Knox squeezed Gabby's hand. "Do you have your gun?"

"Right here."

"Don't be afraid to do what you have to."

"I'm not."

He heard the small, exasperated sigh and smiled to himself. "Then let's keep going."

Clouds moved across the moon, adding incremental shadows, and Knox was grateful for them as they edged their way toward the front of the property. He pushed forward, his hand on Gabriella's back. She came to an abrupt halt.

"What is it?"

"How likely is it Moray has cameras on his roof?"

"I'm sure he has a few. Why?"

She kept her voice low, but excitement tinged the edges of her whisper. "Fewer than down here on the ground?"

"That's likely."

"Then let's go up." Her hand tightened on his before she dropped it and turned to lay a hand on the trellis behind her back.

"Up?" Knox risked moving away from the wall by a few inches to gaze up the side of the three-story mansion. The climb was significant, but her point was more than valid. It was brilliant. "You can climb that?"

One lone eyebrow rose up over the dark orb of an eye. "I have five older brothers. What do you think?"

"I was just checking."

"The real question is: can you?"

"Do you have any idea how many hours of my life have been given over to training and stealth maneuvers?"

"Then we're agreed." Gabriella shoved the gun into the holster he'd given her, then turned and gripped the wood of the trellis. "Let's go."

The trellis was thick and surprisingly strong, and Gabby had to give a mental round of applause to wealth and privilege. Richard Moray might be a devious ass, but the man kept an impeccable home. Nothing was out of place, and the elements that made up the facade of his house were all in pristine condition.

Including the smooth wood of the well-painted and wide-latticed trellis.

Knox kept pace below her. The only audible sound was the two of them brushing their booted feet against the ivy that rose up the side of the house.

While she'd made the joke about her brothers, Gabby hated heights and avoided looking down, other than to keep track of where he paced beneath her. Instead, she focused up as the flat edge of roof that was her goal grew closer and closer. What they did once they got to the top would be a different matter, but at least they were no longer sitting ducks on the ground.

The latticework rose all the way to the top, and she stretched the last few feet, pleased when she felt the firm row of concrete atop brick that made up the edge of the flat roof.

"Do you need a push?"

"You looking for one more chance to touch my ass?"

"Anytime, baby." The words shot out lightning quick, and Gabby couldn't hold back the laugh when his large hand covered her butt, pushing her the last few feet over the roofline.

She swung a leg over, then the other, the gun she'd stuck in the shoulder holster heavy against her side.

But she'd made it. The roof was sturdy beneath her feet, and she could still see a few puddles from where rainwater collected in shallow pools. She leaned back over the roof, her gaze steady on Knox. "Not bad for a caterer."

His answering grin was wide. "Not bad at a—"

A loud crack rent the air, and the trellis that had seemed so sturdy suddenly snapped under the weight of their climb. Knox's eyes widened for the briefest moment before he scrabbled for purchase, his hands slamming against the ivy and the breaking wood.

Gabby moved without thinking, her hand reaching out to snatch his wrist while she kept the other one firmly pressed to the roof wall. The thick concrete was painful where it pushed into her waist. Air whooshed from her lungs at the combination of her bent position and the deadweight of Knox's body, and she fought to keep her focus on the large man whose life depended on her.

"Gabriella!" His voice was strained, but his fingers stayed tight on hers. "Pull!"

She closed her eyes and gritted her teeth against the pain, imagining the short distance he had left to reach the roof. With that her only focus, she tugged hard, pulling backward. Inch by painful inch, she dragged him closer to her and the safety of the roof.

The moments stretched into the longest of her life until the pain and pressure stopped as suddenly as they'd begun. With his free hand, Knox gripped the roof, releasing the burden on their ironclad grip, and she was able to give aid instead of just hanging on. With a few last maneuvers, he was over the roof. Knox collapsed at her feet.

Gabby fought for breath, the heavy weight of the

roofline having already taken what she'd had left after the trellis climb. Stars swam in front of her eyes, but she kept her head bent, focused on his prone form.

"Are you…Are you okay?"

"Me?" He scrambled to his feet, dragging her close. Air had returned to her lungs, but her arm still trembled from the adrenaline and the weight of his body. His arm quivered against her back, knocking against her spine in a matched response. "How did you manage to hold on to me?"

"I won't let you go."

Air buzzed in her ears as her breath continued to whoosh in and out in great gulps. Once again, the lighthearted moments they shared had given away to something darker and far more sinister than she'd prepared for.

He could have fallen.

She could have dropped him.

Or they both could have dropped from the side of the house had the trellis cracked halfway up their climb.

"You held on to me." His words grew stronger, but the audible wonder hadn't fully faded.

"Of course I did."

His arms tightened around her, even as the one still trembled from their near miss. It was a reminder to her that they played a dangerous game against a lethal adversary.

The sooner they ended it, the sooner they could go back to their lives. This wasn't some evening jaunt into the English countryside or a clever game of cat and mouse designed to give her life a spot of adventure.

This was life and death. And with startling clarity, Gabby acknowledged she'd do well to remember that.

Chapter 16

Tremors still racked his body as Knox investigated the roof of Moray's house. Despite their near miss, Gabriella's idea of heading up instead of around was brilliant and provided an entirely different view of the home and estate.

Brilliant and ridiculous, a censorious voice whispered through his thoughts. He'd already given himself a mental flaying for the risk they'd taken, shaken more than he wanted to admit, and his damned hands hadn't stopped trembling yet.

How the mighty fall.

He'd been an adrenaline junkie for so many years of his life it was startling to realize how little he enjoyed the sensation while he feared for Gabriella's safety. He'd never forget the feel of the wood cracking beneath his weight, and it was a short mental hop to imagining her still on the trellis as it gave way.

Clouds wove across the sky, covering and uncovering the light of the moon, and several vanished, providing a view of Gabriella's profile. She had taken up a spot near one of the house's many chimneys and was making notes of the layout in a small notebook he'd stowed in his pack.

He'd already figured out the cameras and had identified a path for him and Gabriella to move around the roof so they'd avoid the four that were perched at various points, mounted on the estate's chimneys. She'd recorded his instructions, then any other pertinent facts he was able to secure from the surveillance.

"The third chimney appears to have a loose covering and no equipment attached to it. It might be a sound point for entry into the house or to get our own camera in."

"Got it." The light sound of pen on paper filled up the quiet air as she captured his directions.

Knox kneeled down, his attention focused on the point where the small half wall that ran the perimeter of the roof met the flat top. He dragged a few tools out of the pack and added a few small firecrackers that could be used as a diversion if needed before settling back on his heels.

The broad, walkable area was unique, yet functional, and he'd already catalogued the two rooftop entrances that bookended the chimneys. If he had to guess, one was likely near the servants' stairs and the other near the master bedroom.

Which put them even closer to their goal.

Was it possible they'd found the ideal way into the house? If they had roof access to the master suite, they might not even need a full search of the rest of the home. Of course, that assumed the gems were not on Moray in person. And it also assumed the security system was easy to bypass.

Knox had some tools from the geniuses at MI5, but he had to assume whatever he had Moray also had or, more likely, could beat.

"You look lost in thought, and you haven't given me anything to write down in several minutes." Gabriella's voice echoed in the cool night air, the soft notes drifting toward him.

"I was thinking about something."

"How we're getting down from here?"

Her comment brought a smile, and he had to give her credit for the quick sense of humor. "We'll get down. I've got the rope and a few carabineers in my pack."

"Clever."

"It will also set us up for our return visit."

"So we're not trying for the rubies tonight?"

The night breeze picked that moment to kick up, and several strands of hair blew wild around her face. The temperature was vastly different from what he'd experienced in Texas, and he had to admit he'd come to like the hot summer evenings in Dallas where the temperature never truly cooled. Darkness might remove the element of the sun, but it still felt like a sauna at midnight.

He'd never experienced anything like it before in his life, and for his first few days in Texas he'd found himself fascinated by the contrast with London.

Pulling himself back from the sense memories and the fascinating flow of Gabriella's curls, Knox shook his head. "This is a recon mission only. Besides, Moray will be back soon."

"Even if we can end this tonight?"

"We can't."

Knox glanced down at Sam's crude map, imagining the rooms below based on his friend's drawing. Although Sam's knowledge had been primarily limited to the first floor, it was likely the upper floors were full of bedrooms intermixed with the occasional sitting room.

Did Moray keep the rubies in a safe? On his person? Knox had to believe it was the former, but even if it was, should they search the master bedroom or a private study?

His urge to get in and hunt for the rubies was as strong as Gabriella's, but he couldn't risk a misstep. After their climbing incident, they needed to finish gathering the intel they came for and go home.

Home.

The thought had whispered through his mind more times than he could count over the past week. It was humbling to realize he didn't have one. He had a place where he laid his head, but he hadn't had a home since the day his father walked out. His mother's mental collapse and Daphne's betrayal had only cemented that fact.

Richard Moray had a home. Lush and well-appointed, the property appeared for all the world like a crown jewel of British real estate. But as Gabriella had so astutely mentioned in the car, it obviously meant very little if Richard was so willing to ignore all he had for what he sought to covet.

Gabriella had a home. And a family who loved her, despite their clumsy way of showing it. He'd like to meet them, he was surprised to realize. Would like to have that enchilada dinner with the sizable Sanchez clan.

Especially Gabriella's mother. Elena Sanchez had obviously influenced her daughter and raised an incredibly strong woman in the process. From the way Gabriella spoke of her, it sounded as if her strength was forged from opposing forces, but Knox wondered if it was something more. Something deeper.

Like the rubies they hunted for, external forces could create great beauty. And like those gems, beauty—something that went well beneath the surface—was rare indeed.

"Did you hear that?" Gabriella maneuvered her way across the roof, careful to avoid the areas he'd already pointed out that were in the cameras' path.

"Hear what?"

"The front gate. It just opened."

"We can't even see it from here. How did you hear that?"

"It creaked."

Knox stilled, waiting for the sound to come again. The gate was on an electronic lock, and if it had swung open it would inevitably close. He strained his ears, listening. Waiting.

Instead of the answering swing of the front gate, he heard the low voice that was as familiar as breathing.

"The front gate's well-oiled, my dear. What you heard was the entrance to the roof."

Gabby felt the weight of the gun Knox had given her against her skin. She'd gotten so used to the press of metal she'd forgotten it was there, and that easy comfort now cost her. If she reached for it beneath the dark, open sweater she wore, Moray would have her down in a matter of moments. She suspected it was only his underestimation of her that made him not yet realize she wore the piece.

They'd have few elements of surprise on Knox's old boss, and she'd take any of them she could get. And while she had no desire to underestimate her enemy, she had a feeling the one thing that would work in her favor was Moray's underestimation of her.

"Move forward where I can see you." He motioned with the gun before adding, "And hands up where I can see them, too."

Gabby glanced at Knox and got a subtle nod. "Do as he says."

Her hands went up, and she used the moment of acquiescence to move beside Knox. The subtle flare in his gaze indicated he understood her message—and the holstered gun that was in easy reach.

"I have to admit, St. Germain. You've made this far too easy for me."

"How is that?"

"Trespassing and intruding on my roof? It's not a difficult leap to theft, espionage or much else, really. The good people at MI5 will be shocked and appalled to find out you were a wild dog I needed to put down."

"No worse than when they find out about you." The words flew from her lips, a hornet's nest of vitriol and ire hurled in Moray's direction. "You've betrayed every responsibility entrusted to you and each and every one of the good people that work with you."

"Ah yes, Miss Sanchez. Knox's little albatross. I can see why he's enamored of you. You've got fire in you. It will be fun to douse that flame." Moray took several steps forward, his gaze never leaving hers. "And make no mistake. Once I'm done with you, I will return to Dallas and make a visit to your family."

Something cold burrowed deep inside her heart. For the first time in her life, Gabby knew a fear that overpowered her ability to reason and think. "They're not a part of this."

"But you are. And that's all that matters." Something

vacant flashed back at her from the recesses of his eyes, and Gabby took a step forward, then another.

"You won't touch them."

That empty stare heated with anticipation. "But I will."

Knox's hand was firm on her shoulder, stilling her movement across the roof and pulling her back from the images in her mind.

"Hands, St. Germain."

"I'm not going anywhere." Knox's voice was a low rumble, his fingers tightening on her shoulder. Reflex or signal, she wasn't sure, but she remained in place. "You're supposed to be in London this evening. Home so soon?"

Recognition lit Moray's eyes. "I thought I taught you better. Never give away your intel."

Intel? Gabby thought the comment odd. What had Knox given away? The two men had an odd shorthand, and even in the midst of her fear for her family, she was sad for it. They had worked closely together for years.

Wasn't that worth something? Didn't that time matter?

"Perhaps I just want this done." Knox said.

Gabby couldn't see Knox's face—she could only hear his words and feel the strength in his hand, secure against her shoulder.

"Done like you are?" Moray waved the gun in their direction, the motion casual but no less lethal. "Like your strategy to take the gems for yourself in Dallas?"

"The stones belong back in Britain. The monarchy deserves to have them returned to their rightful owners. Not go on the market to the highest private bidder."

"The monarchy never appreciated what they had in the first place." Moray's lip curled in a distinct sneer.

"As far as they're concerned, these stones are a blip on the radar of British history. Not even worth keeping in some remote portion of the palace."

"They are theirs to handle as they see fit."

"They're priceless!"

Gabby had suspected a serious degree of instability from Richard Moray, but his violent reaction to being challenged over the jewels was eye-opening.

The force of the man's anger carried him forward, and she took an involuntary step backward at the clear menace in his stance. She stumbled against Knox, and the firm hand that pressed to her shoulder shifted to her waist, pulling her close. She felt his hand lift beneath the sweater. Felt the gun spring free of her holster.

"Get down!"

The harsh whisper was immediately followed by a push to her arm, winging her out of Moray's immediate line of sight. Knox lifted his arm, shooting at a spot near the floor.

Loud popping rent the air and a ready eruption of what sounded like a cross between gunfire and fireworks lit up the air around them. Moray let out a loud cry as something burst into flame at his feet, and he stumbled backward across the roof.

Knox had her hand in his once more and was pulling her toward the rooftop door Moray had left open.

A wounded howl echoed behind them, but Knox kept moving.

"We have to get him. He's vulnerable!"

"We have to get out of here."

She tugged on his arm, but the man was a rock, pushing forward, rushing onward. "Knox!"

"We will keep moving. I'll deal with him later."

"Deal with him now."

But her protests were in vain. Knox never slowed his movements, instead keeping her in a firm grip as he wove through the house, leading them ultimately out through the kitchen.

Fresh night air greeted them once more, but he never stilled.

"Run!"

Never give away your intel.

Moray's words echoed in his mind as Knox raced out of Surrey as if it were the Grand Prix. He cursed himself over and over for his stupidity as he took the entrance onto the A3 at top speed.

Always neutralize your opponent when given the opportunity.

The moments on the roof with Richard replayed in his mind, and he struggled against his personal breach in protocol. He had a chance at the shot; he should have taken it. But taking the shot would have cost precious seconds getting Gabriella off that roof. And she was his only goal—his only focus.

What a bloody fool he'd been, thinking he could manage Gabriella and his responsibilities.

He came back to that over and over, no matter how he twisted and turned this assignment. From their first meeting in the kitchens of Elegance and Lace, he'd been captivated. Entranced.

And now they had both paid the price.

Moray called her an albatross, but Knox knew better. She was a siren; only instead of leading Knox to his death, she was leading herself. He needed to keep her safe, and all he'd done was put her in danger.

Traffic was light at this hour and he kept his eyes on his rearview mirror to ensure they weren't followed on their race back to London. Moray was likely still nursing his foot. The small firetraps Knox had laid on the roof had done their job admirably.

"What was that? On the ground?" She shook her head. "On the ground on the roof."

"A little toy MI5 gives its agents. They're simple and effective."

And a distraction. *Just like the woman beside you.*

"That's what you were doing while I wrote in the notebook?"

"Among other things."

"How did you know he was going to find us?"

"I didn't. The traps were more for our next visit, but they came in handy tonight."

She grew silent once more, and Knox had nearly returned to his mental self-flagellation when she spoke again, her voice heaving out in a great sob. "He's going after my family!"

Her pain sliced through the air like a jagged knife, and he reached for her hand, wrapping it in his own. "We'll stop him first."

"It's too late. He's probably already put something in place."

"He won't."

"I have to warn them. I have to let them know." She shook free of his hand and rifled through the cup holder between them for her phone.

"Graystone is keeping an eye."

"But there are so many of them. My parents. My brothers. My nieces and nephews. Moray could hurt any of them, and Reed can't watch all of them."

Gabriella's hands trembled, the glass screen of her phone catching the light of the street lamps in a jiggling reflection. He snatched the phone from her, his voice harder. "Graystone is keeping watch and has the proper guards in place. You can't alert your family."

"I have to. I have to make sure they're okay. That they are vigilant. That they get away."

The calm woman who'd scaled walls and kept him from falling off the roof was nowhere to be found. The panic and fear broke his heart, even as he knew he had to keep her from making any unnecessary calls.

Calls...

An idea took root and he twisted it in his mind. "I need you to do something for me."

The fretful woman vanished at the urgency in his tone, and Gabby snapped to attention. "What?"

"I'm going to give you some instructions. Type them into your web browser."

As he gave her the secure web address, he switched off his own phone, effectively closing off its digital signature.

"Why did you turn it off?"

"I think this is how Moray found us."

He gave Gabriella the necessary log-in information. "Is it asking for another password?"

"Yes."

"Type in *enchilada*."

"What?"

His face grew warm at the sudden attention. "I have to change my password every few days, and your enchiladas were on my mind."

"Thanks. I think."

He gave her a few more instructions, then walked her through the items on-screen he needed. The city lights were hazy in the distance, and Knox maneuvered them through the toll lanes into the city as Gabriella tapped away at her phone.

"Scroll to the bottom. Does it say *tracking on*?"

"Yes."

"Son of a bitch."

She added a curse of her own. "Do I need to turn mine off, too?"

"No. But I need you to carefully log out." He walked her backward through the process, effectively cutting off each encrypted layer. "We don't want to show you active from that device."

Gabby set her phone back in the cup holders. "He's a monster."

Thick traffic closed them in as he maneuvered through the CBD. Even this late, he had to wend his way, light by light. "That he is."

"Did you know? Before all this started?"

"Know what?"

"That he was so depraved. So soulless? I looked into his eyes. When we were up on the roof, I looked into his eyes, but they were empty."

Knox had seen the same thing and it scared the bloody hell out of him. He'd known Richard Moray for nearly two decades. He'd been on ops with the man and had maintained a healthy respect for his leadership and his willingness to enter the fray along with his team. If that man had ever existed—ever truly existed—he was no more.

"No. Not like this."

"So even with what you do and your knowledge of criminal minds, you didn't know."

"No."

They were quiet as he took the last few turns for his building. "I'm going to drop you off at my building. I want you to wait in the lobby with the doorman while I return the car to the parking garage."

"I'll stay with you."

"I want you in a well-lit place. You'll be fine with them."

"No."

"Gabriella—" He broke off when he caught sight of the immovable set of her lips.

"I know I'm a burden and I know tonight would have ended differently if you didn't have to worry about me. But I'm safe with you. Please don't leave me out in the open with anyone else."

"You give me more credit than I deserve."

"I'm safe with you. That's all I know anymore."

When they walked back to his flat fifteen minutes later, Knox couldn't say he was sorry to keep her nearby. Or to keep a firm arm around her waist as they traversed the three blocks together.

The raw fear for her family hadn't subsided, even after they'd gotten back to Knox's flat and heated up leftovers. A conversation with Reed had gone a long way toward calming her nerves, but those jittery moments of fear—and memories of the cold, lifeless gaze of Richard Moray—continued to haunt her at regular intervals.

She finished washing up the few dishes they'd used and wiped down the counter, determined to try and get some rest. And if she saw those eyes when she closed her own, then she'd have to use that. She'd galvanize the evil and the greed that had overtaken Moray into her personal mission to help Knox and get the Renaissance Stones back.

She left the kitchen and had nearly reached the guest room when she heard labored breathing. Unthinking, she raced into Knox's room, shocked to see him leaning toward a mirror, his shirt nowhere to be found, with a tray of medical supplies on his dresser.

"What's going on?"

"Nothing."

"Let me see." She moved closer. The gash on his shoulder was bright red and stretched against the stitches she'd done a few days earlier. "The roof."

"Sure. Dangling from it didn't do my shoulder much good. I popped a few of the stitches."

"Why didn't you say anything?"

"There was nothing to be done in the car."

"And when we got home for dinner? How about then?" Irritation gave her something to focus on, and Gabriella hung on for dear life. "Come here so I can take a look."

He gave her a sideways glance in the mirror, but moved back to give her a clearer view of his shoulder. She made an inspection, then poked through his medical supplies. "It looks like you've got top-of-the-line here, which should help. Let me go wash up and I'll help you."

As she got in a closer inspection, she could see he'd only reinjured the ends of his wound, so she focused on repairing one end, then the other. "How does that feel?"

"Good."

"That's three times on the same wound."

"Then we'll consider this the charm." His smile fell, the cheekiness disappearing from his tone as his gaze roamed over her face. She could see their matched reflection in the dresser mirror from the corner of her eye and nearly caught her breath. One Knox was powerful enough, but to see him half-naked in what amounted to a visual stereo was awe inspiring. "Thank you."

"You're welcome."

He leaned forward and pressed his forehead to hers,

and Gabby held still, reveling in the small act of comfort. "Don't go climbing any more walls."

"I'll try to keep that in mind."

Images flashed through her thoughts, those tense, endless moments bent over Richard Moray's roof, Knox's hand gripped in her own. She shuddered against the memory.

"Don't think about it."

"It's all I can see. And when I don't relive the grip of your hand and the endless drop to the ground beneath your dangling feet, I see that man's cold, vacant stare and hear his evil words in my mind."

"We will stop him."

"Before he does how much damage? Hugh's already paid with his life. If Moray has his way, we will, too."

"Don't focus on that part. It will consume you whole if you let it."

"This all consumes you. Your life and your work. They're so intertwined I don't know how you can see past the next day or the next week."

"I don't."

Gabby stepped back from his arms, the idea so foreign—and so bleak—she couldn't stand still for another moment. "How do you live like that?"

"It's my life to live."

"Are you?" She searched his eyes, suddenly desperate to find something—anything—to prove he wasn't ultimately on the same path as Richard Moray.

"Am I what?"

"Living it?"

Knox shrank back against the censure and criticism in her voice. She had no right—no right at all—to evaluate him and pass judgment. Nor did she have a right to keep poking around in his head.

"You're here because you asked to be here. Somehow you've forgotten that."

Fire heated her dark gaze, and Knox felt himself being drawn in, even as his every instinct urged him to run from her. She was life and joy, commitment and promise. His heart knew that, even while every survival instinct he possessed urged him to run.

Spending time with her required he give something of himself he believed had vanished long ago.

"That's rich, especially coming from the man who came to my business and inserted himself into my life."

"I shouldn't have come the other night after the drop in the park."

"So why did you?"

"Because I had to see you again!" The words ripped from him with violent force, the tectonic plates of his soul overlapping as an earthquake of emotion threatened to split him in two. "I wanted to look at you and touch you and see you before I left Dallas. Before I went off to capture my boss and dismantle the power structure of my organization or die trying."

"So I wasn't simply a convenience?"

Whatever reaction he expected to his words, that wasn't it. "You're nothing of the sort."

"And me and my shop weren't just an easy spot to hang out and hide for a few hours?"

"No." He hung his head, shaking it. "But now I've put you in horrible danger and by extension your family. And all I can say is, I'm sorry. So, so sorry."

He had no right to touch her—nor did he deserve the absolution to be found there—but he moved into her anyway.

And found waiting, open arms to bring him home.

Chapter 17

Great, galloping waves of freedom enveloped him as Gabriella wrapped her arms around his waist, pulling him close. He didn't deserve comfort or warmth, but he was too tired to move away and too far gone in love with her to even try.

Love.

When had it finally sunk in? And why wasn't he more panicked by that fact?

Because you knew, mate. You've always known.

If he dug down deep and was honest with himself, he knew that avalanche of emotion had swamped him from the very first moment he'd met her. Something had sparked inside him when her suspicious voice had barked questions at him through the back door of Elegance and Lace. He'd been intrigued then, this bulldog of a friend, so loyal to the women who were at the center of the case of the Renaissance Stones.

But when she'd opened the door, he'd been blinded. By her beauty. Her quick mind. Her diabolically good food.

And by her love and loyalty to those she cared for.

"I'm not sorry." The words floated over his ear on a whisper of breath.

He lifted his head from where it rested against her crown. "How can you say that?"

"Because I'm not. I'm not sorry you came to me. I'm glad. And grateful. You've given me something I didn't even know I was missing."

"A death sentence?"

"Life, Knox. You've brought me life. And, finally, a choice. I've searched for one for so long and thought I'd never find it."

Choice?

How could she think that? He'd painted her into a corner, forcing her on the run from a threat that wasn't hers to battle.

"I haven't given you anything. Instead, all I've done is take your choice away from you and put you in Richard Moray's crosshairs."

"That's where you're wrong." Her hands drifted over his chest, then up over the lines of his neck before settling against his face. "You've finally given me the choice to love someone. A man I can give myself to. Who I *want* to give myself to."

She pressed her lips to his, so full of promise he ached from it. "Thank you for giving me the choice to love you."

Gabby moved into his arms, ready and willing to be taken wherever he wanted to go. The words of love had flowed so naturally from her lips, she kept wondering why an answering sense of panic didn't sweep in to ruin the moment. Yet she only felt elation and a deep wellspring of joy that sent a wave of calm through her.

She loved Knox St. Germain.

And if the past few days had taught her anything, it was that keeping good, kind, strong words in her heart were strong armaments against the evil they battled. Life was a risk and terribly fragile, but it was life. And it was good and strong and worthy of the very best parts of her.

If she hid, Hugh's sacrifice was for nothing.

If she avoided the opportunity to live when she had the chance, all her work to escape her family's meddle-some behavior was for nothing.

And if she shunned the chance to reach out and take love when she had it in her sights, every bit of inde-pendence she'd spent her adult life fighting for was for naught.

Knox said nothing in response to her declaration of love, and she had no interest in dissecting it or talking it to death. She loved, and in the simplicity she found strength.

She gloried in the power of their bodies, moving in matched rhythm, an expression of everything said and unsaid between them. Long, quiet moments passed as they drifted across the room to the bed. Mindful of his shoulder, she slipped from her yoga pants and T-shirt, shedding her bra and panties quickly before helping him with his jeans.

Her hand brushed his erection, and she was rewarded with an immediate response; his breath deepened as he pressed against her.

"Gabriella." He exhaled her name on a breath.

"You're so British and so formal." She nipped a kiss

over his heart. "I love how you call me Gabriella. Not Gabby or Gabs. My full name. It rolls off your tongue with such elegance."

She trailed kisses from his chest to his neck, then over his collarbone before pressing one to his lips, a smile on hers. "You could read me the phone book and I'd likely come apart in a puddle on your floor."

"Oh, really?" He smiled back before wrapping an arm behind her and pulling her close. "That one's not in my repertoire, but I'll have to consider adding it."

"You do that."

She followed him down onto the bed. The night wrapped around them as tightly as their emotions, and their teasing conversation vanished, replaced with a sensual exploration of each other. Neither of them rushed, and Gabby marveled at how in tune they were with each other, one languid moment spinning into another.

When their movements grew more urgent—more frantic—Gabby welcomed him inside her body. As their physical connection intertwined with the emotional, Knox set her free.

And as he sent her soul soaring she wondered how she'd find her way back to earth.

Gabby surfaced from the depths of sleep, burrowing her cheek into the soft wash of cotton beneath her head, unwilling to open her eyes quite yet. Her pillow cradled her head, and she could have sworn she floated for the briefest moment before her thoughts brought her back down to earth.

She'd spent the night in Knox's arms, neither of them saying much of anything after her declaration of love. She searched her mind for some reason to be concerned about that, but couldn't find it.

She loved him.

And regardless of his feelings in return, she wouldn't hide from how she felt about him.

Acknowledging her impending return to Dallas was a different matter. However it happened, the cat and mouse game with Moray would end. And in the bright light of morning, she believed Knox had enough resources and credibility within his organization to see the job through. He had to.

Which meant she'd head home soon.

With that thought thudding her firmly back to earth, Gabby sat up and swung out of bed. She'd never been much for lingering, and since there wasn't a large body and endless chest to linger against, she'd do well to start her day.

A quick glance at the bedside alarm clock showed a few minutes after ten, and she picked up the pace, unsure of how long he'd been awake. She slipped back into her clothes from the night before, the soft yoga pants a physical comfort as she braced herself for what the day would bring.

Gabby found Knox pacing the living room, a cell phone pressed to his ear. "I need better plans on the Surrey estate. Your quick map was great, but we need to know the real layout."

He'd put his jeans back on but was still without a shirt, and she could see a fresh layer of antibiotic cream on his shoulder. Satisfied his shoulder had faded from the fiery red of the night before to a fresher pink, she allowed her gaze to follow the lines of his body.

He was magnificent, with lean ropes of muscle visible beneath his golden skin. The same thought that had pulled her awake—that she would head home soon—

had her gaze flicking over that impressive physique, willing it to memory.

He nodded at whatever was said on the other end, then offered up quick thanks before disconnecting the call.

"How long have you been up?"

"A few minutes. You?"

"I got up about seven. I didn't want to wake you." He moved closer and lifted her hand, running his fingers over the wrist that had locked against his when he dangled from the roof. "How do you feel?"

"A little sore. My muscles are tight, but I'll be fine."

His fingers massaged the flesh of her wrist, soothing over the thin layer of muscle and veins. "Clearly rolling all those enchiladas has given you some serious wrist muscles."

"A gal's gotta keep in shape."

"It's impressive."

The resolve that had carried her out of the bedroom wavered in the light of his tender gaze, and again her thoughts drifted to her return to Dallas.

"That was your friend? On the phone?"

"Yes. Sam's my colleague at the Security Service. He updated me on Hugh, and he's digging up what he can for me on Moray's estate."

"You mean you don't trust a cocktail napkin as a map?"

"Hardly."

She hesitated a moment, unwilling to put bad vibes in the form of doubt into the moment. But she did them no good by not asking her questions. "Even if we do get back into the house, how are you going to get the stones? Moray has to have them locked up."

"We'll crack the safe."

"But he already knows we've been to the estate. Is he really going to leave them off his person?"

"Then that works even more in our favor. We lose precious minutes drilling into a safe, but taking the rubies off him is a different matter."

"It's all a different matter. Now that he's seen us at his home, he's not going to let us get close."

"Then maybe it's time I do it. On my own."

Frustration welled up, but she refused to let it color her reaction. He continued to default to shuttling her off to a safe place, no matter how much she argued, and she'd lost interest in fighting that particular battle.

She needed to sway him to her way of thinking, namely, that they needed to get Moray out in the open, on their turf, in their own way. And the longer they waited, the more time they gave Moray a chance to plot and plan.

"Let's draw him out instead."

Moray ignored the pain in his foot and focused on finalizing his plans. He'd spent the night in his study, the throbbing wound keeping him grounded, and planned on what needed to be done through the long, sleepless hours.

St. Germain now had the edge.

Between the burn on his foot and the still-healing wound in his knee, he'd be a fool to go up against Knox directly. Which meant he needed a diversion so he could return the balance of power to his favor.

Gabriella Sanchez would work, but St. Germain wasn't inclined to leave her. Richard well knew the fact he was still sitting in his study with nothing more than a burn on his foot was because St. Germain had prioritized the woman over taking the kill shot.

He could use that.

But he needed something else. A vulnerability Knox didn't even know he had.

Moray scrolled through the data feed on his computer. He'd rigged his electronics years ago to keep tabs on his agents, and St. Germain hadn't disappointed.

But Sam Langston had.

Both men had communicated several times over the past two days, and Sam had managed the retrieval of Hugh Tolliver's body. Richard had believed Langston to be a loyal agent, but clearly he'd misjudged. Despite coming from some serious wealth, the man had always displayed a yeoman's dedication instead of pulling an upper-crust attitude with his superiors.

And now he was a traitor.

Richard scanned the preliminary evidence gathered off Hugh's body, as well as the orders written up for the man's autopsy. The paperwork had already been dispatched throughout the team, and he knew there wasn't anywhere he could intercept it with a small stash of cocaine or a faked email trail.

Bloody hell in a handbasket.

The swift work on Langston's part only added to Richard's frustration. The hands he'd hired the day before had been useless, missing their targets and killing a well-respected and well-loved member of the Security Service.

He'd seen to it they were killed for their incompetence, spending far more time than he'd have liked sending additional resources to deal with their remains.

Clearly Sam had spent the afternoon doing the same with Hugh.

Richard worked through his approach as he tapped into another database that displayed GPS coordinates on all his agents. Sam was at headquarters, his phone signal sure and strong. The man's email had also been active this morning, full of questions about Hugh along with his current caseload.

But it was the phone call that had captured Richard's attention as he sifted through logs. Sam had spent about twenty minutes on his office phone, fielding a burner cell call from central London. Richard didn't need any further intel to tell him who had called Langston, but an image of the city in his mind's eye gave him an idea. He did a final check of his files and confirmed the last piece of information he needed.

With quick fingers, he dialed headquarters and punched in the extension for Sam Langston.

"You can't be serious."

Gabriella's comment still echoed in his ears, and Knox wanted to believe he'd misheard her. Only with Gabriella, he knew that wasn't possible. The woman was more than willing to share her ideas, and they had a frightening layer of well-thought-out clarity to boot.

"The man is a highly trained operative. What part of this don't you get?"

"He's also scared and well aware of the caliber of opponent he has in you."

Her staunch belief in him was humbling and nothing he deserved. He didn't know how to make her understand that, nor did he know how to get through to her. Unless…

He knew there was little upside to giving her the truth of his background, but maybe if he did he could finally make her see why he wasn't the better—or safer—alternative.

"You asked me about my family yesterday. About how they died."

The swift change in topic had her stumbling, her eyes narrowing in confusion. "Which you told me. I'm sorry that you've had to live through that horrible loss."

"I'm the reason."

"You can't be. You told me yourself your father was in an accident and your mother and sister were victims to your mother's grief."

"Only partially true."

"I don't understand." She shook her head, her loose curls tossing around her head in a tantalizing wave. He longed to reach out and capture a curl around his finger, but he held back and willed himself to finish the story.

"I was recruited into an entry program with MI5. Word had reached someone of my father's leaving and the subsequent family issues. Best I can tell, I jingled some database somewhere and someone thought I'd make a good candidate."

"Why?"

"Broken home. High IQ. Stellar test scores. A few other items, likely including the number of speeding tickets I'd ginned up in a few years of driving, proving a bit of a daredevil streak. Who knows exactly what combination drove the connection, but something registered. Richard Moray recruited me himself."

"Knox—"

He laid a hand on her arm, stroking the soft flesh once more. "Let me get through this. You need to hear it from me."

She gave a small nod and he continued. "Mum was difficult in her grief and Daphne was increasingly disillusioned in caring for her. She lost as much, maybe more, than the rest of us when Dad left."

He walked Gabriella through it, his sister's excitement over her engagement to her boyfriend and the months of wedding planning that suddenly dominated their lives. She'd believed herself on the road to a second chance, only to experience the devastation when her fiancé left her after one too many issues with their mother's nerves and outbursts.

"I had work and training and all of the obligatory rah-rah stuff they embed in you as an employee."

"And your sister was left behind, resentful of the responsibility for your mother amidst all she'd lost."

"Yes."

"That's not your fault."

"How's it not my fault? I'm the one who left. I knew how Daphne felt, and I know what she was dealing with when it came to my mother."

"You had an opportunity and you took it. I find it hard to believe two teenagers had the income to deal with a suffering parent who likely couldn't work. How were you supposed to get money? Pay for your lives?"

"I could have found something else."

"No, something else found you, and you took it. There's no shame in that. No shame in going after opportunity."

"I left Daph to deal with my mother."

"No, she chose to stay behind. She could have gotten work, too. Could have juggled caregiving with a job. Your mother wasn't infirm to the point of not being able to stay alone. And some income would have bought some time of a companion, if it was needed, or access to health insurance. You're not to blame."

"But I didn't see. I didn't understand." Again, words he'd never planned to say spilled from his lips.

"Didn't understand what?"

"How far around the bend Daphne was. Or how frustrated she was by my mother. She killed her, then herself."

"I thought it was your moth—" Gabriella slowed before understanding filled her eyes. "Your sister did it."

"An injection to my mother of too much medicine followed by my father's gun on herself."

"I'm sorry. So very sorry."

She reached for him, but he quickly stepped back, unwilling to take comfort or solace. It didn't matter what Gabriella thought; he knew the truth. He'd abandoned his family. And he'd done it all to dance to Richard Moray's tune as a new recruit, shaped and molded into one of the man's minions.

A puppet for England.

She moved forward once more, undeterred by his retreat, her arms settling at his waist. "You aren't responsible."

"I—"

"You're not. And I'd like to believe that ultimately your sister isn't, either. Grief is a terrible thing. A devastating, terrible thing that swallowed her up whole."

In all the years that had passed since losing his family, he'd never considered his sister's actions through that lens. "I have responsibility for what happened."

"You also have to accept she had responsibility, too. For her choices and her actions. Your mother, too. They can't all rest on you."

"But they do. Don't you see that? I made my path, and now that path has brought me here. I need to deal with Moray. Bring him to justice inside MI5 and return the Renaissance Stones where they ultimately belong."

"Your path also brought you to me. Doesn't that count for anything?"

"It can't."

"But it does. You've spent your life convinced you need to atone for your family when they did nothing to deserve your guilt. Yet I'm here, looking at you and telling you I believe in you, and you turn me away."

"You can't matter. Not like that."

She dropped her arms as if burned. "Then I guess we're going to have to agree to disagree. Because I meant what I said last night. I love you and nothing will change that. Long after I go back to Dallas, I will still love you. Whether you want to believe that you deserve it or not, I know it's true."

His heart shattered at her words; the heat of her feelings was layered in each and every syllable. She'd shared her feelings the night before, and he'd breathed them in, reflecting them back on her in their lovemaking. But this was something different.

This was love plus acceptance.

Last night she didn't know the forces that had shaped his adult life. She hadn't known or understood his role in his family's death. She didn't fully understand the consequences of loving him.

But now she knew.

And she claimed to love him anyway.

He was humbled. Awed. And scared as hell.

Knox had always considered himself a man of action, but in that moment, he had no idea what to do. He wanted to say something—wanted to tell her every thought in his mind.

But instead, he did nothing.

And a few moments later, when she turned her back and walked to the guest room, he remained standing as he was, the ghosts of his family pinning his feet to the floor.

* * *

Gabby tossed several items into her overnight bag. She desperately wanted to work up a head of steam and self-righteous fury, but all she'd managed were some frustrated tears at Knox's lack of acceptance. She'd known it was too much to expect he'd have fallen in love with her already, but she hadn't expected her feelings to be thrown back at her with such cold, aloof indifference.

You can't matter.

But she did matter, damn it. And he mattered to her.

She tugged beneath her clothes to find the interior straps that tightened her luggage when her hand brushed over the material of the pantsuit Cassidy had salvaged. Lifting it out, she ran her hands over it, envisioning the woman who had worn the outfit originally.

Did she have relationship issues? A family who made her crazy, even while she missed them to distraction? Had she loved someone? Fought for that love? Or was she the flirt of the party, always looking for the next breathless love?

Gabby traced the material along the neckline, the questions spilling through her mind.

She wanted breathless love, but she didn't have the personality to fall in and out of it. In high school, her best friend had called it fickle and had used it as an insult against one of the girls in their class who dated half the boys.

Gabby hadn't seen it as fickle, but more a personality trait she didn't possess. She preferred to dig in and go deep. She liked knowing people—really knowing them—and couldn't imagine flitting from person to person like a bee who never spent long in one place.

But not everyone felt that way. And there were many who took more joy in the chase than in the having.

She refolded the pantsuit, disappointed she wouldn't have a place to wear it, and considered asking Cassidy if she could buy it when she got back home. Although… She held up the material, considering. It might work for her cousin's wedding. She was partway through evaluating if the outfit would be appropriate for an afternoon wedding in October when a hard knock echoed off her door.

"Come in!"

Knox's face was grim, and something real and tangible danced in the depths of his blue gaze. "It's time."

"For what?"

"Moray's made his opening gambit." He eyed the filmy material in her hands. "And it looks like you've got something for the occasion."

Knox wasn't willing to skip the show, but he was distinctly uncomfortable with Moray's outreach to Sam. In his friend's retelling, the man had been nothing but cordial, inviting Sam to a jaunt through the Tower of London for a catch-up and the chance to get outside the office.

Knox didn't buy the charade for a moment, but he had to admit Moray's selection of the location had a strange sort of symmetry to it.

The Renaissance Stones were smuggled out of London with the fake crown jewels Joseph Brown had been commissioned to create during World War II. Once the rubies were returned to Britain, they'd likely find a place back in the Tower, as well.

A fitting end.

"Why am I wearing this again? Isn't the Tower of

London old and outside?" Gabriella's voice spilled into the living room, and every drop of moisture in his mouth evaporated as Knox took a good long look at her. Black material hugged every line and curve of her body, while a plunging neckline left nothing to the imagination.

There wasn't a single soul who wouldn't notice her at the Tower. She'd stand out, and that was exactly what he wanted.

So don't get distracted, mate.

He admonished himself as those hips swung left and right as she walked toward him.

"The Tower is old but well kept."

"So we're basically going sightseeing in a public place. What are we going to do about Moray? Especially if he has a gun."

"We'll disarm him."

"Do you think he'll have the stones on him?"

"I'm counting on it."

"Why would he do that?"

"I don't think he has a choice any longer. They're captivating, and Sam deliberately mentioned Moray dangled the carrot of something to show him when they set up their meeting."

"He knows you're working together."

"Of course he knows. And he thinks he's going to sway us against each other or manipulate any loyalty we still may have to him."

Gabriella cocked her head, her gaze assessing before she spoke. "Has he ever understood the quality of people on his team?"

"I thought so. Once upon a time, I thought so."

"What happened?"

"I wish I knew."

* * *

The grounds at the Tower of London were busy with tourists. Just as Knox had predicted, Gabriella's skin-tight pantsuit left an impression with others. He saw several men turn to follow them into the Tower, and he'd quelled their interest with a sharp look that suggested they keep to their original plans.

"Why are you scowling?"

"That jerk over there's looking at your arse."

She turned, a pleasant surprise suffusing her face. "He is?"

"Yes, he is. And don't look so excited."

"You wanted me to wear this." She leaned in and pressed a quick, possessive kiss to his lips. "And don't think you haven't been checked out a few times. I nearly had to blind a woman back there."

"What did she do? I didn't notice anyone."

Gabriella let out a loud snort. "I'm surprised your zipper didn't burst into flames, she was staring at it so hard."

He couldn't hold back the broad smile. "One of *those*, eh?"

"Don't make me blind you instead."

"Bloodthirsty." He snagged a hand around her waist and pulled her close. "I like it. And you're in the right place for it."

"The Tower has a long history."

"Very long, all the way back to the eleventh century."

"Didn't they do beheadings here?"

"Among other things."

She shivered beneath his hand, and he was once again reminded of the serious business that had brought them out. While the meet with Moray wasn't far from his thoughts, he could appreciate the lighthearted banter between them as a way to break the tension.

But they couldn't joke away the risk, no matter how much they wanted to.

"I'd like to see the ravens. I've read about them."

They strolled the grounds until they found two of the active six out on display, and Knox pointed toward the birds. "It's purported Britain will fall if the Tower loses all its ravens."

"A silly notion, don't you think? The superstitious idea a few birds could down a country as great as England."

The hard press of a gun suddenly lay against his kidney, and Knox fought to keep himself still. They were in one of the most crowded areas of the Tower, and he refused to put anyone at risk.

"Where's Sam?"

Moray laughed. Gabriella had mentioned the man's soulless eyes earlier. Knox had to admit the soulless laughter shriveled his bollocks. "Turn around, St. Germain."

A sinking feeling gripped Knox in the middle of his chest, and he turned to find Sam standing behind Gabriella. From his position and her stiff posture, Knox knew a gun lay against her back, as well.

"It's powerful symmetry, don't you think?"

Anger clouded his gaze in a wild haze of red, and Knox puzzled over his horrible judgment.

Sam? His friend, Sam?

Unwilling to show just how shaken he was by the news, Knox focused on Moray. "What's powerful symmetry?"

"The Tower, of course. The home of the crown jewels. And the return of the Renaissance Stones to England."

"Don't act so benevolent." Gabriella practically spat the words as she tugged her arm away from Sam. "You don't care about the stones. You just want to sell them to the highest bidder."

"That's where you're wrong. I find I've come to care for them quite a lot. They're incredible pieces."

Knox had never heard such fanaticism in Moray's voice, and it nearly gave him as much pause as the disappointment of seeing Sam in the role of traitor. He flicked a glance toward Gabriella and got an answering acknowledgment in her dark gaze. Her head never moved, but those brilliant eyes flashed her agreement for whatever he needed.

Amazingly, it was her light shrug that put everything into motion. "What's the big deal? My friends showed me the stones in Dallas. They're just some colored rocks."

"These gems are priceless."

Moray's reverent voice was in direct contrast to Gabriella's casual approach, and he watched in awe as she taunted him once more. "Everything has a price. Those rocks have one, too."

Moray ground the gun in his back harder, and Knox arched his spine away from the press of the weapon. "Miss Sanchez prefers cooking to jewelry."

Moray turned his attention on Gabriella. "Then you're even more of a backwoods hick than I'd expected."

"Hey!"

Gabriella cried out until Sam squeezed her arm to quiet her. His glance darted over the open space, his eyes slightly wild. "Richard. We need to move this inside. Now."

Knox tap danced, anxious to get as much information as he could get. Standing out in the open risked too many innocents, but moving inside put him and Gabriella in even more serious danger. Richard and now Sam had the training to deal with them quickly and efficiently, and he refused to give them the chance.

"What do you want? You're both well respected. Well compensated. How can this possibly be the answer?"

"Don't tell me you haven't figured it out." Sam spoke up first. "I'm getting a promotion out of this, and Richard gets his stones. We're both going home happy."

Gabby felt the gun at her back, but didn't feel a corresponding sense of menace. Which was a ridiculous reaction. Just because Sam had been Knox's friend and helped with Hugh didn't mean anything. His true colors had obviously bled on through.

But now he was with Moray? Over a job promotion? *Not your problem, Sanchez.*

She shook off the absurdity of whether or not Sam's goal was a valid one and focused on getting away. Or at least finding a place that gave them a shot at escape, because walking inside the Tower with two armed men for damned sure wasn't it.

Even as she knew her goal, Gabby couldn't resist poking at that edgy madness she sensed in Moray. "The stones have been returned to their home country. What more do you want from us?"

"So attractive and voluptuous, yet sweetly naive at the same time." Moray ran a hand down Gabriella's back. "I'm going to kill you."

She recoiled from his repulsive touch, inadvertently backing harder into Sam's gun.

Which he moved with her, giving her room.

What?

She tested it again, pushing her weight backward on the gun. Once again, it moved with her, giving the appearance of a threat but not an actual one.

Was it possible he wasn't really the enemy?

Tilting her head, she stared up into Sam's eyes and saw the truth reflected back in those solemn green depths.

She'd stake her life on it.

Sam's voice was rough when he spoke, but his eye contact never wavered with hers. "Let's get going, gorgeous. Enough stalling."

Sam pushed her forward, matching Moray's movements with Knox. As they drew closer to the Tower entrance, Gabby understood she was staking her life, as well as Knox's, on a hunch.

She only hoped this weird sixth sense and a pair of trustful green eyes were strong enough to see them through whatever came next.

Knox calculated the odds of disabling Moray and Sam and knew it was a long shot. Moray's injuries might have leveled the playing field, but Gabriella was the wild card. Would she get away or would she get caught in the cross fire?

While he wouldn't bet against her, he couldn't guarantee her safety, either, and that was unacceptable.

He loved her.

Desperately. Fiercely. Madly.

With everything he was, he loved her, and there was

no way he wanted to give up forever with her. Why he hadn't understood that back in his flat, he'd never know.

But he knew now.

But first, they needed to get the hell out of here.

They wove their way past the exhibit room for the crown jewels and continued on deeper into the Tower. Frowning, he took stock of his surroundings so he could navigate them back out. A fresh idea struck.

"Interesting choice for a meet-up. This can't just be about closing a loop or some meaningless symmetry about a few rubies."

"It's about far more than that." Moray kept his tone light and his gun covered by a jacket so, to anyone watching, they looked like another tour group, taking in the sights. "When you're found here, dead at our hand, it will be a small leap to implicate you in the rubies' disappearance. And after we discover the intel you and your girlfriend gathered in Dallas, Sam and I will then uncover the sordid truth that you thought you might take our very own crown jewels to add to your collection of three priceless rubies. Sadly, today's jaunt was a little stakeout that Sam and I were able to intercept before either of you could do any damage to Britain's finest treasure."

"You're mad," Gabriella breathed.

"I'm determined. Never mistake the two."

Moray slipped a small ID badge off his pocket and opened a door sunk into the wall. He pushed Knox through, leaving Sam and Gabriella to follow.

Unwilling to wait any longer, Knox pivoted and slammed his hand into Moray's gun, sending it flying to the side. A howl of pain echoed off the stone walls as Knox kicked at Moray's injured knee, followed by his groin.

"Gabriella! Run!"

Images blurred in front of his face as Sam leaped through the door, gun drawn and pointed toward the ceiling.

"Knox! Get behind me!"

The sense of betrayal that had gripped him earlier vanished as Sam shoved their boss into the small room from behind.

"Behind me, mate! Move! I'm the one with the gun."

Knox shifted to Sam's side as Moray regained his feet, his chest heaving like a determined bull. Before any of them could move any farther, several men and women poured from two other doors at the back of the room, guns drawn, each wearing jackets that declared them members of the Security Service.

Team members he knew and respected rushed the writhing, struggling body of their former boss.

Carl Revere, one of Moray's contemporaries, came forward and clasped his hand. "Knox. We have the deepest gratitude for your service."

"My service?"

The sands beneath his feet shifted, and Knox struggled to make sense of the sudden upheaval of his world. All this time—all the questions he'd had about trusting his colleagues—it was all for naught. "You knew?"

"When you brought your suspicions forward, we created a small task force. I brushed it off but knew that wouldn't stop you."

Carl sheathed his gun, clearly satisfied his team had Moray in hand. "And I didn't want to stop you, but we knew Richard had masked intel on all our technology tools. We needed someone to work the angles and make it look independent."

"So you left me to it."

"I always knew you were a bulldog. It's why I put your name in so many years ago."

"You?"

"You played rugby against my nephew. I saw you in a game. You were determined, athletic. And you played honest and fair. When I looked into the rest, you were a fit."

Gabriella moved up next to him, her smile broad as she patted his back. "I guess that answers that question."

"Miss Sanchez." Carl extended his hand and introduced himself. "You're our most unorthodox agent yet, but you handled yourself admirably."

"So you won't fire Knox over my insistence on coming along?"

"No."

"Will you fire him for this?"

Before Knox could register her movements, Gabriella laid a hand on the back of his neck and pulled him close. As her mouth pressed against his, he felt the curve of her lips as she smiled and the light exhale of her breath. "You're in the boss's good graces."

Carl's hearty laugh only added to the moment. "The woman's right. Take advantage of it while you can."

And so he did.

Epilogue

London
Two days later

The loud pop of champagne lit up their small circle and Gabriella sat back and let Reed do the honors of filling up the ten flutes positioned around their small bar table. They'd set up shop in the Ritz lounge while they waited for Mrs. Beauregard and Max Senior to return from the Palace.

"What was it like?"

"What were they wearing?"

"Did you see the babies?"

Questions seemed to echo from all sides as Cassidy, Lilah and Violet scrambled for Mrs. B's attention.

Mrs. B answered in short order before reaching for Max Senior's hand, wrapping it in her own. "We finally gave the stones back to their rightful owners."

Cassidy let out a small sniff. "I still say you were the rightful owners."

"No, dear. We were entrusted with the job, but the stones were never ours. Now they're back where they belong."

Reed and Tucker passed out the flutes, and Knox took two, handing her one. "You seem quiet."

"I'm still in awe of how quickly everything came together. Reed got everyone here and Carl got Mrs. B an audience with the royal family. It hasn't even been two days."

"Some things have a way of resolving themselves quickly."

She smiled up at him as he put his arm around her. "I guess they do."

She kept her smile in place, but knew not everything had resolved itself. Knox had spent much of the past two days at work, closing up the mess Moray had made and ensuring all details were accurately captured for the record.

And she still had no idea if she and Knox had any future at all. They'd made love for the past two nights as if they had all the time in the world, but she knew there was no future if they didn't discuss it.

Then her friends had arrived, and there wasn't any time to talk about their future even if she had found a way to bring it up.

"A toast." Max Senior held up his glass, his adoring gaze on Mrs. B. "To five determined women who know how to make things happen."

They clinked flutes and sipped their wine before the older man raised his glass once more. "To three magical rubies. Some say they're cursed, but I say they hold an infinitely more mystical power. The ability to bring those who deserve true love together."

Again, a round of clinking, but this round was matched by several sighs as one by one, each couple kissed.

Knox went last, his gaze fully on hers as he bent his head. Gabby kissed him back, desperate to show him all she felt in her heart. Whether it was the stones or fate or the simple reality of finding each other, she loved him.

With all her heart, she loved him.

He pulled back, a twinkle in his eye. "I've got one more toast." He pressed his lips to her forehead. "Raise your glass."

As she did, she saw it. The large emerald-cut diamond he'd slipped into her flute while they kissed.

"Knox?"

"We have five couples and three rubies, but only one proposal tonight." With that he got down on one knee, his gaze turned up to her. "Gabriella, my love. You are more beautiful than any gem. You make me want things I don't deserve, yet you make me bold enough to want them anyway. I love you, and I want to make a life with you. Will you marry me?"

"Yes, I'll marry you. I love you." She bent to kiss him, pouring all she felt in her heart into the moment.

Cheers went up around the room, along with several tinny voices that she knew better than her own name. Lifting her head, she turned to see Tucker holding up a tablet, her family all assembled on the screen. "How?"

As Knox got to his feet and pulled her close, the two of them peered down into the faces of her family. "I called your father to ask permission for your hand, and then we cooked this up."

"You're here. All of you, here with me." She turned to Knox, hugging his arm. "With us."

"Of course, *mi amor.*" Her mother blew her a kiss. "Always."

Tears spilled over, and Gabby didn't know if she'd ever been so happy or felt so carefree.

She was loved. In the roots that formed her and in the future she'd make with the man she loved.

Yesterday, today and tomorrow.

Always.

* * * * *

REQUEST YOUR FREE BOOKS!
2 FREE NOVELS PLUS 2 FREE GIFTS!

⊕HARLEQUIN®

ROMANTIC suspense

Sparked by danger, fueled by passion

YES! Please send me 2 FREE Harlequin® Romantic Suspense novels and my 2 FREE gifts (gifts are worth about $10). After receiving them, if I don't wish to receive any more books, I can return the shipping statement marked "cancel." If I don't cancel, I will receive 4 brand-new novels every month and be billed just $4.74 per book in the U.S. or $5.49 per book in Canada. That's a savings of at least 12% off the cover price! It's quite a bargain! Shipping and handling is just 50¢ per book in the U.S. and 75¢ per book in Canada.* I understand that accepting the 2 free books and gifts places me under no obligation to buy anything. I can always return a shipment and cancel at any time. Even if I never buy another book, the two free books and gifts are mine to keep forever.

240/340 HDN GH3P

Name	(PLEASE PRINT)	

Address		Apt. #

City	State/Prov.	Zip/Postal Code

Signature (if under 18, a parent or guardian must sign)

Mail to the **Reader Service:**
IN U.S.A.: P.O. Box 1867, Buffalo, NY 14240-1867
IN CANADA: P.O. Box 609, Fort Erie, Ontario L2A 5X3

Want to try two free books from another line?
Call 1-800-873-8635 or visit www.ReaderService.com.

* Terms and prices subject to change without notice. Prices do not include applicable taxes. Sales tax applicable in N.Y. Canadian residents will be charged applicable taxes. Offer not valid in Quebec. This offer is limited to one order per household. Not valid for current subscribers to Harlequin Romantic Suspense books. All orders subject to credit approval. Credit or debit balances in a customer's account(s) may be offset by any other outstanding balance owed by or to the customer. Please allow 4 to 6 weeks for delivery. Offer available while quantities last.

Your Privacy—The Reader Service is committed to protecting your privacy. Our Privacy Policy is available online at www.ReaderService.com or upon request from the Reader Service.

We make a portion of our mailing list available to reputable third parties that offer products we believe may interest you. If you prefer that we not exchange your name with third parties, or if you wish to clarify or modify your communication preferences, please visit us at www.ReaderService.com/consumerchoice or write to us at Reader Service Preference Service, P.O. Box 9062, Buffalo, NY 14240-9062. Include your complete name and address.

HRS15

SPECIAL EXCERPT FROM

✦ HARLEQUIN®

ROMANTIC suspense

*Raised apart from his siblings, private investigator
Chris Colton knows what it feels like to miss family. So
when a couple hires him to find their widowed daughter-
in-law, who's absconded with their twin grandsons, this
Colton's on the case. But he hardly expects to find that
beautiful Holly McCay is innocent, and someone's out
to get her—and the family she forms with Chris!*

*Read on for a sneak preview of
HER COLTON P.I.,
the latest chapter in the gripping saga of
THE COLTONS OF TEXAS.*

She didn't want to do it, but Chris's points were irrefut-
able. She suddenly realized her palms were damp, and
she rubbed them nervously on the sides of her jeans. "So
when do we start?"

"As soon as I can coordinate things with Sam and
Annabel—tomorrow or the next day. And I've got to get
Jim Murray's blessing, too." She raised her brows in a
question, and he added, "He's the Granite Gulch police
chief. Sam and Annabel answer to him, so we can't do
this without him giving it the green light. But I don't see
Jim saying no."

"Can he be trusted?" Holly blurted out.

Chris smiled faintly. "He's honest as the day is long.
I've known him since I was a kid, and I would trust him
to do the right thing. Always."

"Okay," she said again. She didn't say anything more, but she didn't leave, either. She knew she should—that would be the safe thing. The smart thing. But suddenly all she could think of was the kiss in her dream yesterday. The kiss that had devastated her with how much she wanted this man she barely knew. And then there was the kiss that wasn't. The almost-kiss in the kitchen last night. She'd seen it in his eyes—he'd wanted to kiss her. Why hadn't he?

Then she realized he was looking at her the same way he had last night, as if he was a little boy standing on the sidewalk outside a store window gazing longingly at something he wanted but knew he couldn't have because he couldn't afford it. As if—

"Go to bed, Holly," he told her, his voice suddenly harsh. But she couldn't seem to make her feet move. "This isn't what you want." Oh, but it was, it *was*.

Don't miss
HER COLTON P.I. by Amelia Autin,
available May 2016 wherever
Harlequin® Romantic Suspense
books and ebooks are sold.

www.Harlequin.com

HRSEXP0416

Turn your love of reading into rewards you'll love with

Harlequin My Rewards

**Join for FREE today at
www.HarlequinMyRewards.com**

Earn **FREE BOOKS** of your choice.

Experience **EXCLUSIVE OFFERS** and contests.

Enjoy **BOOK RECOMMENDATIONS** selected just for you.

PLUS! Sign up now and get **500** points right away!

Earn **FREE** REWARDS
Join Today!
HarlequinMyRewards.com

MYR16R